DRESSED TO KILL

An Anna Harris Short Story Collection

A V IAIN

Contents

DRINKS CABINET   1
HATE MAIL   15
BLOOD. SNOW.   55
DOMESTIC GODDESS   87
THE RANGE   137
BLUE LIGHTS   157
HOTEL PARAISO   203
HEAR ME   237
WHITE OUT   281
VIAL DEBT   319

Author's Note   337

DRINKS CABINET

1

CALL ME UP MYSELF, but I never gave much thought to ever being a waitress . . . and much less to being one to my employer Brian Mathewson.

But I guess that, sometimes, we just can't see what's coming at us.

What's waiting in the wings.

I stand up against the glass of Brian's relentless thirteenth-floor office, set, of course, in the headquarters of Mathewson Media. Though it's beaming sunshine outside, some ambient *thing* in the office is piping out air at a cool eighteen degrees.

That's the thing with alcoholics, they're much more into fridges—and *freezers*—than sunlamps and cookers.

I can smell the whisky cutting through the air with that horrible odour that it has. That smell that's sort of between crumbling, half-burned-up coals and disinfectant.

It dries out my mouth.

Sets my heart beating.

But not with anticipation.

Brian sits over at the other side of the office, with five other men, none of them that I recognise. They're all blabbering about something or other—I have to admit that I lost interest a good decade or so ago . . . at least that's how long it feels like.

They're all sat about the sofa-and-chair set, each of them with their own tumbler of whisky in their hands: four out of five of them with ice . . . no prizes for guessing that Brian Mathewson is the one who will have *nothing* capable of diluting *his* liquor anywhere near his glass.

I glance to my side, to the drinks cabinet: the vodka, rum, gin and . . . of course . . . whisky nestled inside.

There's also a bucket of ice sitting up there with a pair of spring-loaded tongs nestled within. I have to admit that, in the course of the last—impossibly long—hour, I've considered just about six thousand different ways I can use said tongs to batter Brian Mathewson to death.

But Brian Mathewson's not the one I'm meant to kill.

Nope, he'll be the one paying me if everything goes to plan.

If I do a *professional* job.

The one I've got to kill is dressed in a light-blue suit, the one with the wispy blond hair, and the pudgy cheeks that just scream —to me at least—Public School Boy.

I don't know who he is, or what he's about, but I do know that Brian wants him dead.

And he wants everyone here to see it.

All things considered, probably the worst thing about this whole deal is what Brian's got me wearing. Since I'm meant to be looking like a *bone fide* member of the Mathewson Media waiting staff, I have to wear this fairly ridiculous black-and-white maid's uniform.

Pinny apron and all.

And don't get me started on the cheap, white-paper-hat thing that I've got perched in my hair. And how I've had to put in just about a dozen hairgrips to get the thing to stay in place.

I reckon the girls who have to put with this sort of uniform every day deserve a medal.

Or at least a pay rise.

The tinkling of ice in a glass brings me around from my ponderings. Stops me gazing out the window of Brian's office in some sort of daze.

I look back.

See the target, the man in the light-blue suit, shaking his whisky tumbler at me, the ice bouncing back against the glass.

He doesn't *look* at me, of course.

As I approach him, I remind myself not to take it personally.

This is no doubt how he handles all waiting staff.

I clop over there wearing a fairly appalling—and not a little uncomfortable—pair of black high heels. You know the ones that have the heel that could maim someone.

When I reach him, make for his glass, he turns away from the conversation, from the other five men all gathered about chattering away in that happy way of theirs.

His cheeks are all flushed. His pupils dilated.

His teeth look *too* white . . . at least too white to be that white naturally.

"Lovely girl, you are," he says, not quite a question, or a statement really, thinking about it.

I just smile at him politely, consoling myself with the fact that he'll be dead in a couple of minutes or, at worst, half an hour . . .

As I take his glass from him and make to turn away, to head back to the drinks cabinet where I've got everything ready, he snatches hold of my wrist. Quite hard, actually.

His fingers dig into my skin.

When he speaks, he does so out of the corner of his mouth. "Anna," he says, his voice dried from the alcohol, his smile slipping off his lips.

2

HEARING MY NAME said back to me sends a shimmer through my blood. A slight tingle passing down my spine. Instinctively, I look to Brian, sitting across in the group of men, still red in the face from the drink and all the laughing he's been doing.

This man—the target—why does he *know* my name?

Know who I am?

The target's grip slackens just a little, then he takes up his easy smile once more, but keeps his voice down low so the others won't overhear. "Name's Holden Brown," he says, giving me information I really have no interest in, and then he adds, in a kind of floaty voice, "Wonder what Brian's got his very best assassin doing drinks service for."

I feel my heart patter on a little harder.

Flutter up to my throat.

Hang there just for a few seconds.

Leave a sour taste in my mouth.

His smile widens even further, then he casts a glance down at the glass, tight in my hand. "Guess times must be hard, eh? Everyone's got to make ends meet somehow."

He follows up *that* comment with a pretty repulsive wink.

But, finally, he lets me go.

As I pad back over to the drinks cabinet, back to the crystal whisky decanter there, I realise my hands are shaking. That my heart is drumming even harder. I lay *Holden's* glass down on the pinewood cabinet, on top of the many rings that have been impressed there over the years of Brian's drinking.

I look to the decanter.

See it's a quarter full of whisky.

The afternoon London sun, which floods in through the window, gives it a honey-coloured glow.

I turn my attention upwards, to the shelf at about eyelevel.

To the small blue, glass vial.

And to the—seemingly—oil-slick black liquid slopping about inside.

Before the hit, which is to say, before Brian fitted me out in this maid's uniform, he told me that the stuff he was leaving up here was impossible to detect.

Colourless when added to liquid.

Odourless.

Tasteless.

I glance back over my shoulder, back to the men all gathered about Brian's chair-and-sofa set. I see that Holden has turned his attention, very much, back to the rest of the group. And that his shoulders are rumbling with the laughter wreaking itself through his flubbery frame.

I reach up.

For the vial.

Unscrew the lid.

And then pour it into the bottom of the glass.

3

HOLDEN takes the fresh tumbler of whisky from me. Holds it in his hand. I watch on as a little steam rises up off the ice cubes within. I can't help but study the colour of the stuff. Wonder if there's *something* that might give the poison away. That might alert Holden to actually what's inside of the tumbler.

As I retreat back over to the drinks cabinet, I look over my shoulder.

Anxious to see how this'll play out.

Holden brings the lip of the glass to his lips.

My heart holds still.

Stops beating for several moments.

And then another of the men speaks out.

One sitting across from me. Wearing a salmon-pink suit and a —fairly disgusting—frogspawn-silk shirt underneath that shimmers unevenly in the sunlight pouring into the office.

"I say," the man says.

My stomach crunches in on itself.

I see that he's directing his question to Holden.

Holden brings the glass down from his lips.

He hasn't yet taken so much as a sip.

The man's eyes crease a little, not out of suspicion, more out of jubilation. That alcoholic afterglow middle-aged men always seem to get after several rounds of laughter.

"What's she slipped you there?" he says.

My heart does a flip.

My throat feels like it constricts on itself.

I want to disappear, like, now.

Little hope of that happening, though.

Because, from years on this earth, I've come to the conclusion that I haven't got a magical bone in my body.

The man in the salmon-pink suit slips me a look. Inclines his eyebrow in a way that I'm sure—in his mind—makes him think that he might just be James Bond.

If only someone had the delicacy to tell him that nothing could be further from the truth.

Certainty not going to be me, though.

Not till I've done my job.

"Go on then," Salmon-Pink Suit says, "Give us some of what you've given him."

I pause for a long while. Look to Brian. See that he's glaring at me.

There's not many times when I've seen Brian look totally—completely—stumped.

But he certainly is now.

And I really have no idea what I'm meant to do.

. . . Then, right when I least expect it, he gives me an—almost imperceptible—nod.

4

RIGHT ABOUT THEN my whole body just seems to numb. As if all the pores over my skin seal up and prevent me from feeling any longer. But I go about the motions.

I collect up the glasses, all of them held out to me—Brian's too—and then I head back over to the drinks cabinet . . . eye the little vial of liquid there, back up where I'd replaced it on the shelf, and then I set about pouring the whisky—no water, as Brian insists—and then I add into each, Brian's too, a few drops from the vial.

Even though I know that a single drop is enough to make anyone croak.

What else can I do?

Without another word from me, or anyone else, I hand the tumblers back out to the assembled men there, all of them dressed-up smartly in their suits, all of them waiting eagerly to see just what I might be about to give them.

As I stand back, breath hitched in my throat, I notice how Brian's features have all softened up, how he's back into his jubilatory mood once again.

Some of the men swill their glasses, peering into the whisky there, as if trying to make some sort of sense out of it.

I want to warn them—something deep within me . . . perhaps you could call it a conscience? . . . shouts at me to warn them away.

But I say nothing.

I just stand by, as Salmon-Pink Suit says, "What's this, then, Bri? What've you been holding out on us with?"

Brian gives a pout as if he *doesn't* know exactly what's going on here, that these men are effectively staring death right in the face. That he *himself* is staring death right in the face. "Oh," he says, "just this little thing—thought it might add a little spice, that's all."

Holden, who I now see has taken on a steady look of suspicion, slips me a sidelong glance.

Surely he's put two and two together.

Surely he knows *just* why Brian has had me 'placed' here today.

He knows that someone—here—is going to bite it.

The men all continue to look into their whisky tumblers with just a touch of suspicion. But they've got those looks on their faces, those looks that little boys get when they're staring into some sort of a treasure trove: a virgin forest, a muddy puddle, a road kill squirrel to be poked with a stick.

Mean little pleasures.

Holden holds his tumbler down on his lap now, as if afraid to bring it any closer to his lips.

Maybe he's brighter than I gave him credit for.

And then, just when I'm sure Holden's going to say something—to tell them all just who I am and blow my cover, and make life very difficult indeed for Brian—he stands up, raises his tumbler to the ceiling and then says, "To Brian Mathewson and his *wonderful* services!"

The other men all rise, their eyes alive with their smiles, and then they all cry out, "*Cheers!*" as one and clink their glasses together.

Indeed, the *clinks* of glasses are so vigorous that in a few cases some drops of whisky—poison included—slop onto the floor and land to form micro puddles.

And then, heart still tapping at about the same rate as a throbbing car engine, I watch on as they all tilt the liquid down their throats.

Brian too.

5

TEN MINUTES LATER and they're all dead.

Well, that's not *exactly* true.

Brian, it seems, just has a cracking headache.

He sits in one of the high-backed chairs, at the other end of the group: all of them now prostrate in various locales—some slumped on the sofa, others lying on the floor . . . Holden has, somehow, ended up on his knees, head cocked to one side as if he fell asleep while tending to a fireplace.

Brian remains slumped over himself, propping up his head up with his elbows jutting into the fleshy part of his leg just above the knee.

I watch on as his shoulders rise and fall with his heavy breathing.

And then, all of a sudden, he flexes back and I think that the time has come, that he's going to give his death throes . . . but no . . . there are some things in this world that truly *will not* die, and Brian Mathewson seems to be one of them.

He presses his head back into his chair. His eyelids flutter a few times. His fingers still press hard at his temples. And then, ever so slowly, he opens his eyes. Appears to bring me into focus. That same—*familiar*—drunken smile stitches itself across his lips, and then he says, in a slightly croaky voice, "Good life lesson that, Anna." He draws a breath, with seems to shudder its way down into his lungs. "Always—*always*—build up an immunity to your own poisons."

I give him a slight smile, for some strange reason not quite able to shake the grim feeling I have with five dead bodies lying all around us.

And then—*silly pragmatic me*—I turn my mind to what's going to happen next.

"What do we do with them?" I say.

Brian blinks slowly, reminding me a little of a toad—if I can *really* recall ever having seen a toad blink—and then he says, "Be a bit of a clean-up job, eh?"

"Mm."

Brian smiles more widely, which seems even *more* grotesque given the bunch of bodies all piled up around him, and then he says, "Don't worry, Anna, never really did like this lot anyway . . . and if it's any consolation, I think we can safely say that—wherever they are—they're much happier . . . in their own *company*, if you get what I mean?"

"Their own company?"

He gives me a stiff nod.

I look about them. Look to the vast array of loud suits, and even *louder* stomachs, and I think about it.

Yes, what Brian says makes sense to me.

That these men, they're of the same sort.

Those men who enjoy the company of *other* men.

HATE MAIL

1

I GET THE CALL around five in the morning, and it's Brian, the publicist I work for. Brian's an early riser. He tells me that he's got a job. And when he says 'job,' he really means that he needs someone dead.

I hang up then shift off the duvet and stretch. Light leaks in round the fringes of my curtains, setting my room in a kind of twilight. It's one of those long summer mornings. And for me it's going to be longer than most.

When I manage to get on my feet, I tweak the curtain back and look out. It's raining—of course it is, it has done for the past five weeks so why should it stop now? I back up from the window and paw for the towel which hangs from my wardrobe handle, then I head into the bathroom and run myself a hot shower.

I'm fully dressed minutes after getting dried, with a pistol shoulder-strapped beneath my jacket. Those men who claim that women spend ages getting ready have never met me. Then again, most men don't do my job—have no need to be ready at the ring of a phone.

I don't have a car—contrary to popular belief hitwomen don't earn the big bucks—so I'm forced to take the Underground. Luckily enough there's a stop just at the end of my street.

I trot down the stairs of the Underground station, greeting the cleaner—a round, black lady who smiles at me—who's scrubbing at the steps, before skimming through the barrier and down onto the platform. My train arrives within a couple of minutes and I step into a nearly deserted carriage.

A stench of bleach and polish clings to the first Underground train of the day and it stirs me, dries out my mouth and prods me awake. I find a newspaper from yesterday, unfold it and read through the stories. There's always a sense of excitement in picking up a paper on days that Brian calls me because often the client is in the news. I skim through the front pages and onto the political section—where the most likely prospective clients hang out.

The lights are still dim in the reception of Mathewson Media. It's a glass building with a light green tint to it. As the sun rises through the buildings it sets the place in an effervescent light—as if there's something divine surrounding it. And I suppose, to an extent, there is.

I trot up to the front door and press my index finger to the scanner. A light changes from red to green and the lock disengages. I strut through the empty reception area and up to another set of turnstiles where I perform the same fingerprint trick as before.

The only light on the thirteenth floor is the one which trickles from beneath Brian's office door. I say office, but it's probably large enough to fit my whole house—and garden—inside. I give the door a couple of warning raps and then, because there's no secretary this early in the morning, I step into his office.

Brian stands with his back to me, looking out over the city. Although I can't see his face I'm certain that he's staring directly at the sun. He has dark-brown hair which he's kept lush despite his work ethic, and—I think eyeing the half-empty glass of whisky—despite his alcoholism. When he hears my footsteps behind him, he swivels and looks me in the eye, that familiar, carefree smile tracing his lips. "Prompt as always," he says.

"Is this some kind of emergency?"

He chuckles as if what I said was a joke then he collects himself, his eyes turning to the glass of whisky on the table. He walks toward me and stoops down to collect the glass. He knocks it back and then sets it down on his drinks cabinet. "I wouldn't say this is an emergency, but I thought that it might be worthwhile to get you out of bed. Can't abide people sleeping in." He flashes his eyebrows at me. "Did you know we waste a third of our life sleeping?"

This early in the morning my capacity for mental arithmetic is pretty much shot, so I just make agreeable noises and hope he'll be content with that.

"Such a waste," he says with a scowl, pouring himself another glass of whisky.

I consider replying that by the time most people are having breakfast he's on his second bottle, but then I remember my place. Because, for all the ease of our relationship, Brian is my employer—I'm his employee.

Brian sips at his fresh drink then eyes me, as if he's just remembered I'm there. "The reason I got you out of bed so early is because that's how my man operates."

"Which 'man?'"

There's a knock at the door of his office.

Brian smiles. "That'll be him right now." He puts his glass inside his drinks cabinet and closes it.

It looks like this is someone Brian's looking to impress. I don't dwell on that fact for too long—about what it might say about how he views me.

He opens the door and a squat man—perhaps in his late-thirties, early-forties—with straggly, long greasy hair, wearing a waist-high leather jacket and—I notice to my disgust—too tight jeans which show off the inner thigh . . . bulge.

Brian stands aside and the man wanders in.

He looks round in wonder at Brian's room, examining the tall ceiling and then taking in the spectacular view over the London skyline. Finally he turns his attention to me, then nods. "All right?"

Brian closes up the oppressive oaken doors to his office and struts over to us. He claps his hands together like a teacher tackling a problematic pair of students head on. "Anna, Jeffrey"—he gives Jeffrey a sidelong glance—"or is it 'Jeff?'"

"Either," Jeffrey says.

"I'll call you Jeff. Easier, isn't it?"

"Suppose."

"Jeff, Anna. There you go, you're all introduced."

As I stand there, studying this specimen, I notice the rank odour of sweat mingled with coffee emanating from him. He has clearly been out all night. I wonder whether Brian couldn't have scheduled this meeting a little later, to give 'Jeff' the chance to shower. Then again, judging by the state of his clothes, perhaps he doesn't much strive for cleanliness.

Jeff's holding out his hand to me. I note the fudgy fingernails and light yellow tone—suggesting jaundice—of his skin.

I take a deep breath then accept the handshake, shooting Brian a sharp glance to see whether this might be his idea of some elaborate in-joke.

"Let's get down to it, shall we?" Brian says.

"Let's," I say.

He shows us to the sofa-and-chair set which occupies a corner of his office. It faces in the direction of the rising sun. I'm sure that he's spared no expense in interior design—probably had the best Scandinavians money can buy out here.

I take a seat on a chair that seems adverse to angles. It's like the entire thing has been based on the idea of dough. Every time I find myself a seat I catch myself slipping down one of its faces. I realise that I'm going to need to use my hand to support me, and soon get the hang of sitting on the chair, gripping it between my knees. Not the most comfortable piece of furniture in the world I have to say.

"Jeff here," Brian says, "is a private detective. Well, really, that's a bit of an insult. He's not *just* a private detective. He's also an expert in telephony and postal systems."

'Expert' and personal hygiene don't always go hand in hand, I suppose.

"What Jeff's been working on is a very specific case. You see, our client, he's been having problems with hate mail."

"'Hate mail?'" I say.

"That's it."

There has to be more to it than this. I've spent most of my career thus far as an assassin dealing with bigger issues than that: simmering political scandals, kiss-and-tellers, not to mention the whistle blowers. This just seems so petty.

A smile twitches at the corner of Brian's mouth. "I know what you're thinking, but this isn't just your average hate mailer. I mean, this guy, or girl, has gone much further than that. I'm talking a hundred letters a day, phone calls every hour, day or night, emails to accounts round the clock."

"Shouldn't this be a matter for the police, then?"

Brian scoffs. "If this guy catches on to a police investigation then he might decide to act all rash, take his obsession to the next logical step. Problem is that these people tend to be unstable. You can never trust what they'll do next. Whereas the hate mailer knows just who the target is, no one knows who the hate mailer is. Got to remember that they have the upper hand. So we have to seize the opportunity, before going to the authorities, to iden- tify this individual."

"And why shouldn't you just use Jeff? Have him find out who this guy is and then hand him over to the police? What do you need an assassin for?"

"Are you trying to talk yourself out of a job?"

To be honest I do have some bills coming up—payments to my ex-husband, who takes care of our kids. I keep most of my money invested, try to keep as little cash lying round as possible, and so I *could* do with some cash.

Brian continues, "The police will take one look at this and tell our client that he's wasting their time. That they could go to all the trouble of bringing him in—might even get him locked up—but he'll be right out again, back to his usual tricks. That's if they do catch him. It might turn out that he's mentally unstable, and in that case there's nothing we can do to touch him." He swills the remaining whisky in his glass. "And, apart from that, our client has made it very clear that he wishes this hate mailer taken care of *permanently*, and if he's willing to pay for it then who am I to say no?"

"Who are you indeed," I say, glancing over to Jeff who's remained silent throughout this exchange. "And so, why're you calling me in now? Why haven't you just left Jeff on the trail of this before calling me in when I'm needed?"

"It's a question of a logistics," Brian says with a shrug. "We really have no idea where this reprobate is hiding himself, might be up in *Scotland* for all we know." He says 'Scotland' as if it were a swearword. "No, it's better all-round if you two work together, as a team. Jeff finds this bastard and then you take care of him."

I exhale loudly but make no further comment, because I'm nothing if not professional.

I GO DOWN in the lift to the underground car park, getting a fresh waft of Jeff's body odour. I keep myself to myself, feigning a yawn so that he'll think I'm tired or something. In any case he doesn't seem like he's all that keen to make conversation. Just to be polite, I attempt to make something resembling an icebreaker.

"So, how'd you get into this business?"

"Dunno. I've always liked puzzles, investigating things. Started out as a kind of hobby then grew from there."

It seems that's all I'm getting so I take my cue to button my lip.

Jeff owns a battered, boxy estate. I always think of it as a teacher's car—convinced that if I went off to a school I would come across a parking lot full of them. He saunters up to the car and then sticks the keys into the lock. He doesn't even have a wireless fob.

The interior of the car isn't much better. It's just as I'd imagine a private investigator's car—discarded fast food boxes and wrappers, paper cups rolling about in the floor space. He knows how to impress a lady.

Jeff puffs a strand of greasy hair out of his eye then says, "Sorry about the mess. Only got the call from Brian this morning. Didn't think I'd be having company."

I do my best to smile, as I try to find a position for my feet in which I'm not touching any waste. "That's okay," I say.

He grunts then pulls out of the space and drives to the exit of the car park.

The sun beams down on us outside and Jeff rolls down his side window, which has a manual hand crank. I decide to do the same, glad at the prospect of getting some fresh air on the case.

We rumble along the empty road, only a few cars out at this time—early risers like Brian. For a long time we stay in silence. Jeff makes no move to switch on the radio and when I ask whether I can turn it on he informs me that it's broken. I slump back in my seat, feeling a spring coil dig into my spine and feeling the tug of dreariness on my eyes, wishing that I could still be in bed. The hum of the engine and the steady, monotony of Jeff's driving lulls me to sleep.

I wake with Jeff staring right at me. I startle to see him there, hovering over me, wondering how long he's been in that position.

Without the trace of a smile, he says, "We're here."

I rub the heels of my hands against my eyeballs and straighten up in my seat. Out of reflex, I pat the side of my ribcage to find the pistol still there, in its holster. I look out through the windscreen to see a large house—a mansion really. It's painted a powder blue and I can see a balcony growing out of the second storey. The railing is brandished in gold and sparkles in the mid-morning sun.

"Where's here?" I say, feeling the fogginess of sleep still holding my brain in a mire.

"Client's house."

That catches my attention. One of the unwritten rules of my occupation is never to know who's actually behind ordering the hit. Brian prefers that I know as little as possible. Jeff, however, must need to know. So I take this as a nice opportunity to finally have some idea about what's going on—why I've been called upon to kill.

"Who's the client?" I ask, casually.

Jeff studies me and I wonder whether I've overstepped the mark. It might be that Brian has briefed Jeff that I'm to be told as little as possible—when the time comes he's merely to point me in the direction of the target and give me a push. But he casts his eyes back to the house then says, "TV presenter."

"Oh," I say, then, "which one exactly?"

"Sydney Lewis."

Now he's really spoiling me. Of course I know who Sydney Lewis is. He's in his fifties and runs a game show every day on one of the terrestrial channels in the much-coveted three fifteen slot. Being that I spend quite a lot of time at home—when I'm not out killing people—I've seen it quite a few times. It tends to clash with what I dub 'tea and biscuits' o'clock.

The game show consists of two groups of co-workers—four on each team. Their company names are splashed along the front of their desks. The boss is the captain of the team. The format is fairly unspectacular. In turn, Sydney asks each team general knowledge questions and they answer him. Each correct answer means that the team gets a point. At the end of the show, in the event of a tie—which the cynic in me says happens far too regularly for it not to be a fix—the bosses come up against one another and answer questions in a 'sudden death' style. The first to answer correctly when the other answers incorrectly is declared the winner. The winning company receives a special treat—which we, as the viewer, are privy to at the end of following show. This treat consists of a day out somewhere: to a theme park or, in one especially elaborate show, a daytrip to Spain. The hook of this sequence is Sydney's appearance, when he pops up in disguise at some point, grinning—his orange fake tan flawless—to give one of the winning boss a big hug and a kiss on either cheek—hilariously—whether or not it's a man or woman. The game show invariably ends with Sydney standing amongst last week's victorious team as they wave to the viewer through the credit reel while an announcer gently nudges the viewer in the direction of tuning in the next afternoon at the same time: three fifteen.

I take in the mansion with fresh eyes. Sydney lives well, but of course he does. Anyone who gets serious face time on TV must be earning upward of six figures a year—and over the years that all adds up, enough to take out a hefty mortgage in any case. And then there's that generous pension to look forward to. Maybe I've picked the wrong career.

"You ever watch the show?" I say.

A film passes over Jeff's eyes. "When I get the chance."

"And Sydney's got problems with someone sending him hate mail?"

"Uh huh," Jeff says, as he produces a machine—which looks like a chunky walkie-talkie from the eighties—from beneath his seat and taps away at its keypad.

"What's that?"

The machine's screen glows blue and the digits appear on the display. Jeff continues to tap away, entering—for all I can make out—random numbers, one after the other. He finishes whatever technical wizardry he's been performing then says, "I'm dialling into the phone lines, checking up on a system I left out here to scan for all numbers calling the house." He reaches under his seat again and, this time, produces a laptop, which he cranks open and sets down on his knees. He plugs the walkie-talkie device into the laptop with a grey cable and then leaves them both on his lap, his eyes flicking between the two screens. "Just got to boot up the database and then we'll have today's records."

"I thought you'd been on this for days. Don't you already have this hate mailer's number?"

"Nope," Jeff says, "thing is that old Sydney's been a little defensive when it's come to giving us access to his phone, says that there are numbers there that he'd like to keep quiet."

I think about Brian and realise that this is probably a good course of action. From my experience, as one of Brian's clients, it's always better to keep as much of your life secret from him as you can—lest he decide that it's in *his* best interests to share something of yours with another of his clients. Some dizzy blonde might well spell disaster for someone like Sydney who, being in his fifties, must do battle every day to keep brighter, younger things from clinching his sacred, three-fifteen timeslot. Just one scandal in a redtop paper might be enough to ruin his squeaky clean image, the image which brings in those good-hearted old lady viewers. And me.

Jeff taps away at his laptop. "Only gave us the green light last night. So I put it on. Should be a few dozen calls for us if this hate mailer's anything like as persistent as he claims."

Sure enough, when Jeff brings up the database, a series of numbers flashes up on screen. It takes about half a minute before they stop to scroll up. There have been fifty-six calls in the time that Jeff's kept his device monitoring the phone line. He clicks a few buttons and several entries—entries I notice that are all matching—are flagged up in bright yellow.

Jeff claps his hands together. "There we go. We've got our man right there."

"So that's it, then?" I say. "Just have to call up directory enquiries and have them reel off the address?"

"In theory," Jeff says, producing a mobile phone from the chest pocket of his shirt and dialling the number. "But if there's one thing I've learnt scanning the post this guy sends—emails too —it's that he takes care. I've got a feeling that this number won't lead us to this guy's house, or wherever it is that he's calling from, but at least it'll give us somewhere to start looking."

When Jeff gets off the phone with directory enquiries, having noted down the address, we pull out. I turn round in my seat and watch the mansion disappearing round the corner, thinking about Sydney, whether he's really thought out the fact that he's ordered someone dead. Does he believe that it's morally justified? I suppose these sorts of thoughts are the reason I'm not supposed to know who my client is. I might get all judgemental and distracted.

The address is several hours away, off to the east. On the way we stop at a motorway service station and have a silent lunch of fried chicken and chips. I'm already kind of feeling at ease in Jeff's company—almost respecting how he keeps his mouth shut. People who keep their mouths shut are becoming a real novelty these days.

After a quick brush of the teeth, wash of the face and some powdering of my nose, we head on, back to the car park. I notice that Jeff doesn't so much as enter the men's toilets—not even to wash his hands. I'm becoming somewhat obsessed with his lack of personal hygiene and try to tell my brain to just leave it, but that's more easily said than done considering there's not so much as a radio to take my mind off it.

We're well into the late-afternoon glow when Jeff turns off the motorway and leads us along a narrow and curving country lane. We keep on our way, the car's wing mirrors brushing against the overgrown grass verges and the odd squirrel hopping out of our path into the hedgerows. This is kind of the place I've always imagined nutters living—hate mailers—way out in the sticks, too far from anywhere, people frustrated at living miles away and wanting to make some kind of a splash on the wider world. I'm not that convinced by Jeff's claim that this hate mailer is all that clever. In fact, I draw my pistol from its holster and give it a once over, I'm so convinced that I might have cause to use it at any second.

Jeff steers the car round a sheer turn and then eyes the pistol in my hand. "You're going to shoot him, then?"

"That's right."

I wait for him to make some comment as I'm all ready with some response along the lines of me not telling him to do *his* job so he has no business telling me how to do *mine*. But, true to the impression he's already made on me, he remains quiet, not offering his own view. I must confess that I'm starting to like Jeff more and more.

The car rattles along, obviously not used to being in low gear, and a cottage appears on the horizon, out of my side window. A haggard signpost, hanging at an angle from its post by a rusty nail, indicates—in dark-blue hardly legible lettering—the direction to 'Franson Farm House.'

Jeff brings the car to a halt. "This is it," he says.

I peer out my window. A dirt track passes between a pair of dried up fields. It might be that there're in some sort of fallow season or that they're simply neglected, not being a farmer, and having spent my whole life in London, I really have no idea. A whitewashed cottage stands at the end of the lane. It seems crooked, as if it were sinking into the land. And then I realise that it probably is.

"So," I say, slipping my pistol back into its holster, "what's the plan?"

Despite the car being parked, Jeff clings to the steering wheel, squinting as he takes in the cottage. "I reckon we need to have a look round first, get this guy alone and work out whether or not this really is him."

"And how do we do that?"

"Broken down car, that old trick ought to work."

"What's my part in all this?"

"You stay here. You can be my wife."

Repressing the urge to scowl at this suggestion, realising that Jeff really doesn't mean any sort of lecherous offence by it, I nod to him. "You'll give me some sort of signal if you need me?"

"I'll just call out to you. If there's no one there then I'll just return to the car. Got some equipment in the boot that'll be useful for taking a look round the place."

"Okay."

Jeff shrugs out of his seatbelt and gets out of the car. He

wanders up the road and then goes off down the dirt track. It seems to take an age for him to reach the cottage and when he does he's not much more than a blob. I keep my hand resting on my holster, ready to rush out at a moment's notice. I fix my eyes on the front door as he rings the bell.

Jeff just stands there, hands in pockets, waiting. He glances back to me and nods.

I wonder whether this is my cue, but decide to give him a little longer. He said that he would 'call out' if he needed me, and since I've seen no one coming out of the house it's better to stay put for now.

Jeff rings again and again, then he peers into one of the windows. He walks off round the house, then slips out of sight, going round the back.

I look over my shoulder, growing paranoid that someone might come along the road. In a rural place like this I guess that it's common practice to stop and help out strangers in broken down cars, and there wouldn't seem to be any other reason for Jeff's car having stopped out here.

Jeff completes his circuit of the house, emerging on the other side. He rings the bell once again, looks in through one of the windows, hands cupped over the glass, then heads back toward me, where I'm waiting in the car.

Without bothering to update me on the details, he rounds the car and snaps open the boot. He fishes for something out of sight then slams it shut once more. He appears back in front of the car with a beige sports bag hanging from his hand. He glances back at me and jerks his head for me to follow.

I don't need to be asked a second time so I step out of the car and follow him along the dusty path, examining the deep tyre marks which look like they've been made by a tractor. I suppose that must mean the farm's in some sort of use, over the last few months or so anyway, otherwise surely the rain would've washed them out, turned the path into one great mud slick. I almost turn my ankle four or five times, scolding myself over my carelessness each time—I'll be no good to anyone in Accident and Emergency.

We get up to the house and Jeff disappears round back. This time, however, he does give me an instruction. "Stay here, keep a watch out for anyone coming. If they do then play the broken down car game—try to keep them talking as long as possible. I'll hear you talking and wrap up whatever I'm involved with as quickly as I can. When I return I'll feed them some bullshit story about taking a piss round back."

Without giving me an opportunity to raise concerns, he hops to it, beige sports bag and all, leaving me alone out front.

A light breeze blows across the fields. I notice one of those rickety steel windmills spinning away. I've always wondered what they're actually for. The breeze also sends up a haze of dust which gets caught up in my hair and eyes. I spend the next ten minutes combing the knots from my hair while my eyes water away. I'm not made for the country, I've established that much after this brief foray.

The minutes tick by and I think it's been about half an hour since Jeff went off. I wonder whether he might need some help. But I know that I've got to follow his orders—at the moment, with no target for me to take out, we're on his private detective territory. When it comes time to kill then I'll be the one calling the shots. No pun intended.

As I shift my weight from one foot to the other, still feeling a little cramp following the car ride, I hear a distinct, loud *click* from within the cottage. And that's my final warning before the bomb goes off.

3

I JUST ABOUT hit the dirt in time to shield my face from flying pieces of glass and brick. I hear the debris patter to the ground all round me and only about a minute later, with tinnitus clanging in my ears, do I dare look up.

Smoke coils out through the windows of the cottage. Then I think about Jeff, who was still inside at the time of the explosion, and hoik myself up, swaying from side to side as if I've been at Brian's drinks cabinet. When I reach the front door—what was the front door—I peer through the thick black smoke to see Jeff lying face down, arms and legs sprawled.

I bring up my shirt to cover my mouth and nose, then head inside, keeping my head bowed, below the smoke. As I get closer to him I notice the blast marks on the floor. The hate mailer planned on us coming here, drew us here.

I crouch down at Jeff's side and look him over. Blood dampens his face and his body's twitching. I can see that his eyes are closed. Unable to hear my own voice through the shrill ringing in my ears, I say, "Jeff?"

He murmurs something unintelligible.

I grab hold of his shoulders and try to get a grip on him. I'm no medical expert but I'm pretty sure if he's got any hope of recovery he needs to be taken out of the cottage, away from the smoke, as soon as possible. I can't support his weight so I seize hold of his ankle and drag him toward the front door of the cottage. I only allow myself a rest when I've got him halfway along the dirt path, almost back to the car—and only then because it feels like my muscles are on fire. Sweat collects at my temples and rolls down my cheeks in beads.

I kneel down beside Jeff.

His face is covered in ash and his complexion is pallid.

I reach out and touch his cheek. "Jeff? Can you hear me, Jeff?"

He groans and then tries to roll onto his side.

I stop him doing so.

I need to get him some medical help as soon as possible. I glance round the farm, the cottage still smoking away. I can't make out anyone round here—and realise that I'm going to have to take the car, drive him myself to the nearest hospital. But, before I do any of that, being the professional I am, I call up my employer.

As always, whenever I phone Brian with some problem which seems—to me—fairly drastic, he answers in a sombre, almost-bored tone. He reels through the steps I'm to go through: to take Jeff to a private hospital, the address of which he gives me, and then to call him back for further instruction. When I question him as to whether—now that there's a bomber involved—it might be better to call the police in, he just laughs and hangs up. So much for going to the authorities.

I lug Jeff back to the car and, since I now can't get any sort of response from him, I have to haul him into the boot in his reclined position. After I've done all this, he does blink awake, suddenly somewhat lucid. His eyes loll in their sockets. "The bag," he says. "You've got to get the bag."

I glance back at the cottage. More and more black smoke thickens in the air. I let loose a sigh, considering that saving his bacon—making sure that none of his evidence is on the scene for whenever the police turn up here—really falls outside my brief. Then again I suppose, for this job anyway, we're in it together. We're supposed to be working as partners. And so I do the honourable thing and return to the cottage.

As I get there the smoke's billowing out in waves. I keep my head down and look round the doorframe. This place is going to collapse at any second. I enter and skirt round the walls, keeping my eye out for the bag, then I spot it, over on the other side of the room, near to what I believe is the back door. I hunch down and head over. As I do so, I spot a beanie hat and, on impulse, I stoop down to whip it up. I grab hold of the bag—still zipped up and, I presume, replete with its various tools—and then I dash out again, back to the car.

I set the bag down in the boot, alongside Jeff—who's now sitting upright, but hunched over, clutching his ribs. As he watches me back up his stare lingers on my hand. "What's that?"

I examine the beanie cap. It's covered in ash, like myself, Jeff and the bag, but I can make out that it's light-green with a white line round the hem the only design. "Dunno," I say. "It just caught my eye."

Since Jeff seems so interested in it, I hand it over to him, and he takes it from me, turning it over in his hands, like it's some relic from the twelfth century. Private detectives, there's a strange sort.

"You think you're going to hold up okay till we get to the hospital?"

Jeff nods, then hands back the beanie, returning to his grimacing and doubling over. For someone who clearly spends a lot of time alone he knows how to make a scene.

4

W E GET TO THE HOSPITAL round dusk and I drop
Jeff off into the hands of two very capable-looking
doctors, who're already waiting out in the car park, holding a
wheelchair between them. This is what Brian's private medical
plan gets you. So far I've been lucky enough not to have to
sample it. With a parting grimace, Jeff lowers himself into the
wheelchair and the doctors take him away. As he wheels toward
the door of the hospital, he glances back over his shoulder and
mouths *the beanie* to me. Before he gets the chance to elaborate,
he's efficiently wheeled into the building and out of sight.

I presume, following all this, that I've got his car at my
command, so I slip back into the driver's seat and leave the
hospital grounds.

I give Brian another ring, asking him what he wants from me
next—whether he might have a substitute private detective in
mind. He informs me that this is all on me now, that I've got to
do my own legwork. I ask him whether I've got permission to
approach the client—Sydney—and he approves. He doesn't even
make any sort of stink about me knowing who it is. I suppose he's
just as anxious as anybody to get this thing closed up as soon as
possible.

For my next trick, I pull up outside Sydney Lewis's mansion,
unclip my seatbelt and then trot up the path, looking round at the
neighbours' houses which surround me, wondering whether there
might be a photographer sneaking shots from behind a bush
somewhere—all ready for tomorrow's tabloids. At this point a
headline of *Sydney's Young Bit* would come across better than
Sydney Orders Hit on Hate Mailer. Then again I'm sure that Brian
would have a say on anything that gets published. Because if one

of Brian's clients is involved in something an editor of a national newspaper knows to call him up first, for permission.

The front porch consists of a heavy wooden door, painted in the same powder blue—to match the rest of the mansion, of course—and the name of the house: Heresberries, is etched out onto a piece of slate. It all looks very tasteful, which is more than can be said for Sydney Lewis himself. I ring the bell and wait.

Footsteps sound on the other side of the door, someone calls out, and then the door creaks back. I'm confronted with a stony-faced man. He's wearing a tuxedo and has his hair combed off to one side, in a semi-successful comb over. It takes me a moment to realise that this is a butler. An actual butler in the twenty-first century.

He gives me a dour look then says, "May I help you, madam?"

"I need to speak to Sydney."

"Mr Lewis is currently occupied. Perhaps you may permit me to give him a message?"

I attempt to peer round the butler, but the combination of his natural height and, I'm sure, trained stoop, means that the entire doorway is blocked. "It's important and quick. I promise it'll only take a moment."

"Still," the butler says, "Mr Lewis would prefer to hear the subject of the message before permitting a stranger in his house."

"Tell him that I'm here on Brian Mathewson's business."

That does get his attention, finally, and within a couple of minutes I'm sat down on a sprawling, squidgy sofa which groans beneath my slight frame. I'm reduced to waiting for the man, glancing round at the photographs which adorn the walls. All of them feature Sydney at various stages of his career. I can pick out the earliest ones right away, as they're in black and white, as he progresses through the ages the definition of the photographs improves until it's brought up to the present day—with him gurning for the camera, apparently following an especially successful game show. At least the room's theme is consistent.

Sydney saunters in about five minutes later. He's wearing a crimson smoking jacket, the belt of which dangles down at his sides. He has an unlit pipe propped in his mouth. The way his eyes dart about, how his movements are jerky, suggest that he's not quite at ease. He takes a seat on the chair opposite me and meets my eye. "What, what is it? What's happened?"

Hoping that this is an invitation to drop any pretension, that we're safe to speak frankly here, I say, "It's about the hate mailer," then explain what happened at the cottage—the bomb—and then I hand him over the beanie hat.

Sydney twirls the beanie over in his fingers, only realising moments later that it's covered in ash. He wipes his hands on the sides of his chair—I'm sure some poor cleaner will have to scrub that off later. He screws the hat up in his fist and stares at it. After a long period of silence, I decide that it's time for me to step in and move this conversation along.

"Do you recognise the hat?"

"You found this in the cottage?"

I nod.

"Yes, it's familiar. I . . . I remember someone, someone in the front row wearing it."

Slinking back into my amateur private detective mode, I wonder whether I'm supposed to be taking any notes on this. I come to the conclusion that I can remember all the important bits. "And which date was that? Do you remember?"

He purses his lips and hands me back the beanie. He snorts a laugh. "Oh, that person's there every day, never misses a show."

"I see. Can you describe him to me?"

"Chubby, pudgy cheeks"—he puffs out his cheeks and points, as if I might not get the point without the demonstration—"always seems so into it, laughing and smiling along with everything.

Always clapping his hands extra vigorously whenever he's supposed to." He shakes his head. "Just seems so odd, that's all. Sometimes I just don't know who my fans are and who might be pretending. It really throws everything into chaos."

"Hmm," I say, getting an eyeful of his chest hair through the gap in his smoking jacket as he props his elbow up on the armrest of the chair.

Sydney stares me right in the eye—his eyes are a dazzling blue, and I can see how, many, *many*, years ago he got his start in show business. Aside from those sparkling azures, there's an edge to his expression, a ruthlessness. "You should come to the show tomorrow," he says, "that way you can follow him afterwards."

"That doesn't sound a bad idea."

5

TO BE HONEST, it was a bad idea. Did I really expect this nutcase to show up the day after blowing up a cottage out in the sticks? He's onto me, so many steps ahead that I've lost count. As I sit there, on the front row of the studio audience, watching Sydney wrap up the show, I consider how much time I've wasted watching this crap in my life—I'm figuring it at about two days when the woman in charge—with the headset and clipboard—signals that we're no longer recording.

Instantly Sydney's face relaxes, the inane, broad smile giving way to a neutral smirk. Several silver-haired, female audience members bound up to him with pads of paper, pens held out for him to sign. He goes through this ritual before collapsing onto the seat beside mine, as if he's just put in a twelve-hour shift, rather than a solid forty-five minutes.

"No go," he says. "Sorry."

"We'll find him, I'm sure of it."

Sydney straightens the cuffs of his dress shirt. They'll be filming another episode in about half an hour's time. Already I can see a makeup artist bobbing about on the periphery—awaiting her moment to politely dip in and whisk Sydney off for patching up. Sydney flexes his fingers and then cracks his knuckles. "You know, this is the first show I can ever remember this guy going missing."

Again, I think about the cottage yesterday. This guy hasn't managed to keep his identity secret by being clumsy. Of course he wasn't going to turn up.

He sighs. "At least we know who we're talking about now, though."

"You don't keep a record of people who order tickets, do you?"

39

He puckers his lips. "Don't know, maybe. I'd have to ask someone."

Feeling a touch impatient, I say, "Could you, then?"

Sydney collars a near-by stagehand and tells them to get someone called Angela. A matter of seconds later, a mobile phone is brought to him. Apparently a normal occurrence, Sydney takes the phone and holds it to his ear. He only speaks about three words before he passes the phone back to the stage-hand and turns to me. "Yeah, she can get the records."

"Mr Lewis?" someone calls out.

Sydney levers himself up onto his feet. "Well got to go. I never did get your name."

I think about giving him a false one, Hannah is usually my default go-to fake name. But I decide that there's really no point in it. He already knows I'm working for Brian, and with that fact comes a weight of pressure—if he mentions my name to anyone then Brian will dig up some dirt and sink Sydney's career forever.

"Anna," I say. "Anna Harris."

"All right, Anna, good luck in nailing this fool."

I study his words as he walks away from me, into the arms of the relieved makeup artist, and I think about how casual he is with this whole affair. I wonder whether something similar might've happened before. Is this how Sydney Lewis manages all his detractors and wind-up merchants? I know for a fact that it's the first time I've got the call to sort someone out for him. But how do I know that he hasn't had another of Brian's assassins put on a case? Then again, it doesn't really matter because, at the end of the day, he's footing the bill. I'm just the steady hand.

A brunette girl, no more than early-twenties, guides me up several staircases and into a room with a window looking out over the stage floor. There're seemingly hundreds of plastic buttons and levers on a tilted control panel. A couple of men with bulging guts and bald heads—one so hardly distinguishable from the other that I wonder if they might be identical twins—twiddle away at the switches, deeply concentrating on their work. The air stinks of coffee and body odour, which I suppose is par for the course when it comes to television. That sensory detail reminds me of Jeff and I wonder think whether I should pop into the hospital, pay him a visit once I've taken care of this hate mailer. For one thing I have to return his car.

The brunette girl it turns out is called Angela. I don't establish this by way of any formal introduction, but because one of the bald operators shouts out, "Angie!" to her.

Angela leaves me with a computer screen, a database of names and addresses. All those who have booked tickets to watch Sydney Lewis live and in the flesh. I make a mental note that there're far more nutters in the world than I had ever accounted for before. Despite my casual watching of his show, at least I've never had the urge to actually book a ticket, come down here to the studio. And I should be the prime audience for such a thing given the amount of weekday afternoons I have free.

I scan through the list, using the seat number which Sydney pointed out to me—the one on which the man would sit. As I go through the names I see that each week there's a different name registered for that particular seat. Of course there is. That doesn't detract from my belief that it's the same guy, over and over again. I make a note of all the names—on a fresh notepad I bought just this morning for my fledgling career as private detective—and then I buck out of the room, thanking Angela as I go.

Back downstairs, I check in with Brian, bring him up to speed on the whole affair. I tell him that I'm basically onto a bit of a cold trail and that I believe Jeff might be able to shed some light on the matter—also alluding to the fact that I need to return Jeff's car. Brian agrees to sort me out with a new set of wheels from his motor pool, and arranges to have the car brought out to the hospital to coincide with my visit. From what he's heard on

Jeff's condition he should be getting discharged later today. Brian claims he would go out there himself to be there to congratulate Jeff on his recovery . . . but, he's got more important things to do than see that seedy, middle-aged private detectives are back on their feet.

6

THIS TIME, approaching the hospital with a sense of relative calm, I have the opportunity to absorb the scenery. The driveway which leads up to the main entrance, where I dropped Jeff off the day before, is surrounded on all sides by conifers. They're all a vibrant green, not a browned or yellow patch in sight. There are two marble statues of horses standing to either side of the main entrance. I wonder if that's something patients—even rich patients—notice upon being admitted here. I suppose with whatever, surely extortionate, fee they charge here means they can't afford to take chances.

I park up and then head to the reception desk, which is lined with gold paint. A receptionist with pink-painted nails rattles her fingertips along a keyboard, her eyes flickering between the screen and whatever it is that she's copying.

When I strut up to the desk she immediately looks up, plastering on a smile and showing off rows of fine, white teeth. I notice that her top is fairly low cut, giving an ample view of her not-unsubstantial cleavage. "Here to visit Jeffrey," I say.

She beams back. "Have you got a surname?"

"No, I don't," I say, then think the matter over before adding, "I work for Brian Mathewson."

Without missing a beat, she taps keys, clicks the mouse a couple of times then says, "Room Forty-Three A. Fourth floor. Lift's just on your right."

"Thanks," I say, relishing the fact that Brian's name itself springs open doors.

I pad along the corridor reading off the room labels. I'm carrying a box of chocolates in my hand, taking care not to crush them. I have a tendency to grip hard. When I turn the corner, headed into number forty-three, I stumble across a grey-haired nurse plumping pillows of a one-bed room then smoothing out a snow-white bed sheet.

"Um," I say, "I'm looking for Jeffrey."

She startles, apparently not having noticed me coming in. "'Jeffrey?'"

"Yes, the patient who was in this room."

"Oh," she says. "He was discharged this morning. Bruised ribs, nothing serious. Doctor just wanted to keep him overnight to check he wasn't suffering any internal bleeding."

I stand there thinking the matter over. I wonder why Brian hadn't thought to tell me that Jeff had been discharged, he might've saved my trip here. Then I realise that the reason Brian hasn't told me is because he didn't know either. Just at that second, my mobile vibrates in my pocket. I slip it out, see it's Brian and hold it to my ear.

"Excuse me," the nurse says. "You can't use telephones in the building."

"It's Brian Mathewson."

Her mouth forms an 'oh' shape and she skittles out of the room.

I don't think I'm ever going to get tired of those magic words.

"Anna?" Brian says.

"Expecting someone else?"

"It's Sydney Lewis. He just called."

"What does he want?"

"He says that someone's just broken into his house."

Without thinking Brian's reply through fully, I'm already running. I dash down the stairs, and back into the reception. All this time Brian's been blabbering away about something or other. When I get down to the car park, I say, "Whereabouts is the motor pool car?"

"It's a way off," Brian says. "It just left the lot."

"What should I do?"

For the first time during our conversation a note of tension enters Brian's voice. "Christ, woman, just take Jeff's car. He's not going to care. We can work all that out later. First priority's to the client, yeah?"

"Right," I say, barrelling toward the car, keys already in hand. "I'll give you another call when I get to the house."

"Take care," Brian says, before hanging up.

7

EVERYTHING'S QUIET when I pull up outside Sydney's mansion—horror film quiet. The sun's sinking down below the rooftops, catching the leaves of the trees in a tangerine sparkle as it goes. This is the dead time after everyone's got home, either having dinner or sprawled out on the sofa watching TV. I cut the engine and slip the keys out of the ignition. I look the house over. Everything looks normal enough.

I feel for my gun and then fit a silencer. This isn't the best neighbourhood to go firing off bullets. I get out and round the car, then head up the driveway, passing a well-polished, sea-blue car in the driveway. I know next to nothing about cars, but it looks old and rustic—like it's cost Sydney a fair few game show fees. I eye the front door and decide that it's perhaps not the best point of entry, so I slip open the latch on the back gate and sidle up alongside the house before emerging into the garden. Breaking into rich people's houses really shouldn't be this easy.

I step out onto the patio, taking a quick look at the plush lawn —sparing a thought for the gardener who surely has to get down on his knees with a pair of nail scissors, magnifying glass and a ruler. I approach the French doors round the back and try to slide them open. They're locked. I eye the mechanism on the other side of the glass—the key conveniently dangling down from it. I glance round, take a brief look inside, to see if the intruder's anywhere in sight, and then I hammer my fist against the glass.

It shatters and glass tinkles round my feet.

Working quickly, knowing that the sound's going to attract quite a bit of neighbourly interest, if not interest from the occupants of the house, I reach through the jagged glass, turn the key and slide the door back.

As I set foot on the mat just inside, a droplet of blood splatters onto the wooden floor. I inspect my hand, realising I cut it on the glass. I check it out for any lingering fragments and, not seeing any, suck at the wound, shifting the gun to my weaker left hand.

I listen for any sound in the house, but the whole place is deathly quiet. That means one of two things. One, that there's no one in or, two, the more likely, that I've been heard and the occupants are keeping quiet so that I'll think the place is empty.

With that thought on my mind, I remain wary as I stalk along, keeping my back flat against the wall so that no one will be able to sneak up on me. As I round the corner, enter a kitchen, I notice the broken window. That's where the intruder got in. It takes me a few beats to notice the body prostrate on the tiled floor. The butler.

His head lies in a pool of blood. From the wound on his head I can see that he's been struck repeatedly with a blunt object. He probably confronted the intruder, told him that he'd have to kill him before getting to his master, like a faithful dog. Poor bastard.

I put my condolences for the late butler to one side and continue on through the house.

Only when I reach the hall do I get the hint of an inhabitant. I get to the bottom step and hear the distinct sound of heavy breathing coming from upstairs. I raise my pistol and grip tighter, ready to confront whoever it is up there.

I climb the stairs with my pistol pointing to the floor, so as not to blow a hole in anyone I don't want to blow a hole in. I reach the top step before the first bullet flies, whistling right by my ear and plunging into the wall.

I leap forward, landing in a forward roll, and find cover in a room. I wait there, back to the wall, listening for any sound of footsteps. Not hearing any, I risk a glance round the corner.

Crack.

Another bullet flies, missing my forehead by no more than an inch. Whoever this person is they have no qualms about not using a silencer in this residential area—which demotes them to an amateur in my book. But a *dangerous* amateur, nonetheless.

My shoulders stiffen as I try to get my plan of action straight. The way things are at the moment this guy's got me pinned down in this room. I look to my right and see the window there. I think about the narrow window ledge, which I might be able to sidle along. Not without alerting the gunman, I won't. Before I get a chance to think of a second option, the gunman speaks.

"Anna?"

That voice, it's familiar. Another second and I know just who it is. I tilt my head in the direction of the landing. "Jeff? What the hell are you doing?"

Jeff stays quiet then says, "I'm the hate mailer, in case you hadn't guessed."

My mind floods and I think over our interactions in the past twenty-four hours. How could he be? It can't be right.

Jeff sniffles, like he's got a cold. "I set up that bomb to throw you off the trail. I've been plaguing my friend Sydney here for months now. I even managed to convince the great Brian Math-ewson to take me on."

"But . . . why?"

"I enjoy it," he says.

I can sense that fanlike tone in his voice, the one which yearns for something or someone to cling to, something to make a life more than a mere mediocrity. And I actually believe him.

"And you're going to kill him?" I say.

"Yes," Jeff replies. "Don't you see? It's all part of the game—the endgame. It has to work like this, *this* is the natural conclu-sion. He wanted to kill me, but I got to him first. Isn't that ironic?"

"Let's talk this through, Jeff, okay? There's no way out of this for you if you kill Sydney Lewis. That's not what Brian employed you to do. He won't protect you when the police come knocking."

"Oh, don't think that I don't know that."

"Then you just want to destroy yourself?"

"It seems that there's no other choice really. Not now."

How're you supposed to reason with a deranged maniac? Is there any way to do it, any way to work out what it is that they want? Maybe that's the hard part—that all they want they already have, ready to throttle their victim to death.

The only way that I'm going to get a chance here is to keep him talking. If I manage that then maybe he'll present me with an opportunity. I curl my finger round the trigger and say, "But that bomb, what did you put in it?"

"Does it really matter? I just made sure that there wasn't anything that would cause lasting damage. Just a big bang and lots of smoke."

"You must be pissed off that I managed to get here so quickly, before you had a chance to kill Sydney."

"No," he says, "it's just another obstacle. Nothing can prevent me from going through with it."

"Go on, then," I say. "Go through with it."

There's a long silence.

I sit there with bated breath knowing that I'm not going to get another chance. This is my chance to call his bluff. I won't have another opportunity. I squeeze my eyes shut and when I open them again I've flipped the Kill Switch—I'm feeling cold-blooded, and single-minded. I leap round the corner, landing on my side and pick out Jeff's plump forehead. I shoot.

His head jerks back and his body tumbles.

Sydney, previously in his grip, stumbles forward and lands face down on the landing carpet. He crawls away on his elbows, panting and sweating.

I get to my feet, keeping the gun fixed on Jeff's fallen body, but he's not getting up, I've killed him. I step through his sentient legs and stoop to snatch up the gun lying in his lifeless fingers. I pocket it and then glance back at Sydney. "You might want to invest in some more robust security round here. Place's got more holes than a rat's nest."

Sydney cowers up against a radiator as if he might be my next target.

8

POLICE STREAM THROUGH the property while I stand off to one side. Already about five of them have come up to me, demanding to know who I am—and each time I've fobbed them off by telling them to speak to Brian Mathewson. Eventually word gets round and I'm left in peace, watching the men cart the bodies—Jeff and the butler—out of the house to the waiting ambulances.

Brian arrives on the scene a little after. He gives the supervising office a firm handshake, patting him on the upper-arm, before he heads over to me. He kisses me on both cheeks. His breath has the warm odour of whisky on it. "Bit of a sticky one this, wasn't it?"

"You could say that," I say, watching the supervising police officer steering a forensic officer away from the staircase, arm round his shoulders, as if he were a coach giving advice to one of his players.

"Still," Brian says, with a grin. "I knew you'd come through it. You always do."

"You know how to tell a girl exactly what she wants to hear."

He gestures to the front door, and his waiting car—a stretch limo with tinted windows.

After waving goodbye to a bewildered Sydney, who stands on the front doorstep with a foil blanket round his shoulders, Brian ushers me into the back seat of the limo and closes the door. Once inside, sitting on the plumped up leather seats, each of us with a glass of champagne—mine non-alcoholic, as Brian knows I like it—he turns to me, holding up his glass. "To bigger and better things."

I strain to smile then chink my glass against his.

He replaces his glass of champagne in its holder in the door.

I do the same then say, "There's one thing bothering me, if I'm honest."

"You can always be honest with me, my dear."

"Right," I say, clutching the stem of my glass. "It's just that Jeff said, before I shot him, that he'd managed to convince you to take him on—to hire him as a private detective."

"He did, did he?"

"Yes."

"And what about it?"

"Well, I guess I just wanted to know"—I search for the appropriate phrasing, not wanting to deliberately insult my employer —"did you make an . . . error of judgement in employing him?"

Brian simmers into silence. The car rumbles round us, takes corners at breakneck speed, and I get to thinking that Brian's forgotten all about my question—or worse, he's found my question so insulting, such a mark of disrespect, that he's going to give me the silent treatment. All at once I'm fearing for my job, worrying that he might turn me into his police friends, as I've always thought he would after I'd finished working for him. But then, long after I'm sure he's forgotten my question, he turns to me and says, "Sydney, yes, Sydney. He's been getting a bit big for his boots lately. At least," Brian says, examining his champagne, "he's decided that I'm little more than an assassin agency, ready to put out a hit on every Tom, Dick and Harry that crops up insulting him—sending him rude letters or making prank phone calls." He looks at me with steel in his eyes. "I knew about Jeff, don't you think I didn't do a background check? I knew that he wasn't a private detective, that was all guff, quite frankly—no, I suppose, in employing Jeff, I was somewhat hoping that a situation like this one might crop up, something to make him think twice before picking up that phone again."

"So you knew he was dangerous—that you were putting me in danger?"

"Isn't that why I pay you so well?"

I don't suppose I can argue with that.

"No," he says, "I trusted that you would keep Sydney safe from any sort of harm—God forbid that I lose a well-paying client, even if he's got a bad case of tail-shaking-dog—and, while I did have a few doubts at the end, that unfortunate disparity what with you at the hospital and with Jeff breaking into the house, it all turned out for the best."

"What about the butler?"

"Collateral damage."

My skin chills. I've always felt uncomfortable with the way that Brian considers human life, the lack of value he places on it. Without fail, after every hit, I go through mental torment, feeling terrible about what I've done. I wonder if, deep down, Brian feels something similar. But that's a discussion well outside the employer-employee framework, so I don't even consider asking.

Brian reaches for his champagne, gives me the sliver of a smirk then raises the glass to his lips. "Chin, chin."

BLOOD. SNOW.

1

I GUESS that I should've been honoured for my invitation to Brian Mathewson's Annual Christmas Party. After all, it's not every day that a humble employer sends his most trusted assassin an invite to a very public occasion. But, then again, I would've been a fool to think that it was a gesture of kindness. Nope, that wasn't it at all.

Brian wanted someone dead.

So that's why I stand here in Function Room Three.

Brian assures me this is the *largest* function room of Mathewson Media, though I can't say the name is all that catchy, not as catchy as Function Room One or Two, in any case.

Anyway, I've got a flute of nicely chilled orange juice in hand the colour of which at least seems to go *some* way to complimenting the dark-blue, shimmery, silk number which I'm wearing for the evening.

When Brian wants something done, he orders it done properly.

So, not two hours ago, I opened my front door a very smart-looking man, dressed in a tuxedo, and sporting several dresses all wrapped in sheaths that put me in mind of body bags . . . or something like that.

The man was about in his seventies, and had those birdlike features of older men. He was obviously still trying to cling to the rest of his flimsy, grey bird nest that was the remains of his hair.

No wigs for him.

Still, his sense of style wasn't anything to be brought into question.

But, then again, I've never been all that great with anything involving fashion.

In fact, I'd sooner murder fashion than embrace it.

He was the one who picked out the dress for me, and the matching shoes, and the handbag which now dangles from the crook of my other arm . . . the arm that's not hauling the flute of orange juice.

. . . Oh, and he was also the one that gave me this nifty little handgun: a short, snub-nosed thing.

But I only really found that *after* he'd handed me the handbag, slipped away to the car purring to itself, waiting on the curb.

I really have no idea how to blend in here, which probably means that I'm doing a good job.

You see, the main issue with the sorts that Brian hangs out with is that they all tend to be either celebrities or people in great power, and then there are those who are sitting somewhere in between: either on the way up or on the way down— and the ones most likely to want to take out an assassin's services.

Anyway, the bottom line about these functions, and the people they attract, is that *everyone* is doing their very best to stand out, to be the loudest voice, to have the most garish laugh and . . . with those who are *really* struggling . . . be the one who makes the *worst* drunken spectacle of themselves.

I'm not going to be the latter at least.

I'm teetotal.

. . . Or so goes the theory.

But I really can't get away from that itchy feeling I get, right beneath my skin, the way that these kinds of do's really make me feel uncomfortable.

Maybe it's the size of the room. The way that it seems about five or six storeys up to the towering, corniced ceiling. Or perhaps it's the way that *everything* appears to be carved out of marble . . . and polished-up within an inch of its life.

It might just be the red, velvety—can't be *real* velvet, surely?

—carpet that runs about the whole place as if it was as cheap as toilet paper.

Or, at least, the toilet paper that *I* buy.

A string quartet squeaks about over in the corner of the place, so much as Function Room Three can be said to *have* corners, seeing as it's pretty much a circular affair.

They're playing something classical, which is just about as far as my musical knowledge stretches.

The air absolutely *reeks* of both perfume and cologne.

There are so many different odours, each and every one of them screaming *Look at me!* that I'm really having a tough time so much as separating each one.

I wonder if some scientist, somewhere, might've invented a sort of screen that can see odours, and then think about just what *this* room might look like through it.

No doubt nuclear green puffs all over the place.

I take a sip of my orange juice.

Finally.

Just enough to catch the spike at the end of it. To know that it's been laced with vodka.

I catch the eye of a passing waitress—dressed in a simple black-and-white, and not a *little* degrading, maid's uniform.

She seems well practised, and receives my full flute of orange juice on her silver tray. She swerves on through the crowd: through the cummerbunds and high heels, striving for the entrance on the other side of the room marked out only as: *Kitchen Access*.

That leaves me with nothing to do with my hands.

Nothing except shift the weight of my handbag in the crook of my arm.

Feel the gun that's nestled inside.

I turn my mind to the hit.

And when it's supposed to happen.

Three in the morning, Brian said. When no one's expecting it.

When everyone's too drunk to notice or—more importantly —*remember* anyone.

Just as I'm thinking about dashing to the little girl's room for the fourth time that night—not because I have any sort of a bladder complaint, but because I can't handle this amount of colour and noise and false *enthusiasm* for longer than fifteen-minute-at-a-time doses—I feel a light touch on my shoulder.

When I turn around, I see Brian standing there.

He's grinning.

His cheeks are rosy.

Drunk, no doubt.

Like just about always . . . and yet, at the same time, I really don't think that I've ever seen Brian *really* drunk, not so much that he gives anything away—some days I've speculated as to whether Brian might be playing up a persona: the absent-minded alcoholic so that he might lure people into his trap, learn their secrets while they learn none of his.

Or maybe he simply wields so much power that, really, he can act however he damn pleases and not be worried about *anyone* coming after him.

His lush, dark-brown hair is swished off into a side part-ing. Like everyone else in the room, he is wearing a tuxedo, and I see that he's wearing a fluorescent-yellow—not at all Christmassy—bowtie and cummerbund, adhering to the theme of 'loud dress' . . . and, quite amazingly, he even seems to have surpassed a great many of the invitees standing in this room.

I look about Brian, on instinct, thinking that maybe he has someone—his wife?—on his arm. But I see that he has no one. He has approached me all on his own.

He continues to grin like a drunk idiot. He grips my shoulder just a little too tight . . . at least for my comfort in this employer-employee relationship we've got going on here.

"Lovely to see you here," he says, a slight slur to his words.

I smile back at him weakly. "Pleasure to make it."

He grins even wider, and his cheeks seem to become more rosy with blood. "You haven't got a drink."

The way he phrases it, it's not a question at all.

Just a statement.

But certainly a *pointed* one.

I shake my head. "Juice has been spiked."

Brian latches his mouth open wide, brings an open hand up to his forehead, and slaps it out of mock despair. "Oh, goodness, that's *right!* You don't drink."

I keep quiet, look beyond Brian, to the door of the room.

Just as I do, I see a couple swagger on in.

'Swagger?' . . . Yes, that's *exactly* the right word.

I recognise them right away, of course: Grant Flowercut and Jimsy Earthheart.

Just their names alone make me want to puke.

Actors.

Americans.

Both of them.

Before they had their overblown, celebrity wedding they had different names. But, from what I've read in my gossip mags, they decided, for some undisclosed—or *unfathomable*—spiritual reason to rechristen one another.

And while I can understand a gal not wanting to take her husband's name—I never took *my* ex-husband's, after all—I think you need to draw a line somewhere.

And I think if you have 'spiritual advisor,' or words to that effect, anywhere close to your list of wedding expenses you might be better served being taken outside and shot at dawn . . . just my opinion, of course.

Perhaps Brian has been watching me the entire time. Or maybe he snatched a quick glance over his shoulder to check. But it's now that he leans into me and says, "Grant Flowercut."

I feel my stomach crunch in on itself, and suddenly I wonder if I made the right choice to send back my spiked orange juice.

2

BRIAN leaves me alone soon after.

I wonder if I should be trembling.

If I should be *just a little* apprehensive about what I'm about to do.

After all, Grant Flowercut is A List . . . very much so . . . his adoring, lady wife too.

But if Brian says he's got to die, then who am I to complain?

When I check the large minimalist clock up on the wall—minimalist because it's my way of saying it doesn't have any numbers—I see that we're approaching midnight.

These celebrity types are all the same.

Another of their competitions.

Who can arrive the latest?

Make the biggest scene?

Cause the biggest splash?

Grant and Jimsy win tonight's round . . .

I shift along with the crowd, not really sure what I'm going to do to kill time till I . . . well, have to get to *killing* . . .

The stench of perfume seems to get stickier in the air. And the champagne—spiked orange juice too—seems to be flowing pretty much without stopping.

I have to admit that I'm feeling just a little queasy at this whole thing.

And I'm looking forwards to getting back into my bed tonight.

Tucking myself up.

This thing done.

Pretty much as soon as Grant and Jimsy arrive to the room, I notice a whole swell of people forming up around them, all of them with those same eager, smiling-too-hard faces, apparently wanting to please them.

Grant and Jimsy both assume a standard expression.

Their eyes crease into slits.

Their mouths make inroads on their cheekbones.

And their arms remain crooked at ragged angles, both of them holding their flutes of champagne tight to their chests as if that's what these vultures really want.

But even I know that's *not* what they want.

No, these people—the people jostling the two actors—they want to get close to Fame, they want to experience that glow no doubt coming off them, to know what it really is to meet someone transported from the big screen to the little real world.

Okay, I have to admit that I do feel *just a little* fizzle through my blood at the prospect of seeing them here. Live in the flesh. But that doesn't compare to the sensation of my handbag.

And the weight of the gun nestled inside of it.

I hang back some more, keeping myself close to one of the elaborate, white plaster walls. As I'm staring at Grant and Jimsy, I accidently catch the eye of one of the waiters. He gives me one of those curt—*professional*—smiles, and I notice him swaggering on over towards me.

That silver tray of his twinkling in the yellow light from the chandelier that hangs over our heads.

And just like that he's standing before me.

A whole tray of champagne glasses nestled there.

The bubbles twinkling away in the light.

He gives me another thick smile then lowers the tray slightly, brings it just about level with my elbow—perhaps a trick they all get taught in waiter school: make the guest feel comfortable, make sure you're approachable, totally *non*-threatening.

In a way that's just what my job description is.

Right till it's the moment to strike, that is.

Though I want to tell him that I don't drink, that he doesn't need to offer me champagne, he leans into me, his voice gruffer than I expected, more worn in than his buzz-cut blond hair—and his youthful, wrinkle-free features—suggest.

"Room Forty-Six C," he says, and then backs up again.

When I breathe in, I catch a distinct waft of peppercorn, and only then realise that it's the waiter's cologne.

For a few seconds it strikes me as weird—a *really* weird odour.

But, after another few moments, I kind of get used to it, and I start thinking about it as a *warm* and *reassuring* smell.

Actually, truth be told, it sends just a little tremble of hunger through my gut.

To be honest, I thought that there'd be something a little more substantial at a buffet put on by Brian Mathewson than some wafer-thin salmon slavered over wholemeal crackers.

Then again, I guess most guests didn't come for the food.

They came for the *connections*.

The blond waiter gives me another light smile, nods to his tray of drinks, and I realise I'm not going to have the option of *not* taking one.

So I snatch the stem of one of the flutes of champagne.

The waiter ducks away, that same smile smeared all over his lips.

As he walks with his back towards me, I can't help but notice how well those jet-black trousers of his fit snug up against his rock-hard buttocks.

I have to remind myself that I'm here for *business, not pleasure*.

And then I remind myself that Brian Mathewson has no way of reading my thoughts.

Not that I *know of*, anyway.

3

THE PARTY boils down to its constituent elements.

Grant and Jimsy slip off somewhere . . . though I keep my cool, remind myself about just what the waiter said to me, that my interests lie in Room Forty-Six C.

Brian slips out too, and without wishing me Goodbye.

Then again, I suppose that manners might tumble down the list since I'm the one who's going to kill according to his orders . . . probably for the best that he gives me a wide berth even if this *is* his building.

I watch on as the hulking masses of muscles—the bouncers—wander in to kindly help haul out several dozen of Brian's guests who have ended up the worse for wear.

What strikes me as amazing is the way that, though these people have obviously had far too much to drink—are totally out of control—no one pukes up at all.

Not in Function Room Three.

Sure, there's a lot of staggering, lots of drunken blabbering, wives and girlfriends generally looking on with cross expressions on their faces, arms folded over their chests.

But that's it.

And I wonder if this might just be *another* act.

Another competition that I really have no idea of at all.

I only realise that I've brought my flute of champagne up to my mouth when I feel the cool glass touching my lower lip, and feel those bubbles jostling to get up my nostrils.

I put my still-full, untouched flute of champagne down on a cornice, just a few paces away from a collapsed forty-something man who has one arm flailing out over his stomach, the other wrapped back, lying on the red carpet, behind his head.

Only as I shift my way towards the staircase, do I notice the bald-headed bouncer headed my way, apparently intending to help this gentleman to the door of Mathewson Media—and no doubt into a cab too.

As the bouncer approaches me, I see the slight look of weariness attached to his eyes, and I look to his full, purply lips. "You with him?" he asks.

I shake my head.

He takes another few steps. Up to the prostrate man. Then, squatting down with a practised motion—surely one that he's perfected in some gym *somewhere*—he shovels the man up in his arms, and begins to cart him towards the exit of Function Room Three.

Over his shoulder, as he goes, the bouncer says, "Party's winding down, gonna start chucking out pretty soon."

And that—I think—is the cue for me to get moving towards Room Forty-Six C.

4

I WATCH the bouncer slip around the doorway, and then I head for the stairs which lead upwards. There's no one standing there—why does there need to be? Brian's got the entire setup wired for sound and video, no doubt.

I do bet there're twice as many security staff tucked away in some unknown nook or crevice of Mathewson Media who're watching a whole wall of CCTV footage.

Who've got the entire building covered—top to bottom.

I push on through a weighty—oak?—door, and emerge into a corridor.

The lighting is a little dim, not much more than a slight orange glow, and I wonder if Brian maybe has one of those fancy systems where the interior lights emulate night and day . . . or something like that.

I shift on through that corridor, and out through another.

After two or three more flights of stairs, I reach a floor . . . I really have no idea *which* floor seeing as to get to Function Room Three in the first place I must've had to climb at least half a dozen flights of stairs.

But I do know that this is the floor with *those* numbers.

With the number that the waiter gave me.

How do I recall that number so readily—know *exactly* which room it indicates?

Because Room Forty-Six C is where me and Brian met, where he brought me in for what, for want of a better term, was my interview.

I keep my pace even and swift, pacing along the thinner carpet. In the dim orange glow of the lights, I can see that it's either a pale blue or a grey shade. The sharp stench of carpet shampoo clings to the corridor, and it makes my mouth feel even drier.

Sends a slight pang to the pit of my stomach.

When I step on *this* carpet, I can feel the heavy-duty cement —or whatever it is that holds this building together—through the soles of my shoes.

I make as little sound as I can—glad that my heels don't make that giveaway *clack-clack* that they seem to make just about everywhere else.

Just another reason to hate heels.

As I bring the door into sight, that number: Forty-Six C, I reach for my handbag.

Fumble the zip.

Finally feel it draw back, and bring the mouth of the handbag gaping open.

To reveal my miniscule gun nestled inside.

I look over my shoulder, then check up ahead of me.

I'm standing in front of the door now.

This is the moment of truth.

. . . If I wanted—if I *really* wanted—I could just back up the hall, head back down to Function Room Three, and then stride my merry way on out of Mathewson Media.

I could be back home within the hour.

All of this forgotten.

Till Brian's call on Monday, of course, him wanting to know just what happened.

Why I called off the hit.

Nerves, I know on instinct, isn't an excuse for an assassin.

So, taking down a deep breath, right to the very pit of my lungs, I hold the gun to the ceiling and then reach out for the brass doorknob.

5

I T'S DARK INSIDE—I mean, totally *black.*
  I can't see anything at all.

The blinds are drawn so no light gets in from the outside—not even the dribbling, steady glow of the streetlamps.

I draw a quick breath.

Another.

Feel my pulse quicken.

I try to peel back the darkness as fast as I can.

But I can't.

The darkness is just *too* complete.

Any second I'm expecting someone to tell me to drop my gun, for me to surrender myself. I wonder in a dizzy moment if —*maybe*—this might be some kind of an ambush.

Then I realise that I'm just being paranoid.

Yeah, that's right.

Paranoid.

When no voice comes, I carefully step about the darkened room, trying to piece it back together in my mind's eye—to remind myself of how it vaguely is.

I remember the simple four—or were there *five?*—chairs all set about the fairly cheap-looking, laminate wooden table.

A boxy room.

Only just about big enough to fit those four, or five, chairs.

Those four or five *people.*

I sat here at this table: Brian Mathewson, my contact AA, and a pair of Brian's most trusted aides, neither of which I've seen again in all my years of working with him.

Sometimes, when I'm lying in bed at night, staring up at the ceiling, unable to sleep, I wonder just who that man and woman —both in their fifties or so, *Brian's* age—really were.

. . . It'd probably make for a shorter list if I simply thought over what I *haven't* imagined them being.

I tread about the room, still being careful not to make a sound.

Nothing at all.

No one's here.

Just me.

No one else.

And it's right then that I hear the voices drifting along the corridor.

That rumbling laugh that I've heard maybe a dozen times before.

That girly laugh . . . only difference is that whenever I've heard it before it's always been up on a big screen, or on a DVD . . . and whereas before it kind of had a slight jubilatory effect on me, now it sends a tingle rushing up my spine.

Jimsy Earthheart's laugh.

I duck down behind a filing cabinet.

And wait.

6

I LISTEN for the footsteps getting louder. Drawing closer to the door.

I hold my breath like a little girl playing hide-and-seek—one who's afraid of getting caught.

They come closer still.

I expect the doorknob to turn at any moment.

For Grant Flowercut and Jimsy Earthheart to come strolling in.

Flipping the lights as they go.

Washing the place in that clean, sterile *fluorescent* office light.

Right at the moment when the sound of their footsteps is loudest, I listen in to them growing quieter again. Listen to them *moving away* from Room Forty-Six C.

Shuffling on, along the corridor.

For a second I'm sure that someone has made a mistake. That someone has made a *big* slip with the details. And then I wonder if, maybe, this is different.

If this might really be some sort of a setup.

If this *was* planned all along.

Then I reach the most likely conclusion yet.

The one that *I'm sure* is the one in Brian's mind.

He expects me to hunt.

To track them down.

And kill them.

7

I COUNT their steps away from the door to bide my time—twenty—and I think about how I'm going to do it, how I'm going to make sure, one hundred per cent, that I go through with my task as cleanly and efficiently as possible—thirty—because if there's one thing I've built up with Brian, one thing that I've got down at this point in time, it's a reputation for *not* messing stuff up, though I guess that there's *always* a first time.

Forty.

The footsteps stop.

I cock my head back.

Grip tight to the gun.

Still hold it pointed up to the ceiling.

My heart ticks by in my eardrums.

I do my best to flip my kill switch.

To blank out all other thoughts from my mind.

And focus on the task at hand.

That done, I unfold myself out of my crouch and reach for the doorknob.

8

THEY'RE GONE by the time I peep out into the corridor. Disappeared from view.

But I know just how to find them.

Forty paces.

That's where they are.

That'll lead me right to them.

I shift along the corridor, keeping myself close by the wall as if it might keep them from spotting me if they decide to glance back over their shoulders.

No, my best bet, if they were to spot me, would be to hide the gun.

There'd be no way of hiding myself.

I count out the paces.

Ten.

Fifteen.

Twenty.

Twenty-five.

Thirty.

Thirty-five.

. . . I stop.

Feel my heart tickling my throat.

I have the urge to cough, but I refuse to give in.

I must be silent.

And deadly.

I can hear their voices.

Their *tittering* voices.

Just beyond the door here.

I can't quite make out the number in the light from the hallway.

But I guess that it really doesn't matter.

I know *just* where they are.

So, with a final, deep, cleansing breath, I curl my fingers into a fist and rap my knuckles against the wood of the door.

Then I take a few steps back till I feel my shoulders press up against the wall behind me.

9

A T FIRST it feels like they haven't heard me at all.
I think about knocking again.

I realise that I'm shaking now—all over.

I tell myself to snap out of it.

I squeeze the grip of the gun tighter.

My heart drums in my ears, and I can taste blood in my mouth.

The footsteps continue to shuffle towards the door.

Then I watch the doorknob jiggle a little in its place.

Then turn.

The door draws back.

Jimsy Earthheart stands there.

Looking slightly bemused.

Her eyes alive with alcohol.

She glances from one side, then to the next.

Finally she locks her glance back onto me.

Her mouth parts, in question, or out of shock?

I know what I have to do.

I know what I *need* to do now.

I raise the gun.

Squeeze the trigger.

Shoot her square in the chest.

10

S HE STAGGERS BACK.

I feel more assured now.

Less of the shaking going on.

I take a step forwards.

Another one.

Then another.

I keep the gun pointed at her.

The gunshot seems to hang in the air, almost bouncing back from the walls of the corridor. I wait for my moment. Know that the *real* target will soon make an appearance.

He was the reason that Jimsy had to die.

As she lets loose a gargle as the blood swills into her chest, I step over her body.

I feel her limp hand snatch at the hem of my dress.

But she can't grip at all—has no strength to do so.

I pass over her, step into the room.

11

UNLIKE Room Forty-Six C, the blinds are all pulled up, and the light orange glow from the streetlamps below gets into the room.

The room, it turns out, is pretty much a carbon copy of Room Forty-Six C other than the opened blinds here.

Small, a little boxy, just enough space for the table and four or five chairs.

I see him, pretty much straightaway, sitting in one of the chairs, his back to me, apparently staring out the window, looking down into the street outside.

I wait out the time.

Count the seconds as they tick on by.

Try to keep my cool, try to keep my palms from getting too sweaty, and the gun from slipping right out of my hand to clatter down onto the floor.

I keep my breathing light, certain that he must have heard the gunshot.

. . . Or maybe he didn't . . . maybe he's sleeping . . .

And then I round his chair.

Take one look at his face.

The position of his neck.

And his slippery, purple-blue complexion.

And I know that he is dead.

12

I T'S ONLY when I see the cord from the blinds, wrapped around his throat, that I realise what has happened. And only when Jimsy splutters over my shoulder do I remember that she's there with me.

That *she* must have done this.

I back away from Grant Flowercut's corpse, a thousand questions on my mind and really no answers forthcoming.

I look back to Jimsy. See that the blood dampens her chest where I shot her. And I know that, in a matter of minutes, she'll be just as dead as her husband here.

Jimsy's sparkling blue eyes slowly incline to meet mine. Her eyelashes flutter a few times. I see her lips quiver, and the blood draining out of them. Soon she'll have that same purply-blue complexion too.

She grits her teeth at me—almost a smile, an *approximation* of a smile—and then she says, "You came here . . . to . . . to . . . k-kill *him* . . . didn't you?"

I feel a numbness rush over me. Consume my nerves.

The only thing I can think to do is nod.

She sucks in hard, and I hear the rattle of blood in her throat as she does so. When she speaks again it's like she's trying to gargle water while talking. "You . . . you killed *me*."

Again, I nod.

Not really anything else for me to say.

Her eyes loll back in their sockets. I get a glimpse at the whites of her eyes.

And then, just like that, she's gone.

She slumps over, onto her back and her chest relaxes as she breathes out her final breath.

I stand rooted to the spot for what seems an awfully long time.

And then I hear more footsteps.

Coming towards me from down the corridor.

13

I ACT QUICKLY, think about what I'm going to do.

There's no question about protocol.

The way things sit here—the way that I *just happen* to be standing right in the middle of two recently deceased bodies—it means that whoever comes up here, whoever pokes their nose in around the doorway, they're going to get a bullet in the forehead for their trouble.

I wait.

And wait.

Hear the footsteps get louder and louder.

Then they stop.

I hear a voice.

Thin, reedy.

And, somehow, familiar.

"I'm coming in, okay?"

My heart bounces in my chest. I think about my options. Nothing else. I'll have to shoot whoever puts their head around the doorframe . . . or else my only plan of escape will be to hurl myself right out of the window.

. . . Not much chance of me surviving *that* fall, anyway . . . and I don't imagine Brian would appreciate the bad press which would come from having someone *apparently* throw themselves out of the window in an act of suicide—it'd probably take him a good *hour* of phone calls to clean it up, to keep it out of the papers.

I scan that voice. Try to place it.

But it's only when the face peers in around the doorframe.

Only when I *know* that I have to shoot.

That I recognise just who it is.

The old man.

The man in his seventies.
The one who fitted me out in my wardrobe for the evening.
The one who handed me the gun.
He gives me a light smile.
I allow the gun to fall down to my thigh.

14

A PAIR OF BOUNCERS, wearing sunglasses though they're indoors and it's well past three a.m., trail in behind the old man.

They each carry a body bag and I watch on as they work busily, going about folding all the limbs inside the tight case, making sure that everything fits snug before zipping up as if they were doing nothing more than pack a suitcase for a weekend away.

I stand to one side as each of them lugs his bag on out of the room, and I know that it takes *some* strength to be able to lug a dead body *anywhere*, and I can't help admire them for that.

Even though the bodyguards are obviously complicit in all this killing that's gone on here tonight, I can't help but stay silent till I'm certain they're out of earshot.

And it's then that I turn to the old man and say, "She killed him. Before I got here."

The old man's birdlike features shake just a little. He looks so frail. So out of place here, in the middle of this murder scene.

I find myself looking about the carpets, seeing the way the blood's got all mottled into them, and I wonder dizzily whether Brian will even bother to pay for the carpets to be cleaned or if he'll just order a fresh batch brought in.

"Funny lot, the rich," the old man says, his eyes slipping away from mine, looking about the room as if he'd only just discovered the blood all matted about the place. "Never *really* can tell what they're going to do." His eyes suddenly snap back onto mine. "Good thing that *assassins* can always be trusted, eh?"

I blink a few times, not quite sure whether or not he's taken in just what's happened. "I was supposed to kill Grant Flowercut— Jimsy just got in the way." I pause for a moment, allow my heart to rap itself down into a steady rhythm once more, then I continue. "She did the job for me."

"Hmm," the old man says, and then he cocks his head to one side. "You're quite sure about that?"

"Uh, yeah, why?" I say, with just a little spike at the end of it.

The old man's mouth slides back just a little to reveal rows of crooked, yellowed teeth—teeth that seem just a little at odds with his frail appearance, and which hint at perhaps a misspent youth . . . and, come to that, a misspent *middle age* too . . .

It's right then that he reaches up to me. Lands his bony fingers on my bare shoulder. Gives me a friendly pat.

I might suspect him of lechery if it wasn't for my assumption that, as far as downstairs is concerned, his race is run.

"No, Anna," he says. "It is *funny*—terribly *funny*."

I really don't like the way he says *funny* and get the stirring sensation at the base of my gut which tells me that if he dares say it again then I might be forced into taking some sort of action.

If just to preserve my sanity.

"Brian," the old man continues, "he has *plans* for everybody. He plays them all like, uh . . ."

As he appears to search for the word, I decide to help him out.

"Idiots?" I put in.

The old man's grin widens. "Well, I would have said *marionettes* myself—but, yes, I suppose that 'idiots' carries about the same sentiment."

"Then what's Brian up to?"

"Oh Anna, you know what they say about having to ask . . ."

"I was always a slow learner . . ." then I glance down at the gun, still hanging from my fingers, resting lightly against my thigh ". . . but I have my ways."

The old man sighs hard. He peels back the sleeve of his tuxedo, glances at the golden watch he conceals there. Squints at its face, gives me another pat and then heads for the door of the room.

Just as I'm certain he's about to breeze on out into the corridor, head on out of the building and—hopefully—out of my life for good, he turns back to me.

Meets my eye.

"All right," he says, "just this once . . . but don't let Brian know that *I* told you."

I glance about room. Know that we're being watched, even if I can't see where the camera is . . . having the audio recorded *too*.

"You know as well as I do," I say, "Brian's been watching us this whole time."

The old man gives an arthritic chuckle, and then he cocks his head to one side. He seems to get a slight sparkle in his eye . . . I don't linger too long on just what the meaning of it might be . . . don't *want* to linger on it . . .

"An agent," the old man says. "Brian and an *agent*—they had a bit of a fallout, and this is the result." Then he gives me a shuddering wink. "Let's just leave it at that, shall we?"

I decide that's fair, and I watch him out of the room.

As I stand there, in the room with the blood still seeping into the carpet, I think about what I've done, and all that I've been responsible for here.

Then when I get into that old moral thinking about what's *normal* for one human being to do to another I make myself stop.

I flip my kill switch and it all goes away.

Blank mind.

No thoughts.

Just the snow piled up outside.

Up on the pavements, up against the building of Mathewson Media.

I try not to think of the blood at all.

. . . And mostly fail.

DOMESTIC GODDESS

1

I PLUCK OUT a rogue sock from beneath my bed, give it a sniff—it's pretty much clean—and then stuff it into my sports bag, which is already packed full with my gear for the weekend. My ex-husband, Arnold, rang about an hour ago and declared that he was heading out for the weekend, him and his sweetheart, Kate, and he needs me to look after the kids. He claimed that he told me about it a week ago, but I don't remember. It's been something of a packed week. Three hits. Maybe for some assassins about town that might be par for the course. Not for me, though. Call me a part-timer if you like.

As I make it to the bottom of the stairs, I notice Lizzie, my tortoiseshell cat, peering around the kitchen door, looking at me expectantly. It's probably dinnertime. Then I realise that I haven't thought of what I'm going to do with her while I'm off at Arnold's for the weekend. I consider leaving her at home and coming back to give her a lashing of food but, knowing my forgetful streak, I decide that I'm better off just taking her with me. So I dig through half the kitchen trying to locate the cat carrier, which I finally locate beneath the kitchen sink. A bit of spitting and clawing later and Lizzie's in the carrier, all ready for her weekend outing.

I stand at the front door, hand resting on the latch with the feeling that I've forgotten something. I wait out a couple of seconds and then look back up the stairs to my bedroom. I plump Lizzie's carrier down at the front door and dump my sports bag on top of it and then trudge upstairs. Jesus I really am a nutcase. What the hell am I thinking? Still, I keep on moving, taking the steps, getting into my room.

I open the creaking wardrobe and drop to my hands and knees. From within I tug out a cardboard box and tear the lid off, discarding it behind me. I peruse the contents. I've got to be a bit more careful that I used to be. Before I'd just stash everything in the box, no attempt at hiding it away. Nowadays, though, I have a series of shoeboxes each seeming only to contain photographs of my children, Ben and Josie. There are four shoeboxes in all and I flip one of them open. A small handgun is nestled inside— a silencer beside it. I shake my head at myself, my poor, old paranoid self. Who takes a gun to spend the weekend with their kids? Despite my apparent consciousness of this personality quirk, I do take the gun out, load it up, strap it to my calf, concealed beneath my jeans, and then shove the box back in its place—back in the wardrobe. And then I'm away. All set for the weekend.

2

I ROLL UP with cat and sports bag—and my hidden companion—around half an hour later, which is how long it takes me on public transport. As I reach Arnold and the kids' house I notice the prim little garden they've got going on—surely one of Kate's innovations. From my non-expert, *abotanical* perspective I can see a few roses, all nicely trimmed out of the garden path, the grass has the quality of a lush carpet, that too-green-to-be-true look, and a garden gnome has appeared at the perfectly blue pond, fishing away with an inane grin stretched across his face. I do my best not to vomit and strut up to the front door where I give my standard, smart ex-wife pair of knocks before standing back and waiting for the inevitable fallout.

There's the *patter* of footsteps within the house and, just that sliver of a second before the front door opens, I know that it'll be Kate that'll do the answering. Sometimes I wonder if she does it to wind me up—consciously does her best to maximise our face time. I mean, she knows that I'm coming so why not leave the door to Arnold, or one of the kids? It seems like she's on some sort of relentless mission to get me onto her side, to count me as being some sort of 'friend.'

Kate does open the door. She's looking glamorous, as ever, her skin looks cleaner, whiter, her hair blacker—if possible—and her blue eyes more sparkling. I get a faint waft of rose petals as she drinks me in with her pleasant smile and I wonder whether she got that particular fragrance from crushing the roses in the garden. I'm not going to ask her. "Annie! Lovely to see you."

I strain to smile back, giving up after the first second or so, in the end just settling for a steady wince, and then say, "You all set for the weekend?"

Kate does that thing where she simultaneously rolls her eyes and shrugs her shoulders—that weird girlish thing that I'm sure keeps Arnold wrapped around her little finger. "It's all a bit of a shambles, as ever."

I know that her idea of a 'shambles' is wildly different from mine.

"Always find it tricky," she says, "working out what to pack for just a couple of days." She leans into me conspiratorially. "All very well for men, isn't it? They just chuck in a couple of fresh shirts and some underwear and they're set."

Finding the combinations of the stench of roses and the sight of her slight frame beneath the floaty white dress she's wearing a little overpowering, I take a step back. At first I think that she's detected my subtle movement and taken offence—not that I would care—and then I see that she's staring at the cat carrier that's still hanging from my left hand.

"Oh," she says, her mouth etched in the closest thing I've ever seen approximating a frown, "I didn't know you had a cat."

I glance down at the cat carrier as if I'd just remembered that I had it with me. "Didn't you? I thought I'd have to bring her with me, can't leave her at home for the whole weekend."

Kate's cheeks flush slightly and then she brings her china fingers up to cover her nose and mouth. She emits the weakest little sneeze I've ever heard and then turns her head away.

I take the opportunity to get a little smug grin in. "You're not allergic to cats at all, are you?"

Kate continues to tilt her head, to cover her mouth with her dainty little hand, apparently unsure whether or not this partic- ular sneezing fit has passed her by. Seeming to be more confident that it has, she meets my eye, and gives me the sliver of a smile. "Just a bit," she says, then she catches herself, worried that she might've offended me in some way, and says, "But we'll be out of here in a few minutes so no need to worry." Her easy smile returns and she stoops down to the cat carrier, sticks a tentative finger through the wire mesh and strokes a tuft of Lizzie's fur. "You're a pretty girl, aren't you?"

Despite my mental imploring for Lizzie to take a swipe, or at least have a hiss at Kate, she decides to go down the purring route. I guess all friends stab you in the back at one point or other.

A few seconds later, Kate straightens up and retreats into the house, ushering me inside.

I take her up on the offer and cart cat and sports bag in. I feel the reassuring weight of the handgun at my left calf and follow her upstairs to the guestroom. Kate looms in the doorway as I get myself settled. I set Lizzie down on the foot of the bed, and toss my sports bag in the direction of the bedside table.

"I'll just leave you to get settled," she says.

I shrug. "I'm fine, that's all the unpacking I planned on getting up to this weekend."

Kate seems torn for a moment, unsure whether or not that was a joke. Instead of looking for clarification, she slinks from the room with a parting smile.

To say that me and Kate have a bit of a history might be a fair statement. To put it bluntly, I broke her arm. Under great duress, I would add. Ever since then she's been—understandably, I guess—somewhat wary of me. Even though neither she, nor Arnold, know about my current occupation—I believe that they think I'm most likely a benefit scrounger—they do know about my Army record, that I've killed people. Lots of people, in fact. And I guess once you know that someone's killed a person, never mind lots of people, that has a way of skewing your judgement of them. I have to say that, so far, it's only been to my benefit. Sometimes it's a good thing to have people a little scared of you.

I can hear muffled voices carrying along the hall and so, after taking care to look twice before crossing the threshold to the spare room for any sign of Kate, I slip out onto the landing. The door at the end of the landing is Arnold, and Kate's, bedroom. The door's been left open about an inch—that polite gap which is left when guests are in the house: not quite as cold and unwelcoming as the thoroughly private closed door, but just clear enough to communicate "Stay out" to said guest.

Although it's tempting to put my silent assassin moves to use and sidle up to the door and eavesdrop on their conversation, I decide that, one, that would be an intensely creepy thing to do and, two, I'm really not all that interested in what they've got to say to one another. Not *that* interested, anyway.

And so I step up to Ben's bedroom door which, as I've noticed on my visits more and more lately, is smartly shut. I come face to face with the various posters and pictures he's stuck up there: a collection of superheroes, all hugely muscled, some flying, some caught in the middle of a demonstrative swipe, others just standing there with their arms crossed looking smug. Hopefully, like everything else with twelve-year-old boys, this is just a phase: the superheroes and the shut doors.

Not wanting to get into trouble, like last time, I knock on Ben's door, and listen to the weary, "Come in," which follows. I take a final glance up the landing, to Kate and Arnold's almost-closed bedroom door and then step inside.

Just as I'd imagined, Ben's perched on the foot of his bed, eyes glued to the television screen, gamepad clasped in his hands, fingers mashing away at the buttons. He doesn't so much as say a word as I sit down on the bed behind him and stare at the television screen side on. "How was school?" I say.

Ben murmurs something, which I guess suggests indifference.

"Where's your sister?"

"Out with her friend."

Be still my beating heart, it does speak. "Who's that, then?"

"Who'd you think?"

Perhaps I was a little hasty in declaring this specimen to be civilised. "Francesca, then?"

"Uh huh," he says, as he plugs a neon-green lizard between the eyes, in the videogame, and blue-purple blood splashes all over the place, some of it appearing to stick to the inside of the television screen.

"You haven't got any plans for the weekend?"

"Nah."

"No friends you want to go hang out with?"

"Uh-uh."

"Got much homework to do?"

He gives me a shrug, pulls out a machine gun and peppers about a hundred of those lizard creatures apart. Blue-purple blood near enough covers the entire screen. This doesn't seem to throw Ben at all, however, and he simply marches on, continuing to wage war on the lizards.

"Annie?" I hear drifting along the hall.

I squeeze my eyes shut and press my fingertips into my canthi —those are the inner corners of my eyes, I have quite a bit of spare time between contracts and the internet's a big place, go figure—and hold them there for a few seconds until my mind clears a touch. When I look up, I see Ben staring back at me, the game paused, a light smirk on his lips.

"What's so funny?" I say.

"He's calling you that again."

To be honest, this time I really hadn't noticed. But Ben's right. I cannot stand Arnold calling me Annie. It drives me berserk. Always has. Glad to have got some sort of a response out of Ben, I reach forward and ruffle his hair. "Ten more minutes of game time, kiddo, all right?"

Without another word, Ben pivots around and resumes his lizard genocide.

I get up from the bed, already feeling weariness seeping into my body at the prospect of this conversation with Arnold. I bring Ben's door closed behind me, just as he likes it, and then find myself staring down the twin barrels of Arnold's sable eyes. As always, he's grinning at me as if I'm some sort of postie standing on the doorstep having brought him a train set he's been waiting weeks for—Arnold likes model railways. His light brown hair swipes at his shoulders—he's grown it quite a lot since I last saw him, which I quickly calculate to have been about two or three months. I do go out of my way to avoid him when I come around to pick up the kids.

"You brought your cat," he says.

"She's called Lizzie."

He dials his smile up a notch. "I know," he says, "Josie told me once, I think."

I gaze off along the landing to see that his and Kate's bedroom door is now wide open. I can just see the foot of the bed, the neat bedspread tucked in beneath the mattress, a pair of suitcases stacked one on top of the other. It *does* look like a lot to be taking just for the weekend. I turn my attention back to him. "So you all packed up and ready to go?"

"Think so, Kate's just putting her contacts in and then we'll be off."

Well, it's nice to know that Little Miss Perfect isn't quite as perfect as she makes out. A small deficiency, but a deficiency nonetheless.

Kate rounds the bedroom door, blinking away, but still smiling. "All set, dear," she says to Arnold.

"Want me to help with the cases?" I say.

Kate scrutinises me for a couple of seconds, as if scanning this offer for any sign of malice, then, finding none, she hits me with yet another grin. "That'd be lovely, Annie."

I cast off the urge to bite her head off and then stride into the bedroom. Despite my slight frame it's something of an open secret that I can hold my own physically, having been in the Army gives that away somewhat—even if I hadn't gone to the trouble of breaking Kate's arm that one time. I've got well-hidden, tight and efficient muscles. Sometimes my strength surprises even me.

I shovel my hands beneath one of the cases and check myself, realising that it's somewhere around the thirty-kilo mark. Unbelievable. I lug it just above the floor under the gaze of Kate and Arnold.

"I can give you a hand if you like," Arnold says.

"No," I hiss, through gritted teeth.

Arnold watches on for a moment then slips past me and goes to get the other case.

I'm still aware of Kate keeping her eye on me as I descend the stairs, pound out through the front door to where the car waits, boot already open. I let the suitcase go and it thumps into place in the boot. My muscles flare up and I feel the blood burn through my veins. Heavy lifting wasn't in the job description for this weekend, then I remind myself that I *did* offer.

Arnold emerges from the house, puffing out his cheeks. I get out of the way just in time for him to lurch forward and drop his case into place in the boot. He leans back against the car, sweat streaming down his face and then wipes his forehead with the back of his hand and turns to me. "Don't know what you're doing at the moment, but you're certainly staying in shape, aren't you?"

I do my best to hide my own exertion, keep my breathing steady and then say, "A lady does try."

Somehow Kate has managed to extract Ben from his bedroom, managed to peel him away from the television screen, and he now stands on the doorstep, arms crossed over his chest, expression somewhat reluctant but, still, *there*.

Arnold gives him a hug then a pat on the head, before

climbing into the car, giving me a wave over his shoulder as he goes. He brings the hefty door shut behind him with a weighty *slam*.

Kate approaches Ben and, to my horror, ducks down and plants a kiss on each of his cheeks. To my more extreme horror, Ben blushes slightly. I clench my fists down by my sides and then find myself confronted with Kate myself. My outrage at her interaction with Ben is side-lined for a moment while I face up to my own personal etiquette crisis. Kate stands before me, holding back a moment, before she rushes forward and wraps her arms around me in a hug. My body goes stiff all over. Before I know it it's finished with and Kate's rounding the car to the passenger seat. "See you both on Sunday," she says, blowing a kiss to me and Ben as she drops into her seat.

Feeling that my personal space has been somewhat trodden on, I trudge up to the front door and stand beside Ben. Together we wave them off in the car, which powers up the cul-de-sac and then out of sight.

I think about letting out a sigh and then remember that I'm supposed to remain neutral, to be an adult. However, just as I think this through, Ben lets out his own elongated sigh then says, "Glad that's over with. Those two bloody drive me nuts."

I stay serious a few moments then break out in an ineffaceable grin before giving him another ruffle of the hair for good measure. I shepherd him back into the house. "Come on, kiddo, I think this is going to be a long and glorious weekend."

AGAINST ALL ODDS I manage to extract Ben from his video game console and get him downstairs with me, where I seat him at one end of the kitchen table and myself at the other. Cup of tea each. I don't know what it is about boys, but, from what I've noticed in my experience, for some reason between the ages of twelve and eighteen they're almost impossible to look in the eye. Ben plays with his teaspoon, twirling his mulchy tea around in endless spirals. I wonder, if I don't utter another word, whether he'll ever look up at me again. I don't quite have the patience to put my theory to work, so I say, "What about your mate, Kevin? What's he been up to recently?"

Ben continues to play his avoiding-my-gaze game.

"Are you still"—I pause, then close my eyes in recognition that I'm going to have to lay down some trademark 'mum' lingo —"hanging out?"

"Nah."

"Why not?"

He shrugs.

"I thought you were playing football together. You know, going to play for the school team."

"Yeah, well, I don't really like football. I was rubbish, anyway."

"But if you practised I'm sure you'd get better pretty quickly."

"Can't be bothered."

"Fair enough."

He sips at his mug of tea.

"So who're you hanging out with now?" I say, again flinching at that expression.

"No one, really."

"That doesn't sound like much fun."

He stays silent.

"Don't you ever get lonely at all?"

He mumbles something under his breath.

"What was that?"

"Dunno, I mean, I don't mind being alone. It's fine. Doesn't bother me."

My stomach twitches a little and, somewhere off upstairs I hear my mobile vibrate. I consider leaving it, but then decide I'd better not. As a rule, I'm supposed to keep it on me at all times, twenty-four hours a day, so that my boss, Brian Mathewson, can call up at a moment's notice if there's someone that needs taking care of. As I get up from the table I do catch Ben's eye. I stand still for a long moment, feeling the beating of my heart, the breath blowing in and out of my lungs, then I say, "You know, I was a bit like that at your age. I mean that I didn't mind being alone. It was normal for me."

"Has much really changed?" he says, getting up from his seat and placing his mug so quietly in the sink that I ponder that this must be some sort of etiquette Kate has impressed upon him.

As he passes by me, heading out of the kitchen, I almost reach out and grab him, but, in the end, I just step aside and let him go by. I listen as he treks back up the stairs, goes back into his room, shuts the door behind him with a *waft* of air. I break from my daze, remind myself of the phone and climb the stairs, back to the spare room.

The first thing that strikes me, being back there, is that I still haven't released poor Lizzie from her cat carrier. She doesn't seem all that phased by this oversight as she lies on her side, sleeping, her furry flanks rising and falling with her gentle breathing. All the same, I crouch down and slip open the latch of the carrier, opening the door with its familiar *squeak*, before making for my sports bag and my mobile phone which is packed into one of the front pockets.

As I fumble the mobile out and shoot through the screens to read my new messages, I realise that I'm sweating just a touch. I rang Brian before leaving home to inform him that I'd be pretty much out of action for the weekend—off the hook to anything less than an absolute, die-cast emergency. So now I know, if the message is from Brian, that this will be an emergency. Already, as I finally get to my inbox, a thousand scenarios flash through my mind—that I might have to look through phonebook, bring in a nanny. And what would Arnold say once the kids had inevitably told him that Mummy had snuck off without much explanation and left them with a total stranger? It might be the final nail in the coffin, the action which leads him to take steps for the good of Ben and Josie, to keep them away from me.

My blood's running cold when I read the message at the top of the inbox. For a second my breath hitches in my throat and then the suspense is vanquished. It's not from Brian. It's from Adam Alderknot, or AA as he's affectionately known.

I almost want to toss the mobile against the wall of the spare room in rage, for him having the nerve to contact me, no doubt with some frivolity or other, to get me all wound up. Doesn't he see that when my kids are on the line it's no laughing matter?

I take a few seconds to calm myself down, telling myself that it would be completely irrational that AA would, one, know that I'm with my kids for the weekend and, two, want to wind me up so soon after I've been responsible for putting him in hospital. We're coming back around to that having-people-scared-of-me thing again, aren't we?

AA's the one responsible for getting me involved in all this hired killing so he sees himself as something of a firm hand on the shoulder. I choose to see him as an occasional best friend and, more often than not, a massive annoyance of big-brother proportions. Still, I've come all the way up here now, so I might as well read whatever it is that he's got to say:

Call me, Anna.

Not even a kiss following on from his message or anything. He does know how to make a girl feel put out. I listen in to the house for any sign that I'm urgently required. I can hear the lizards being blasted into little pieces coming from Ben's room. Lizzie's still sleeping in her carrier, unaware that she's now been turned free. With a sigh of acceptance, I reel through my contacts list and dial up AA. It rings only twice before he answers.

"Anna?"

"Yeah, what's this about?"

"Where are you?"

"Look, that's none of your business. What do you *want*?"

"Are you at home?"

I stay quiet, sticking to my guns. Why should I spill information about my private life just because he has me call him up while he's all in a tiff? I've known him to break into my house at all hours, drunk and stinking horribly, looking for someone to cry with. Well, today he can go cry with someone else.

"Anna? You still there?"

"Yes. You've got five seconds to make some sense or you can give me a call back on Monday when I'm back on the clock."

AA emits something between a cough and a laugh, then says, "Anna, that job this week—"

"Which? I did three," I say, at the same time regretting having surrendered that information without much—any—fight.

"Does it matter? Look, they're coming for you Anna—"

An ice cold sensation runs up my spine and my shoulders stiffen. "What're you talking about? Who's coming for me?"

"Some men. Your cover's blown. They know where you live."

I almost break into a giddy laugh as I process the fact which

AA's just dropped on me. "I'm not at home," I say. "I'm with my kids this weekend."

"They know," he says. "I don't know how . . . I . . . Anna?"

"What is it? You're starting to scare me now." My heart pounds in my ears. "My god, I have to get the kids out of the house!"

"No, Anna, no . . . you—"

Already I'm running the various scenarios through my head, how I might get them away, get them to safety somewhere. "Maybe if I act now I can get them out."

"Anna, they're watching you. I wouldn't do anything rash."

"Jesus, that's easy for you to say, they're not your kids."

AA takes in a long, dry breath—I imagine him with his fingers pressed to his temples as he thinks this out. Then he says, "I tell you what, Anna, how about I come to you? I might be able to, you know, help out."

"But, AA, I just don't get this at all. How did you find out?"

"I'll be there in the hour, okay?"

Now my mind's caught in a full-on panic and it feels like my blood's itching inside me. I feel the weight of the handgun at my left calf and, on impulse, reach down, flap up the leg of my jeans and slip it from its holster. I feel much better with it in my hand, squeezing the rough grip, supporting the sizeable weight.

"Anna?"

"Yeah."

"It's going to be okay, all right?"

"Fine," I say, and then, catching my breath, "How did you find out?"

But AA's already hung up.

4

I MOOCH ABOUT THE HOUSE, feeling somewhat like an intruder. My heart's going at a rate of knots as I inspect the various porcelain statues which line the kitchen windowsill. They're all dogs: a beagle, a terrier, a sheepdog in a sitting position. I notice that there's not a speck of dust anywhere to be found.

Lizzie brushes up against my leg and I almost have a heart attack. I startle, my shoulders stiffening up and my breathing going shallow. I bend down and whisk her up into my arms: my great big ball of fur. I stuff my face into her warm belly and hold it there for a while. A great big shudder runs through my body and I take it as nerves, for the men who are coming for me, and then I realise that it's a bigger reason. Josie.

I set Lizzie down hurriedly and she gives me a jabbering half-purr, half-yowl at having been cast off so unflatteringly. I shuffle up the carpeted stairs and bound into Ben's room. Even Ben, despite the lure of his television screen, the exploding lizards, cranes his neck back and looks at me, eyes wide—all at once seeming like a young boy again, scared by a roll of thunder, a flash of lightning. "Josie," I say, just about getting it out from my breathless lungs, "when's she coming back?"

"Uh, later tonight, I think."

"But, when?"

"I dunno," he says, already half-turning back to the television screen now that he can see no immediate explanation for my all-out panic. I suspect that Arnold and Kate have had talks with him and Josie from time to time about my irrational behaviour, about how it's nothing to get alarmed about—it's just who I am.

I linger in the doorway to his room telling myself that I might well be acting nuts, but there's no other option. Josie might be in danger. If they're watching the house, they might snatch her away before she so much as skips up the garden path.

I break out of my daze and cross Ben's room. I sink to my knees and, with the sound of Ben's protests in my ears, yank out the power cable to the games console. The screen flashes silver a couple of times before settling on pitch-black static.

Open-mouthed, Ben stands, his controller falling from his grip. "Hey!" he says. "You can't do that!"

I stand up to him and glare into his eyes: sea-green, just like mine, nothing like Arnold's, then say, feeling the sound of my voice hoarse in my throat, "Do you have Francesca's mum's number?"

Ben bears up to me, still out-raged that I've pulled him out of his virtual reality world. "How should I know?"

"She's your sister."

"She's your daughter."

I side-step the sting of this remark and break into action. I snatch Ben by his wrist and drag him, hissing and snarling, behind me, down the stairs, into the kitchen, to the wireless telephone which sits smugly in its cradle—a red light blinking intermittently every couple of seconds. I grab the telephone from its cradle, flip the green 'Call' button and shove it into Ben's chest. "Call her up," I say.

Ben rolls his eyes. "Really," he says, "I have no idea what the number is. What do you think I'd want to call Francesca's house for?"

I judge him for a few moments. If only I could reveal the reason behind my panic. I decide that he's telling the truth, that his logic is sound. Why *would* he want to telephone the house of one of his sister's friends? I scan the walls looking for a piece of notepaper hurriedly stuck up there with various phone numbers of children's friends. But, of course, this being Kate's domain there's nothing at all approaching 'hurriedly.'

No giveaway scraps of paper anywhere. I curse under my breath.

"What did you say?" Ben says, lips slightly parted, for the first time actually looking taken off guard by what's going on.

I shake my head. "Forget it."

The upshot of this is that Ben seems to catch the drift, to realise that this is something more serious that mild 'Mum panic.' He ducks down below the phone cradle and slides out a pristine phone directory. "Maybe we could try in here."

"Do you know Francesca's last name?"

"Smith, I think."

I curse again.

Ben flinches and then, several seconds later, his mouth worms into a sly grin. "What's this all about?"

"Doesn't matter."

I think about all the times that I've told Arnold that I wanted the kids to get mobile phones—and all the times he told me, "Next year, next year," and now it might cost Josie her life. I try to put that to one side, to try and think through what I'm going to do now, with this situation that I've found myself in. Is there anything I can control with Josie? It doesn't look like it. I feel the weight of the gun strapped to my calf and have the impulse to reach for it, to feel the steady weight—I know that it would have the calming effect of a long-drawn cigarette on me. I can't do that, of course, because Ben's standing right here beside me and while he's used to Mum throwing the odd temper tantrum, it would be a whole new level for her to pull out a fully-loaded, silenced handgun.

And then the doorbell goes.

5

B EN MAKES A MOVE toward the front door.

"No," I say. "I'll get it."

He opens his mouth as if in protest, but then gives up.

As I rest my hand on the latch, I look to him and then say, "Why don't you go upstairs and continue with your video games?"

He lets out a sigh and slumps his shoulders. "Well which is it, then? Am I allowed to play or not?"

"You're allowed to."

"And what if I don't want to now?"

The doorbell goes again. My pulse increases. "Just go up now, okay?"

"No. You can't tell me what to do in *my* house."

That one does burn a bit, but I leave it alone, like the restrained, fully-mentally functioning parent that I'm trying to be. "Fine," I say. "You just do exactly what you want." I test the weight of the latch, pause another moment and then, in a single action, open both latch and door to reveal AA standing there, on the doormat, a suitcase in hand.

AA's black hair is slicked to the side, in a way that I always tell him makes him look like The Great Dictator. He's wearing a beige overcoat with his shirt collar poking out through the neck. The collar looks a little twisted, his face is flushed and his eyebrows unusually wiry. Strangely, for AA, he looks tired, a little under stress. However, his familiar smile appears and he curls his lips back to deliver, no doubt, some typical biting AA greeting, when he's stopped in his tracks by the sight of Ben at my shoulder. He breaks off whatever it was he was about to say, rounds me, holds out his hand and says, "Adam Alderknot, pleased to meet you. You can call me Uncle Adam, if you like."

Ben looks to me and then to AA. He accepts the handshake, looking thoroughly bemused, then meets my eye once more, as if to ask who this weirdo is. It's a fair question.

"Go on, Ben," I say. "You can go back to your room now, if you like."

Ben appears to have slipped into some sort of stupor. But he soon breaks from it, catching my eye as he climbs the stairs, pads back up along the carpet, returning to his lizards and virtual bullets. I wonder if he realises how close he is to real ones right now.

Once Ben slips from sight, AA's easy smile disintegrates and he leans into me. "I thought the kids would be in bed," he says.

"It's six thirty."

"What time do kids usually go to bed?"

"Later than six thirty."

"Right," he says, looking lost a moment, twirling around to take in the hallway. He looks back at me once he's completed his spinning tour. "Well, aren't you going to take my coat?"

I do take his coat, and he leaves his suitcase down at the door, before we go through to the kitchen. I surprise myself how well I manage to keep my bubbling emotions under wraps as I relay the situation with Josie. After I've wrapped it all up my hands are shaking, though, and I find myself looking upwards, as if Ben might be listening in on the conversation. But the same sounds come from upstairs, the gentle mashing of buttons, the occasional burbling scream as another lizard succumbs. I lean in across the table and keep my voice down. "So, what's really going on?"

AA's wearing a waistcoat and he brushes a couple of creases out of it as he considers my question. "Not got much else to tell you, Anna. I got an anonymous call a few hours ago and I thought I'd do you the favour of relaying the information onto you."

I look out of the kitchen, into the hall where the briefcase sits beneath the coat stand. "So when are you going to show me what you've got in there?"

"In time," he says. "First things, first, though, we have to work on securing the perimeter, and sorting out how we're going to keep an eye on what's going on outside."

"Forgive me, but I'm more used to breaking in than 'securing.'"

"Don't worry, leave it to me. I know what I'm doing." He gets up from his seat, carries his emptied cup of tea over to the sink, gives it a quick rinse then leaves it to dry on the side. "Got any cameras in the house at all? Any outside, ones that would capture anything?"

"How am I supposed to know that? It's not even my house."

"Just asking," he says. "You know, it's for your own benefit to help me out as far as possible, so if you could keep the lip to a minimum I'd appreciate it."

Wow, someone is a little grumpy today. "I'll bear it in mind."

"Now, if what you say's true then there's nothing we can do with the Josie situation for the moment. We've just got to play that as it happens."

The mention of Josie is like setting my heart in a vice then ratcheting it a couple of notches.

He lays his hand on my shoulder. "You all right, Anna?"

"Yeah."

"You're gonna be fine. No one's going to mess with us and live to tell the story."

"I hope not."

6

A A GOES ABOUT the work like he does this sort of thing every day. Considering how little I know about AA's job and, in principle, how little he knows about mine, then, for all I know, he does. Maybe he spends a decent portion of his time setting traps for fellow assassins.

Inside the suitcase AA has a laptop and a set of six wireless cameras, each with a clip to attach to foliage, drainpipes or whatever else is handy. He goes to work straightaway, patching the cameras into the laptop interface, and soon enough he's got them all broadcasting simultaneously in the same window, so we can keep an eye on various locations around the house. My job is to position them all. As I go to do it, he grabs hold of my forearm and stares me in the eye. "You are armed, aren't you, Anna?"

I nod back to him.

"Keep an eye out."

I allow myself the sliver of a smile. "Thanks for the advice."

Deciding that I want to get a camera up at the front of the house, looking along the cul-de-sac in case Josie comes back home, I snoop my way out through the front door, handgun dangling down by my side so as not to alert any curious neighbours. I fix the camera to the wooden post of the garden gate and then, after a quick look around, I dash back for the front door.

The sun's dipping down below the horizon now, twilight is coming toward an end and it'll be night soon. Night, an assassin's best friend. That's when they'll come.

I run a couple of quick logical scenarios through my head, trying to speculate as to when Josie will be on her way back. She's only ten years old, so surely Francesca's mum will see to bringing her back before eight—at the latest. I check my watch. It's already seven thirty. My heart lodges in my throat.

I stick another camera down at the base of the front door, angled upwards so that I can get a good look at whoever comes knocking, not that I'm holding out hope that the men that are coming for me will do that.

Done with the front of the house, I go around back, where I'm sure the attack will come from. I stalk about the garden, keeping to the foliage, working to stay out of any potential sniper sights, or at least to make it difficult for them, and place the remaining four cameras in various positions, so as to give a full view of the garden and a few of the gardens beyond too. I stand back to examine my good work and then I hear the giveaway *thwap* of a silenced shot ripping through the air. The shot bursts a plant pot, sending dust and porcelain scattering into the air and then tinkling down onto the concrete patio slabs.

Before I've even completely rationalised what's happening, I hit the deck, planting my front into the grass. I seize the handgun tight and scan the area around me, trying to work out where the shot came from. My ears ring with tinnitus, not from the sound of the shot, but the built up fear and expectation coming to fruition. There's nothing more terrifying than having someone shooting at you from some unknown location. I want to scream out for AA, but know that's not an option. I can't alert the neighbours, or Ben, to what's taking place out here. I hope that AA might've seen what's just happened on the computer feed from the cameras, but I don't hold out too much hope. You can't rely on other people when guns are involved.

I test out the gunman's vision by crawling a couple of centimetres in the direction of the back door of the house. *Thwap*. Another bullet races by my ear. But the fact that he didn't hit me suggests that he doesn't have a clear shot.

I have to take my chances now, to not give him another chance to re-aim and, this time, find his target, so I leap up and rush for the cover of a nearby tree trunk, which I shove my back up against. Another shot smashes into the tree, sending wood dust flying through the air. The bullet buries itself in the trunk. I dare a quick glance around the trunk and think I get a shade of movement in the dark. Trusting my assassin instincts, I fire off a couple of my own suppressed shots, and then hear a narrow, almost silence *groan* in the night air.

The hair raises on my arms at the exertion of picking out my target. The only problem now is that I have no idea how badly I've wounded my opponent. Worse still, he might simply be faking, be waiting for me to burst from cover before taking a pot shot. I have to be patient. I count out the seconds in my mind, telling myself that I'll go on sixty, a full minute will surely test my foe's patience as much as mine—he will reach the conclusion that his ruse hasn't worked. And then I go.

The grass whispers against the soles of my trainers. I keep my movement smooth and as quiet as possible. I look out before me, while taking a quick look around for any of this guy's friends, they might well be waiting in the trees, waiting to pick me off. As I draw closer I can make out the slumped form in the darkness. With each footstep, my confidence increases, and I begin to believe more and more that I have managed to down my target. After a while you get accustomed to what a dead body looks like —what distinguishes it from a live one, lying in wait—and I'm sure that this is a dead one.

I'm only a matter of steps away when my complacency bites back. All of a sudden the hunched form breaks from its stasis, prone into what can only be a shooting position. The *thwap* comes and I close my eyes, knowing there's no hope.

A few seconds later I realise that I'm still very much attached to my mortal coil and I look around. There, standing right beside me, silenced pistol still outstretched before him, eyes still fixed to the target, is AA. He maintains his posture then turns to me, grinning. "Don't mention it, it's what friends are for."

7

A A HAS THE LAPTOP all set up in the living room, night-vision mode engaged on the cameras. He tells me he saw the man there the whole time, just after I'd placed the first camera. He claims that he was just giving me a test, giving me the chance to stand up on my own two feet. But I reckon the real reason was because he was in the toilet, judging by his trouser zipper flying low.

I leave AA to surveillance while I go check on Ben. He's still there, in his room, blowing up lizards. I bring his door shut again with a faint *click*.

When I get back down into the sitting room, AA stares back at me, his lips slightly parted.

"What? What is it?" I say.

He gestures to the screen. "You see that," he says, pointing out some movement on one of the cameras from the front of the house—difficult to make out even with night-vision mode engaged.

"Yeah," I say.

"That guy's been crawling his way through the bushes for the last few minutes."

Something on another of the cameras catches my attention. One of the cameras in the garden. I glance over to it. "Look," I say, "there's another one there, coming down over the fence."

And then another three pile down over the fence, each of them, in turn, stopping to examine their fallen comrade. Pretty soon all of the garden cameras are showing up movement, it seems like they've sent half a battalion here to get me.

"Anna?" AA says, his complexion paling by the second.

"What?"

"Have you seen what's happening out front?"

For a moment the only man I see is the same one, the one who was slowly making his way through the bushes, and then the whole scene appears to open up and I realise that there're another two of them, moving through bushes, making their way toward the house.

My heart skips a beat. "They've got us surrounded."

And then all the lights cut out.

8

WHENEVER THE WORLD seems to fall apart, my body outthinks my mind, pushing me into action, getting me moving, out of harm's way. AA just about has time to grab the laptop and clutch it to his chest before I've scurried out of the sitting room and begun to leap my way up the stairs in the pitch-black darkness. When I get to the top of the stairs, I feel something touch my leg and, on impulse, let out a shrill scream. Only when I watch the furry form darting down the stairs do I realise that it was only Lizzie—only Lizzie heading right downstairs to where the men are all preparing to break through the periphery. I turn on my heel and make to head back down.

AA catches me with his free arm and says, through gritted teeth, "What in hell's name do you think you're doing?"

I consider an explanation and then drop my resistance. I have to protect Ben first and foremost. He's my priority. Which isn't to say that my heart's not bleeding for Lizzie, what those brutes might do to her, as I drag AA into the spare room. I bring the door closed behind us while AA sets the laptop up on the bed—running off its battery.

I prowl back and forth at the door, wondering whether I should just cut free, bring Ben in here with us. But if I do that then my cover will be blown. He'll see the cameras, the men. I'll have to tell him the whole story. Maybe if he were a little younger I might be able to make it pass as if nothing at all, but at twelve years old I have no chance of pulling the wool down over his eyes.

"Mum?"

I hear the voice coming along the landing and know that there's nothing I can do. I have to go out there, go and reassure him. If I don't he might wander downstairs. As I get up, AA stirs from the bed and says, "Where're you going?"

"Out, I have to get Ben."

"You're sure?"

"I've got no other option, have I?"

AA gives me a half shrug and then returns to monitoring the cameras.

I can't really blame him. How's he supposed to know how it feels when Ben's not his kid? "Shut the laptop," I say.

"What? Are you crazy? That's like putting on a blindfold before dropping into a pit of snakes."

"I'm bringing him in."

AA lets out a long-held sigh and snaps the lid shut.

I wander out of the spare room and onto the landing. I almost bump into Ben as I go. I touch him on the shoulder gently. "Over here," I say, doing my best to keep the outright panic out of my voice.

He jumps. "Jesus, Mum! You almost scared me out of my skin."

"Sorry. Look, why don't you come into the spare room. I'm in there with Adam"—I pause for a fraction of a second —"*Uncle* Adam."

Even through the gloom I can see that Ben's shooting me an are-you-serious glance.

"Come on," I say. "Power will be back on soon. I'm sure."

He comes without any further protest and pretty soon it's us three: me, AA and Ben, all packed into the spare room. AA's dug out and lit a candle from who-knows-where and it sheds a little light, sending wonky shadows scurrying all around—like a scene from a hundred years earlier. Only the knowledge of those men skulking about downstairs kind of ruins it.

And now it comes down to it I have to decide whether or not I'm going to spill everything to my son. I look at him, hunched up on the bed, staring at his fingernails. This could destroy every-thing. Surely if Ben were to relay the information to Arnold, he would ensure that I never see the kids ever again. That would be the rational course of action for any sensible adult. Just as I'm on the point of reeling through an explanation of what Mummy does for a living, AA reaches into his waistcoat pocket and produces his mobile. He rummages about some more in another pocket before withdrawing a pair of headphones. He turns to Ben. "You like video games?"

Ben lifts a corner of his mouth in a smirk. "Yeah."

"Then you want to play on my phone for a while?"

Ben looks to me, then back to AA. "All right," he says.

"Just one condition."

"What?"

"You've got to find some music on there and turn it up to the max."

"Why?"

AA shrugs. "You never listened to music on full volume and play video games before?"

I stand there watching them, my head moving between the two of them like I'm at a tennis match. I want to break through this and tell AA that, whatever he's doing, it's not going to work. But then Ben takes the phone and headphones from him and says, "All right, I'll give it a try."

AA sneaks me a wink and then says, to Ben, "Just one more thing. Me and your mum are going to try and sort out this power cut, okay? So if you hear any screaming that's probably just one of us getting a bit of a shock."

Ben's not sure whether to take this as a joke, decides it is, then plonks himself down on the floor, stabbing an earphone into each ear and tapping his way through AA's phone with a hunger I've never seen before. I guess that's what we get for not letting them have mobile phones for so long—when they do get hold of them it's like the best day of their life. At least it'll keep him occupied.

Music buzzes out of the headphones and Ben loses himself to the mobile phone game.

AA swivels the laptop around, then snaps it open. Both of our eyes fly around the various cameras scattered about outside. From the one positioned in the garden I can see one of the men jimmying open the back door silently, while, at the front, I see the men crawling their way through the garden.

AA digs into his waistcoat yet again and removes an earpiece which he hands to me. "I can be your eyes. You're going to have to do something for me first, though, okay?"

"What?"

"The plan should be for you to take care of those men coming in the front, snatch those cameras and then place them inside. Way I see it, those men trying to get in through the back door are coming in whatever, so we'd better take measures for when that happens—so you can see what you're shooting at in the darkness once your inside."

My nerves jangle a touch. I look back over to Ben, merrily tapping away at the phone, music still croaking away. I turn my attention back to AA, take the earpiece and smush it into my inner ear. I give him a nod to let him know I'm ready, then step out, yanking out my handgun as I go.

I drift along the hallway, ear sensitive to AA's breathing down the microphone. I have to place all my trust in him now. It's like I'm a blind woman. A blind woman clutching a lethal weapon skulking about her ex-husband's house.

Under AA's guidance, I find my way down the stairs.

"Still pressing to get in through back door," he says. "You've got a bit of time."

I get down to the hallway, look left and right, despite AA's assurances that I'm still alone, and then I reach out for the latch on the front door. I still my breathing, listen to my heartbeat in my ears and then, in one slick action, I push downward and sneak out onto the front doorstep.

The whole neighbourhood's out, of course. They've left the entire cul-de-sac steeped in darkness. Now it'll come to *my* aid. I press my back up against the wall, trying my best to see through the gloom, into the front garden to where I know the men are sneaking their way forward. All of a sudden, I spot one, I aim and fire without so much as a second's thought that I'm ending a life. I hear the *whiffle* of my shot then the stilted breath followed by the earthy *thud* as the body tumbles onto the lawn. One down. Who-knows-how-many-more to go.

AA gets into my ear. "There, Anna, on your right!"

I don't need telling twice. I plug the sucker right in the chest and then, for good measure, his shooting hand. Looks like my eyes are adjusting to the darkness now. This might just be a walkover after all.

I move around to the front of the house, still keeping myself as flush as possible to the wall, gun raised to the sky, keeping my elbow at a perfect perpendicular angle.

"Just one more out there," AA says. "You see him? Lying there, by the wall. On his belly."

I make my first mistake, stopping and gazing out into the darkness. Call it overconfidence, or whatever you like. We all make mistakes.

The shot burrows in the brickwork inches away from my thigh. I drop onto a knee, then onto my front where I wriggle behind the plant pots lining the edge of the flowerbeds. I try to ascertain where the shot came from. I'm scanning the wall, as AA suggested, but I'm just not seeing anything at all. I peer over the peach-coloured porcelain and suddenly I see him, the man, he seems to have lost me in the darkness too. I wonder why he didn't bring night-vision goggles on this particular foray. Guess it's going to cost him his life.

Once he's done with, I rush up to the garden gate, whip the camera off its wooden post, then do the same with the camera at the front door. Then, without much time for hesitation, let alone thinking, I'm back inside, front door closed behind me—another three kills registered on my account.

I check my gun, reload and then set off through the house, putting up the cameras so I'll have the upper-hand on the intruders. Just as I plonk the second camera down, I hear the back door go, an almost indiscernible *snick* that no one but a borderline maniac like me would notice. I get down on my haunches, trying to make out what I can of the back door from where I am in the kitchen.

AA gets into my earpiece again. "Two of them have got night-vision goggles. The rest are goggle-less, as far as I can see."

Guess not all of these guys are amateurs, then.

They don't seem that switched on tactically, either. I plug the first one as he steps in through the back door. He drops down, this time making quite a racket. I curtail his screams with a shot to his throat. I hear the unmistakable *slop* of flesh coming unstuck, blood splattering about. This is all going to take some serious cleaning up.

As if ignorant to his companion's fate, another steps over the threshold, I take him down too. He lands on top of his unfortunate friend, making much less fuss, though.

"Five to go, Anna," AA says.

"Did I get any of the goggled guys?"

"Nope."

I swear to myself then get my mind back focussed on what's about to unreel before me.

The guys have learnt their lesson, that I've got that back door well and truly covered. So this time they decide to fire off several shots. I have to duck, of course, a bit annoyed that they've worked out a way to force their way in before I'd got the chance to pop off another two or three. I hear their rugged boots now, on the slatted wooden flooring. I feel my chest heaving, the adrenalin poking about in my body, my muscles seizing tight with tension, my stomach churning. I close my eyes for a fraction of a second.

"Hey! Anna," AA says in my ear. "What're you doing? Catching up on some sleep? Come on, there're guys less than five yards from you. Engage them."

Although they've managed to force their way into the house the men are all, understandably, fairly reluctant to move much further inside. I take my chance and pop up from behind the kitchen counter. I let off a whole round into the room, hoping to scare them if nothing else. When I get to the other side, another place of cover, just behind the kitchen door, I hear AA in my earpiece again.

"Nice work! Three of them down. You got one of the guys with the goggles."

"Look like there are any more outside?"

AA pauses while—I guess—he checks his cameras. "Seems clear for the moment."

I reload the gun again, then set off. I prowl through the room with the five bodies. It sends a shiver up my spine to know that I killed these men. But they deserved it. They threatened my children. I can see no sign of the remaining two—one with night-vision goggles. I have to take care. I speak to AA again, trying to get a fix on the location of the final two, but he's lost them from the cameras, a beat later and he tells me that the battery on the laptop's gone.

I tap the butt of my handgun against my thigh as I scour the room, looking for any sign of the intruders. Nothing. I can see nothing. And then I do see one. Over there, crouched in the corner. I only have time to see the muzzle flash.

A roaring pain splits my skull. I fall forward, somehow managing to keep the grip on my gun firm. I fire off a shot and, just as I hit the ground, I'm aware of the *grunt* the guy emits—that that will be his final sound. As I lie there, trying to force the pain out of my thoughts, the pain beating through my shot thigh, I think to myself that there's just one left. I can hear heavy breathing just above me.

There's a husky chuckle and then, "Thought you'd get away with killing Gus, did ya?"

I think back to one of my hits this week. Three men I've taken care of. I didn't know any of their names. Gus could've been any one of them.

The weight of his boot comes down on my back.

I resist the urge to scream out, both at the bullet lodged in my thigh and the pain ripping through my spine. I manage to turn over onto my back, to force my way out from underneath the man's steady tread, so as to get a look at him.

In the darkness all I can make out is a bald head, round black eyes. He has a pair of night-vision goggles dangling around his neck. I guess he doesn't need them now. He has me, right here. "You killed a lot of people tonight," he says. "What they said about you was true."

"And what did they say about me?"

He snarls. "That you were a real, hard bitch."

"Thanks for the compliment."

"But," he says, bringing his gun sight up to his eye and peering through it, right into my eyes, "if there's one solution for bitches, it's to have them put down."

My grip loosens on my handgun. I try to refind my hold but it's gone. I just don't have the energy left. I close my eyes and say a silent prayer to a god that I don't believe in. And that's when I hear the roar from the man, the clatter of a chair being hurled to the ground.

AA again, I think. *He's saved me again. Second time today.*

As my vision wobbles in and out of focus I get a snatch of something that I can't quite believe is real. It's Ben. He's standing there, shoulders hunched, fists clenched, looking over the fallen man, who's still rubbing his head, coming around from his unexpected tumble. Even with all the pain, all the confusion flushing through me, I manage to get to my feet, to stand up alongside Ben and to fire the shot into the man's skull. He recoils at the impact, immediately dead.

We just stand there, mother and son, for a long time. I don't know what to say—what am I supposed to say standing there with my son and a roomful of seven men that *I* killed?

Ben turns his head to me. "Mum?"

"Hmm?" I say, feeling almost like I'm floating.

"You're bleeding."

As if I'd forgotten, I gaze down at my thigh and see my blood dripping steadily into a pool on the floor. I need to get myself patched up quickly or this could twist into a serious problem indeed. But, I manage to gain a few more lucid moments, enough to say, "Where's AA?" anyway.

"AA?" Ben says, deadpan, still deeply affected by the spectacle before him.

"Someone say my name?" AA says.

I turn my head to look, into the sitting room. I see AA standing at the door, looking a little sheepish.

I know I should be angry, but I just don't have the energy, and all I can summon is a kind of dreary, "Where . . . where were you?"

He scratches the back of his neck and takes in the rest of the room. "I lost contact on one of the cameras, went into another room, thought I'd get a better connection there. Then the battery went like I told you."

I look back to Ben, put my arm around his shoulders and—with a touch of resistance—manage to steer him away from the mounted bodies. I walk with him across the sitting room, back into the hallway. Then I hear some low-level muttering, followed by a pair of knocks at the front door.

9

STILL FEELING DAZED, and still holding onto Ben, I open the door to find Josie standing there, looking a little drawn, tired after a long day's play. Francesca and her mother—a lady done up in power blue all over, from her skirt and shoes up to her earrings and mascara, beam back at me. Francesca's mother says, "Looks like you've had a bit of a power cut around here, huh?"

My heart sticks in my throat. I look out past her, into the garden. I see Francesca's mum's car sitting on the curb outside the house. A little closer in I can see the dim outlines of the bodies lying on the grass.

Josie drifts over the threshold, into the house.

"Well, they've had a lovely time. Not much squabbling."

"Oh?" I say, feeling faint from the blood loss.

Francesca's mum squints at me. "Are you all right, you look a little bit . . . well—"

"I'm fine," I say, a little curtly.

Francesca's mum seems to take momentary offence—her smile slipping from her cheeks—before being fully-restored to its former glory. "Well, I should be getting back. Sorry for coming over so late—it's just that we were baking cakes, and you know how that can take longer than you think."

I manage a sweet smile and it seems to do the trick to calm any fears Francesca's mum might have. She gives Josie a parting, girly wave and then waddles off with her daughter, up the garden path, unaware of the dead bodies sprawled out there. Slightly unbelieving and feeling increasingly woozy, I watch them go, start the car and then trundle back off, up the cul-de-sac and out of sight.

"Mummy?" Josie says, rubbing her eyes with weariness. "Did you cut yourself?"

"Yes, dear. But don't worry. Mummy's going to be just fine."

10

I PUT BEN IN CHARGE of Josie, helping her off upstairs, both of them getting ready for bed. I know that I should tell him not to tell her about what he's just witnessed, but I've got the feeling that he already realises—that he understands far more than I ever could.

AA sees to my wound in the kitchen, once again showing himself to be a man of many talents—although babysitting unfortunately isn't among them—and before I know it I'm feeling much better, all plugged up and ready to heal. Then comes the more perplexing task of what to do with the dozen-odd bodies scattered about the house. AA tells me that he's "Got it covered" and I trust him. He tries to fob me off with a painkiller but I turn him down. He tells me to go up and see to my kids, which I'm only too glad to do.

As I make my way up the stairs, I feel the familiar brush of fur against my leg. I stoop down and bundle Lizzie into my arms, hold her against my chest. She purrs and purrs as I climb upward, feeling the stiffness grow in my thigh with each passing second. I get the feeling that my wound's going to hurt quite a bit tomorrow. Not that I haven't got the stomach for it.

When I go in to check on Josie I find that she's already in her pyjamas, teeth brushed, beneath the covers and letting out little-girl snores. I lean forward and give her a tiny peck on the forehead. She stirs a little at my touch, turning over on her side to face the wall. I steal out from her room and onto the much more daunting task of saying goodnight to Ben.

I ditch Lizzie before I get to his room, letting her loose to go and take up her position warming the bed in the guest room. As I round the door into Ben's room, I notice that this is the first time for ages I haven't seen the television going, no lizards are being blasted into an early grave, most likely because the power's still out . . . Ben stands at the window, leaning on the ledge with his arms crossed, looking out down on the street. I go over to him and follow his gaze. Outside the house, on the curb, a midnight-blue van has rolled up silently. I can see AA below, having an equally silent conversation with the man in the driver's seat. When AA looks back over his shoulder, both me and Ben get the hint and leave our place at the window.

Without a sound, Ben gets himself into bed, pulling the covers up to his chin and then lying on his back, staring at the ceiling. I sit on the bed, taking care not to sit on his adolescent legs. "I need to explain—"

He jerks his head to face me, almost violently, and then, as if aware of the effect this gesture had on me, he tries his best at a warm smile. It gives way after a few seconds, though, and his steely, traumatised gaze returns. What have I done to my son?

"You see," I say, starting out without having any idea of where I'm headed, "those men wanted to kill me. They . . . they wanted to kill Mummy."

Ben nods, but I have no way of knowing if my words are finding any sort of penetration into his skull, making any mark on his consciousness.

Downstairs, I start to hear light *scuffles* and *scratches*, the sounds that mice might make, as AA's clean-up crew goes to work. I try to put it out of my mind as much as possible. Just as I'm about to speak again, I feel another wave of nausea seep through me. I manage to get a hold of it before I lose my dinner, swallowing the bile back. "Listen," I say. "If Daddy finds out about this, he'll stop me seeing you, do you know that?"

No response from Ben.

"You . . . what I'm trying to say is that this is something, a part of me, that I . . ." But my words just trail off after that and I find myself sitting there, on the edge of the bed, sinking into a big nothing. Minutes tick by. Maybe hours. I lose all concept of myself and my surroundings. Only when I hear a sure *thump* outside the house do I think to get up and go over to the window.

I watch on as the midnight-blue car rocks off, up the cul-de-sac and out of sight. Soon after I hear AA's shoes scuffing their way up the stairs, and then he peeks into the room, catches my eye. Only then, when I look back to Ben's bed do I realise that he's drifted off to sleep while I've been doing all my zoning out.

AA speaks in a near whisper. "Left you some painkillers on your bedside table. Take two, three if it's really bad. No more than twelve in a day. Got it?"

I nod weakly in reply.

He backs up from the doorway, back out onto the darkened landing. "Called up the electric company for a report, say they've found signs of vandalism in the system and are investigating. Lights should be back on by morning.

My throat dries up and I feel tears prick the corners of my eyes. Maybe it's the pain, maybe it's the trauma that I've put my son through, but I have no control over the word which slips out between my lips. "Stay."

AA cocks his head to one side, as if he's not sure whether or not to take what I've just said seriously, then, deciding that I did mean it, he backs up some more. "Call me if you have any problems, yeah? I've got some good people looking out for you. Any more problems, any stragglers hanging about round here and they won't have a chance." He pauses, as if unsure whether or not to divulge the next piece of information, that in my current state I might not be ready for it. "I called Brian, let him know what happened. He's behind this now. He'll take care of the security around your place. Says he'll see you on Monday, 'bright and early.'"

He makes the last remark with a slight smile and, despite everything, I find myself smiling along too. It's funny how sharing some quirk of a shared boss can cut through everything else and relieve tension whatever the situation.

"See you, then," AA says, then disappears off down the landing before I get the chance to implore him not to go. If there's one talent that outshines any other of AA's it's his escape artistry. Any situation, no matter how intricate or emotionally charged, and he's off like a rocket.

I stand over Ben's bed another couple of seconds, pause, then plant a kiss on his cheek. He makes no motion. I wonder whether he's really asleep, but decide not to press the matter. He needs time and space to make sense of things. Then, maybe later, we can talk.

I crawl into bed with Lizzie and drop into a profound, death-like sleep.

11

W E SPEND THE REST of the weekend as if nothing at all happened on Friday. To be honest it's probably among the more successful that I've spent with the kids. On Saturday we go to the zoo, then the park, ice cream afterwards before going bowling in the evening. On the Sunday we have a lazy day around the house, watching films, eating mountains of popcorn. Sometimes I catch Ben's eye, catch him looking at me, and I'm unsure whether or not he's ready to ask me some question—to put me in my place. But the day passes by without so much as a whisper between the two of us, beyond the necessary.

Kate and Arnold's car drones into the driveway in the early evening and Josie skips out of the sitting room to the front door to welcome them. Ordinarily I would feel a touch irate at her happiness at welcoming Arnold and Kate back home, as if I weren't enough for her. Who am I kidding? Children need a mother *and* a father. But that does beg the question: why should the mother be me?

As Josie skitters about outside, loudly greeting the two of them, Ben turns on me, his eyes serious, expression unmoving—like a marble statue. "Those men," he says. "All the men who were here, they . . . they were dead."

Before I get the chance to reply, Josie barrels back inside, Kate and Arnold trudging in on her heels, each of them lugging a suitcase each—this time Arnold's taken it upon himself to commandeer the suitcase I had to carry out to the car on their departure. Both of them look a touch drawn, faces reflecting a long drive, but they raise a smile to me. And I do my best to reciprocate.

Arnold hunches his shoulders and drops the suitcase with a rare scowl. "Kids behave all right?"

"Yeah, they were fine," I say, feeling my nerve shaking, knowing that if Ben chooses he can cause a storm here.

"Minor miracle, then," Arnold says, brushing his hands together then wiping them on the sides of his trousers. "Cup of tea?"

"Uh, no, it's okay. I should really be getting back home."

"Okay."

Kate wanders into the sitting room, bends down and gives Ben a kiss on the cheek. "You look like you've had a good weekend with your mummy, anyway." She straightens up and meets my eye. "Looks like you've had him hard at task—getting all his homework done."

To be fair to Ben, he hoiked himself off mid-afternoon to do it all by himself. But I don't want to disappoint Kate's expectations so I smile in reply.

Kate shimmies out of the sitting room and faces up to the garden. As she looks out there, hand resting on her hip, something catches her eye down at her side. She crouches down to inspect further.

My heart flutters.

"Oh, dear," she says, half-turning, looking mildly concerned. "There's a bit of a stain here. Is that . . . is that, blood?"

My mouth dries up. I want to run, kicking and screaming from the house, right there and then—not caring if I get committed for doing so.

Ben sparks up, showing animation previously unseen. His whole body seems to lighten up. "Mum fell," he says. "She was just coming in from the garden and she slipped. Caught her leg on the ledge, just there," he adds, pointing out the area. He turns back to me. "Show them the cut."

Feeling a numbness seize hold of my body, I find myself easing down the waistband of my jeans to show off the bandage.

Kate looks to me, frown lines marking her forehead. "That

does look nasty," she says, I think with a touch of genuine satisfaction. "You have to be careful around here." She breaks out into another of her famous smiles. "They always say that the home is one of the most dangerous places."

"Yeah," I say, "I guess they do."

Ben gives me a long stare and then passes me by, climbs the stairs and heads back up to his bedroom—I wonder if he's going to blow apart some more lizards.

I do my best to make the always-awkward farewell to Arnold and Kate go fairly quickly and I succeed, for the most part, managing to cut loose with cat carrier and sports bag in hand—handgun still strapped to my calf. As I wander away, up the garden path, and onto the pavement, I have the urge to look back over my shoulder, and I do just that.

Up there, looking out of the first floor window is Ben. He stares down at me. His features are sombre, he rests his arms on the window ledge.

My heart beats hard against my ribs. I set the cat carrier down and then give him a faint wave.

He remains there, in the window, his moochy look, until—apparently—someone calls to him from inside the house. He gives me a parting glare and then he's gone, slipped out of sight.

I wait there for a while for him to get back, but I know that he's gone. When that fact hits home, I retrieve the cat carrier and make for the Underground station, glad to be getting away from the house, all of this.

12

I DON'T KNOW what I expect back home. I guess I just wasn't prepared for the stillness following that hectic Friday night—the fallout between myself and my son. Is there any way to fix it? Who could I go to for advice? I know that, really, I have no one but myself. My job is my life—and as long as it is my job it will bring everything and everyone I love into extreme danger. I need to stay distant, be more responsible, not sleepwalk through my life as if it's a normal one.

I pull up a chair at the kitchen table then let Lizzie loose from her carrier. I inspect my mobile and find that I've got a few missed calls, all of them from AA, except for one, which is from Brian Mathewson. As I bring the phone up to my ear I feel my hand shaking. I give myself a moment, the shaking stops, and then I'm ready to go again.

THE RANGE

1

THE ROOM is overwhelmingly grey, and stuffed from floor to ceiling with steel lockers. They all have card-swipe locks keeping them snugly secure.

And with good reason.

This place, the Range, membership here really doesn't come cheap at all.

The patron of the Range has stuck one of those fragrance squirters up on the wall, and every five—maybe ten—seconds, it lets loose a fine spray of something that smells somewhere between lavender and peaches.

But, more than anything else, it tastes acidic, and it burns the back of the mouth to breathe it in a little too far. Burns right down to the lungs.

The sound of the squirt is a sharp *hiss*. Vicious. And deadly.

Effective.

Which is just what the Range is all about.

AA finishes his sweep of the place. Not that there's likely to be someone like him . . . an *assassin* . . . lurking off in the shadows somewhere. It's just a habit. Nothing more. Like a dog curling round on itself before lying down on a rug.

Hiss, goes the fragrance squirter above.

And the fine mist of peachy-smelling lavender drifts down in the harsh fluorescent light that floods the room.

Lands cool on AA's skin as he shrugs off his denim jacket, chucks it off onto the sleek wooden bench, like the ones from gym at school. It lands there, without slipping, in a crumpled heap.

Next he looks over the lockers. Finds the one with his number on it.

Number forty-six.

He's spent a lot of time wondering just why, back years ago, when he got asked to choose a number at the main desk, he chose that one.

But he's come up with nothing.

It's just a number.

He removes his cardkey from his moleskin wallet and slides it through the reader.

The lock mechanism twitches, and the door bucks open an inch or so.

When he brings the steel locker door wide open, all that's nestled inside is a single, unmarked attaché case. No locks. No point. No one would *dare* steal it from him.

Not if they know what's good for them.

He slips the attaché case out with a teeth-grinding *screech* as it passes over the base of the locker, and then he brings it down on the steel table which sits in the middle of the locker room.

Brings the case down on the table with an almost careless *slap* and then flips the catches.

They open with a smart pair of *snicks*.

AA peers inside.

The interior of the attaché case is lined with a turquoise-grey foam.

And nestled within the mould of the foam rests a pistol.

His favourite.

The Hotflush .34.

His very own customised handgun.

He breathes the inside of the case in. Breathes deep into his lungs. That wondrous, synthetic odour that comes from sealing foam away for a long while. And letting it get all sun warmed out in the boot of a car.

Just *wondrous*.

He reaches forwards and slips it out from its mould in the

foam. Feels its weight in his hand. Though not weighty enough. Because it's not loaded, of course.

The magazine, polished to a dull shine, lies in its own mould.

Fully-loaded and ready for action.

Time to hit the Range.

Just like always, AA loves to chew gum while shooting. While in target practice. And so he jostles his jacket, still draped over the wooden bench, and slides out the pack of gum nestled inside there.

The packet of gum has a garish yellow-and brown design. With the brand name: Pearler's, and a parrot with gleaming white teeth.

Liquorish flavour.

His favourite.

Good for concentration.

When he *needs* to concentrate.

He slips the gum out from its silver paper pouch and slips it between his lips. And he chews on it for a full minute, feeling all the juices in his mouth mingle with the liquorish flavour.

And it brings him round. Wakes him up. Better than just about any coffee in the world.

He brings the empty attaché case shut with a solid *snap*, and then replaces it in his locker. He yanks the hanger out from inside the locker and prods it through the sleeves of his jacket. Hangs his jacket up inside. And then he slams the door shut.

The locking mechanism reengages.

And AA is ready for action.

2

A PRODS the fingerprint scanner and watches its red light blink to green. Several locks inside the soundproofed, reinforced door all snick back.

The door slides open.

He steps over the threshold.

Hears the door slam shut behind him.

And finds himself trapped in a small space, only large enough for two people to fit. And at that, it would be a squeeze.

None of that peachy-lavender scent remains. All that's gone now. Steel and fired shots stink out this tiny area. And those scents wander their way up AA's nostrils. Fire him up from the inside. Draw his muscles taut. And clear his head.

Things are much simpler with a gun in hand and some time to kill.

As he waits for the time delay on the door, for the next door to open, he snaps the magazine into place in the Hotflush, and then primes it. Everything ready. A deadly weapon now.

His heart beats thick in his throat, gives a kind of bloody taste to his mouth, and makes his brain seem to throb against the inside of his skull.

This is excitement.

What shooting a gun can do for a man.

An upbeat *bing!* sounds from somewhere and the door springs open. Sliding into the wall. An array of shots ring out in the air. One after another. Like fireworks.

But louder. *Much* louder.

And the air feels tense with that feeling that only bullets can cultivate.

Real, live, *killing* bullets.

There aren't many places like this in London. Or, at least, the people that find out about these places don't tend to live very long.

But AA has lived.

And *Much* longer than most.

3

SIX SHOOTING GALLERIES. Three people. Two men. A woman.

Beyond bulletproof glass.

AA takes in all of them. He peers at them, noise-excluding headphones clasped about their heads, and all three of them—without exception—with their hands grasping tight to the grips of their pistols. The barrels are hot. Smoking hot. And send up tiny plumes of smoke with each shot.

All of them have their eyes fixed on the targets ahead of them. Staring long and hard. At those mocked-up diagrams of a head and shoulders, and the black-and-red rings which spiral about. And the little black holes constantly appearing in them —*puncturing* them as if someone was behind there with a hole-puncher doing all that.

But no one's there, it's all the bullets.

AA scans their faces. One of the men is much older than the other. Grey-haired. A bounding beer gut that flaps out of his tight-fitting shirt. And he has a pair of sweat patches at his armpits.

Though AA can't possibly smell him from here, he can imagine.

Imagine the sour, salty sweat pouring off the man.

What will his wife think when he gets back home? Or perhaps she knows about this little sordid habit of his.

The woman, she's slim, and wears a business-like blouse, with cuffs that open out like lampshades, and which she refuses to roll back as she fires off round after round.

She has on purple-blue tights which gleam in the fluorescent light.

Or maybe it's her sweat sticking to them.

Dripping out through the tightly knit material.

AA recognises her as a lawyer. A woman he's seen about town. She has neat blond hair which is done up in ringlets. And it remains flawless despite her firing off bullet after bullet. Her eyes never shift off the target she's shooting at.

The last man, well, he looks to be about to same age as AA.

Late-thirties. Approaching the forty train.

And he wears a V-neck t-shirt, untucked, and a pair of stone-washed jeans. Like the other two, he's dripping with sweat. It glistens off his brow.

He has a firm set of abs as AA can wells see through his tight-fitting shirt. And several, wiry coils of fair chest hair poke up out of his V-neck. Just as he takes another shot, his eyes glance off the barrel of his pistol, and lock onto AA's.

Laser-green eyes.

To go with that honey-glazed hair.

And AA thinks he might just be in business.

4

WITHOUT A SECOND GLANCE, AA ships off to the hooks where the noise-excluding headphones all hang. He slips a pair off, flexes the headband and then brings them down carefully over his ears.

Instantly the world slips underwater.

The shots become just distant *pops* among a distant and persistent sea. Its tides seeming to lap at his ears. He strides his way along the channel which runs behind the shooting galleries, and he slips his way into the booth right at the end of the Range.

The one which is located beside the laser-eyed man.

AA chances another sidelong glance. Through the bullet-proof glass to the man still firing away apparently totally oblivious to AA.

AA examines how the man takes his shots. How his eyes flicker for a moment before he squeezes the trigger. How the muscles in his jaw tighten and then slacken off. How his shoulders rise with tension just before the shot, and then drop immediately afterwards.

This is an experienced shooter.

Someone who has spent some serious time here, at the Range.

Not someone to be messed with.

AA turns his attention back to his Hotflush, which he holds down at his thigh. He gives it another check over, drags the magazine back out of the base, then slides it back inside.

And he's ready.

He lines up the shot on the head-and-shoulders target presented him, and then he lets fly.

Again.

And again.

And again.

Till he's made a great big yawning hole of the head of the paper target.

And he allows himself to breathe again.

Lets himself rest.

The doctors all tell him to take things easy. That he shouldn't exert himself . . . though, what was the *exact* word they used?

. . . *Overexcited*, that was it.

He shouldn't get *overexcited*.

But it's very hard when you make your living killing, plugging real-life targets with bullets.

How is it possible *not* to get overexcited?

Still, as far as the doctors are concerned, AA is a simple office worker. That those bullet wounds he caught in his flesh were all a simple matter of crossfire.

If only they knew.

Because he can't tell them the truth.

Though, if he did, it might allow them to make a better assessment of his health.

AA never did know how to help himself.

Never did know when to stop, or when to pass on *anything*.

And—goodness—it's difficult to stop. When all the blood is pumping. And the heartstrings are all pulling. And the muscles are taut.

And when there's another *guy* watching on.

AA slams the switch to bring the target groaning along its roof track. Over to him. Just for fun. So that he can see that great big hole in the target's head up close.

Because he can see it just fine from here.

But there's never anything wrong with indulging a bit of ego, is there?

As the target whirs its way along its track, AA slips a sidelong glance to the rest of the gallery. He sees that the man with the beer gut and the lawyer woman have both left.

Got to get back to their wife, or their clients.

AA knows they come here to practise their self-defence. No real *professional* reason. But they need to *know*. Because, if AA ever gets the order to take care of one of them, to take care of either this lawyer or this guy with the beer gut, they're going to need much more than a little time spent on the Range.

They'll need luck.

And prayers.

AA narrows his gaze to the booth beside his, where the other man, about his age, has been firing away.

Empty.

AA flips his chewing gum about his teeth. Bites it between his molars. Feels the last of the liquorice flavour washing about his mouth, allows some of the flavour to slip down his throat to his gurgling stomach.

The air's filled with a metallic stench. And AA breathes it in hard.

He feels the heat rising in his cheeks, and the gentle *whir* as the paper target continues to swivel closer to him.

Alone on the Range.

Doesn't get much better than this.

And then, just as the paper target, as that head and shoulders, grinds to a halt in front of his eyes, there's a distant *pop* and yet another hole appears in the target.

In the chest.

A *smoking* hole.

5

AA SPINS ROUND, the Hotflush gripped tight in his hand. And he has his finger lingering over the trigger only to find himself facing off with the man who was in the booth alongside him.

Who has his own pistol raised.

AA's heart patters against his ribs. His blood flows fast. And cool. He tells himself to relax his muscles, to ease the tension out from his shoulders. And his body obeys him.

Just as it always does when he asks it nicely.

He waits out the time. His eyes on the laser-green eyes of the man.

Both standing with their pistols raised.

Neither one wanting to back down.

AA looks to the man's expression. Sees the stone complexion, and the fair-few, worn-in wrinkles about the nose, and at the corners of the mouth.

And then, slowly, the man's mouth curls back to reveal rows of pearl-white teeth. Beyond the cracked lips. And the man lowers his pistol.

But AA keeps his raised.

Just for the time being.

Just to be sure.

It's never wrong to be sure.

But it can often be *too late* to be sure.

The man nods at AA, to his pistol still clenched in his fist. "What's that you've got there, eh? Not like anything I've ever seen."

AA holds his pose. As he well knows, anybody that frequents this place has some *in* with somebody . . . has a connection with someone high up in either politics or business, or both.

Handguns are no laughing matter in London.

Not unless you're a solid twenty-feet underground, and hidden behind some pretty sturdy security. And given no small amount of protection from people in suits.

Ipso facto, trust in a place like the Range is for idiots, or people who have a death wish.

And AA has neither.

In fact, he clings to dreams of growing nice and ripe and old with his soul mate.

Not much in the way of originality, but a clear-cut dream nonetheless.

"Custom-made," AA says, answering the question about his gun, pinching his gum between his teeth and the inside of his mouth.

The man waves his hand downwards, indicating for AA to lower his gun.

But AA has no intention of doing so.

At least not quite yet.

"Come on," the man says, now switching his pistol over to the other hand, and holding it by the barrel, "we're all friends here. You really think if I tried anything here—with *you*—in this place, that I'd be allowed to get even over to that door without someone dropping me?"

He swings his free hand casually to the door where AA walked onto the Range.

AA keeps his eyes on the man's gun. Just where they should be. He doesn't care that he's holding the gun by the barrel. He's seen chatty customers before, and it's usually because they're trying to bluff—trying to pass themselves off as novices, amateurs.

But this man doesn't have a good poker face.

And, besides, AA has seen him shoot.

He can shoot just fine.

As far as AA knows, the man could flip the gun back into his shooting hand in the blink of an eyelid. And then blow AA away.

And AA would know nothing about it.

That's the thing about getting shot, it has a habit of refocussing your mind. It doesn't make you jumpy, not when you've got a gun in your hand.

On the contrary, it makes you steadier. More risk averse.

Because, quite simply put, you don't *want* to get shot again.

And so AA keeps his eyes well and truly fixed on the man's gun, and doesn't buy the bait of those laser-green eyes, no matter how attractive they might be.

Or how *ripped* that midriff is too.

The man shakes his head. His grin widens, and gives a little shrug. "Fine, then, guess you've left your manners at home or something, huh?"

"My manners are just fine. It's my clumsiness that's missing in action."

The grin gets wider still. The man nods to the target behind AA, but AA's certainly not falling for that trick. "You did a pretty good number on that fellow there, eh? Left him in tatters as far as I can see."

"You didn't do so badly yourself."

The man chuckles. "So you have been watching after all?"

"I *always* keep an eye on my surroundings. No other option if I really want to stay alive."

"In a place like this?"

"Especially in a place like this."

The man shakes his head, apparently out of disbelief. "All I wanted was to check over your gun, is that too much to ask?"

AA feels his heart throb. Those laser-green eyes are hard to ignore. It's like they burrow right through his skin. Down to the bone. Rip right through him. But he has to stay solid.

Has to take care.

Because he's been betrayed before . . . and not so long ago, so it'd be folly for him to trip up again so soon.

"Yes," AA says, and then adds, "it's too much to ask." He nods to the gun in the man's non-shooing hand. "Now take yourself back to your own booth and get on with your own session, deal?"

The man's grin wilts a little, but doesn't disappear. Remains there, like a throbbing vein pulsing just below the surface of the skin. "You said your gun is custom-made? And how's that, then? You had it all built up from scratch, got someone to make it for you?" He lets go of a tuneless whistle. "That's gotta cost quite a bit."

"Do you really think that someone who comes to the Range is struggling for money?"

The smile returns to its former glory. "You've gotta point there."

AA wiggles his gun—the Hotflush. "Go on, time for you to be getting back to your own shooting, don't you think?"

The man holds up his hands, his gun still gripped in his non-shooting hand. "Come on," he says, "you know as well as I do that they'll take you down just as easily as they'll take me if you decide to take a shot."

At this AA feels a warm flush rise in his cheeks. "You think so?"

"Sure," the man says, but with a slightly raised pitch.

"I wouldn't be so confident if I were you."

"Why's that?"

AA thinks it over long and hard. Thinks about revealing just who he works for. Telling this guy that, if AA wanted—if he *really* wanted—he could plug the guy with the whole magazine, and no one would bat an eyelid.

Not once he tells them who he's working for.

"Last chance," AA says. "Just turn round, go back to your

shooting, and I'll just go back to mine."

At this, the guy tenses up, and his smile finally gives way for good. He still grips his gun hard in his fist. "Come on, lighten up a little, won't you? I just wanted to check out what you're packing there." He nods to the Hotflush as if it wasn't totally obvious what he was referring to. "Is that so impertinent, or what?"

"Yes."

"Yes, what?"

"Yes, it's impertinent. I'm very particular about just who I introduce my guns to."

The man closes his eyes. He holds his free hand up to his forehead. He shakes his head.

AA still keeps his eyes fixed on the man's gun. Ready to take the shot at any time.

"Come on," the man says, "I mean, if you really thought that I'd come here to kill you, or *whatever*, don't you think that I could've just plugged you from behind? Shot you right through the back of the skull? Wouldn't that have been way cleaner? I mean, look, now I've spoken to you, and you know as well as I do that it makes a hit far more personal."

AA scans the context of the man's sentence with great care. So this man is an assassin too or, at least, he wants to keep up the pretence that he is one.

It would be better to be cautious whatever his plan is.

"Why else would I have done that thing to get your attention? Think about it, it doesn't make any sense otherwise."

AA keeps his gun raised, pointed right at the man's forehead. "I'll grant you that it's unprofessional what you're up to right now, speaking with your target, way against any pro conduct I'm familiar with, but the fact remains: You waited till those other two cleared on out of the Range before coming up to me. That's what gave you away."

"Won't you at least tell me who you're working for?"

AA stays still, keeping his finger lingering over the trigger.

The man's eyes seem to bulge out from their sockets.

AA notices the gun in the man's non-shooting hand swivel about.

The man grips the gun. In his left hand. Brings it round.

Ready to shoot.

But AA beats him to it.

6

THREE BULLETS LATER and AA stands over the man's body.

The man fell down on his knees, his back arching backwards, and his gun clattering to his feet.

A nice, clean kill, considering.

Now it'd be all right to tell him who his employer is.

"Brian Mathewson," AA says as he steps away from the corpse, hearing a dozen alarms all clang out on the Range.

He hears stomping feet.

And hurried voices.

The door to the Range slides open all of a sudden. A group of five security men. Dressed in blue-and-black camos. They all carry semi-automatics as they strafe into the room.

One covering the other.

They stick to the walls.

One calls out to AA, tells him to drop his gun.

AA does what he's told.

When they come close enough, see the man lying dead on the floor, they demand AA gets down on the floor beside him. That he lies himself face down.

Again, AA does just what he's told.

The floor of the Range is cheek-numbingly cold, hard cement. And AA can feel his heart pulsing away inside his mouth.

When one of the security men asks him who he works for, he tells them.

They ask him kindly to get to his feet. And wish him a pleasant day.

AA trudges off the Range with the Hotflush tight in his grip, and a smile pressed onto his lips.

Killing. It's what he does for a living.

And if your job doesn't make you happy, then why're you doing it?

At least that's the credo AA has lived by his entire life. And Brian Mathewson makes AA very happy indeed. Gives him the flexibility to simply do just what he does best.

And pays him well for it too.

BLUE LIGHTS

1

I DRIVE LIKE A MADWOMAN through the mid-morning traffic, cutting off old ladies, men in business suits, looking extremely serious, and mums with carfuls of kids on their way to wherever kids go in the holidays. I guess I should really be a little more empathetic with that last one, considering that I've got two kids of my own.

I'm not usually this bad of a driver, what with this weaving in and out of lanes, ploughing up the dirty, exhaust-strewn backsides of lorries, but I'm on an urgent mission, and I need to get there as soon as—

There's a loud *honk* at my tail and I check the rear-view mirror. It's a police car. Of course it is—just my luck. I glance up at the rear-view mirror again, then think to myself.

My employer—Brian Mathewson, owner of Mathewson Media, which provides both media and publicity services—has cleared me to break whatever traffic laws I want to get to my destination as quickly as possible. Brian holds the sort of power that turns most presidents of banana republics green with envy. So I clamp my fingers around the steering wheel, my fingers falling into those plastic indentations, and grit my teeth, the faint scent of toothpaste still there from my hurried morning brush. I press the accelerator right to the floor, like I've seen in films, and I get a little buzz from doing it in real life.

I swerve out of my lane, undertaking a bright red sports car before me, enjoying that disbelieving look from the fifty-something man in a suit driving it. Then I buck back in front of him, and the fast lane's all clear now. I really open up the accelerator and hear that shrill, high-pitched snarl of the engine, feeling the vibrations pass through my body, send shudders up and down my spine.

Once I see open road up ahead, I glance in my rear-view mirror. All I can see are the cars at my tail, slowly rolling back into the horizon. No sign of the police car. I guess they had bigger fish to fry than a reckless speeder. All the same, I reach across my dashboard where my mobile sits in its cradle and hit the speed dial. A few phone burbles later and I'm being connected to Brian. He picks up and says, "Anna? That you?"

He always likes to pull these games, make it seem like he doesn't check that caller ID every time he gets a call—thing with Brian is that he *knows* when or when not to take a call, who or who not he *needs* to talk to.

I allow myself a little grin before I say, "Yeah, I might need you to flex some muscle with the local constabulary—think I might've pissed off a patrol a few seconds back."

I hear tapping in the distance and I just know that he's triangulating my exact location from my phone's signal, or something. "Forgot to say," he says, "there's been a bit of a change of plan."

I roll my eyes at this. If I had a penny for every time I've been told 'there's a change of plan' or 'something's come up' . . . well I think I'm just going to start screaming every time it happens from now on. Okay, starting next time.

Brian continues, "Look, I've pulled the strings, but there was only so much I could do. I gave the police your details—registration, description, all of that. They said they were sending someone with you to make sure you wouldn't contaminate the scene."

When he says 'scene,' he means murder scene. I know, this is where it gets a little messy. But, from where my job's concerned it's not that big of a deal. Well, considering that I'm used to working with live bodies this should be an easy one. There's no one to kill.

With Brian's words still crackling around my car speakers, I glance back into the rear-view mirror and, surprise, surprise, there's the police car, blue lights all lit up, flashing away. "So," I say to Brian, "you're absolutely certain this is going to be fine— that I'll pull over and it'll all go all right?"

"I give you my word," he says, and then, amidst the buzzing of another of the dozen mobiles Brian keeps, he hangs up.

I breathe in deep, that new car scent still lingering in this car which I took out this morning from the Mathewson Media car pool. I eye the police car, bombing closer by the second, lights all flashing, and then, with a slight sigh, I check my mirrors—there's nothing behind me of course—and then I swoop across the lanes and onto the hard shoulder where I, reluctantly, pick my foot up off the accelerator and apply the brake.

My stomach drops as I brake hard and I listen to the sad *whine* of the car slowing down, the light scrabble of loose gravel flying beneath it, some pieces leaping up and pinging off the bottom. And then, just like that, I'm stopped. A brief, silent pause and then traffic rushes by me once more with a *whoosh* of air and the *roar* of engines.

As I undo my seatbelt, peel it away from my shoulder, I glance out the window and see the suit in the red car passing by. In that fraction of a second I get to look into his car I'm sure I can see him smirking, going on his way satisfied that justice is all balanced in the world.

And now I turn my attention to the police car, the opening door, and the policewoman stepping out of it. I sink my teeth into my lower lip and taste a little gloss there. Just my luck that I get a woman—still there's always a chance . . . but I'm clutching at straws now.

I turn in my seat and just hope—blindly hope—that Brian's not going to steer me wrong. This time.

2

I LOOK INTO MY WING MIRROR. The police officer has neat blond hair, gathered up into a bun at the back of her head, the rest of her hair pressed down by her trim, navy blue hat. She's quite small, but bunched up, muscular, and I know that —all things being equal, no guns involved—she could quite easily take me in a fight. When she draws level with the car, she reaches out and raps neatly on the window, that glassy *thunk* of her knuckles against the thick glass—which, like all windows in the Mathewson Media car pool, is also bulletproof.

I reach forward and depress the button. The window winds down with its distinctive mechanical *whine*, and I turn my head to look up at her.

I catch a whiff of the dual carriageway behind her, the exhaust. Just as she opens her mouth, the words are stolen away by a passing lorry, which sends the suspension of the car rocking and my heart suddenly racing. With an annoyed pout, she glances back over her shoulder, as if calculating whether or not she can race to catch up with that lorry, and then turns her attention back to me. This time there're no interruptions.

"You must be Anna Harris," she says.

I get a small rush of blood to the head, and can't resist a smile, feeling like the naughty girl at school who's just been caught by the deputy head creeping through the corridors five minutes after the bell.

The police woman, however, doesn't return my smile. "You know you were going at a fair rate back there, don't you?"

"Was I?"

She nods glumly.

Several lorries rumble by, that stench of exhaust becomes almost overwhelming, and the police woman coughs several times, before getting a hold on herself and looking at me through narrowed eyes. She waits for the sound of the lorries to dissipate, and then says, "Know where you're going?" she says.

I nod in reply.

"Fine, but I'm going to lead the way, okay? Some of us have rules we have to follow."

The police woman turns on her heel and I watch her—again in my wing mirror—returning to her car, wasting no time before slipping back in behind the wheel. As she turns the ignition I hear the faint couple of beats of the siren and watch the shimmer of the blue lights on the roof. And then she's pulling out into the road again. Remembering myself, I do the same, following her lead.

3

A S I FOLLOW HER, I grip the plasticky wheel tighter, burying my fingers deeper in its grooves, gritting my teeth too, tasting my slick tooth enamel. I try to work out what it is about this lady I'm not quite keen on. Maybe it was her tone, the way she spoke to me in that schoolmarm way. I don't take kindly to people belittling who I am or what I do just because I'm not affiliated to any union, or because I'm not subscribed to any pension plan.

We swoop through a built-up area, all great towering sand-coloured constructions. The windows are all tinted blue. It's a fairly modern area, and I can almost smell the cement mixer still churning, hear flatulent builders bellowing to one another.

The police woman sticks right to the limit as we pass through the residential zone. We pass a school, which I see is deserted, just a bunch of wooden chairs standing on the tables. I always thought that was the reason why the tables at school were so covered in graffiti, chewing gum stuck to the underside. Any cleaner who dared take a spray can of polish and rag to that thing would be facing an avalanche of chairs at any moment— taking her life in her hands. Guess that's another reason to be cheerful that I'm not a cleaner.

She indicates to pull off into a cul-de-sac, and I watch her, very clearly through her rear window, jerk her head from side to side, doing it all by the book, checking all the angles, before she actually does the turning. In a way it's useful, because she's done my looking for me, so I just need to plough around the bend without letting off the accelerator much at all, and I certainly don't stray anywhere near the brake.

Houses spring up on both sides. The cul-de-sac is marked by trees too, great big green, leafy fellows. It's the kind of street you see in films when you're a kid, what with a great big wide road, lots of room for ball games and hijinks. Shame that, for most of us, it's just a fantasy.

I remember, from my own briefing, that we're meant to be looking for house number forty-three. Before I've even had a chance to glance along the house fronts, I see the police woman applying her brakes, the bright red lights shining back, just about burning the backs of my irises. And I roll up behind her. When I see through her rear window I see that steady bluish glow of a monitor, a GPS map running. Clever bitch. Or maybe I'm just a dumb one.

The house itself isn't all that remarkable, which is to say—just like the rest of the houses on the street—it's just your standard five-bedroom place, what with twirling ivy crawling up the walls, thick . . . *bushy* bushes and a neat gravel driveway. There's a white-washed back gate, too, which I imagine leads to a fairly expansive garden. Lawn pristinely cut, of course.

I reach over into the passenger's side. I snap open the glove box and look to the pistol I slipped in there this morning, nestled inside in a crimson piece of velvet. Just in case. Sometimes it pays to have a gun close. I shove the glove box shut again then lock it up, checking twice to see that it's truly secure.

As I step out of the car, I take in that fresh-cut-grass smell, that woody, sap smell of the trees, and listen to the steady silence, only broken by a faint hum—way in the background—of the dual carriageway we travelled along to get here. I'm sure I can, somehow, taste strawberries in the air.

I take hold of the car's thick, heavy door and give it a *slam*. It makes that reassuring, snug muted *slap*, the one that tells you that, however hard you shut it, however angry you are, it's such a feat of engineering that the hinges'll never buckle, let alone break off.

Without so much as casting a glance in my direction, the

police woman struts her way up the gravel pathway, the gravel crunching beneath her steady bootfalls. When she reaches the front door, she glances back over her shoulder, then waits patiently as I take my time in walking my own way up the path.

The truth is, doing this, visiting the scene of a death, I'm feeling just a touch inexperienced, unworthy. This isn't really what I do. So I'm determined to take everything I've seen on TV and in films, heard on the radio, and put on a good private detective impression. To be honest, it looks like, detective impression or no, the police woman hasn't noticed.

"Have you got the key?" she says, with a short, sharp tone.

I dig down into my pocket and withdraw the key I found this morning, in a white envelope stuck beneath the windscreen wiper of the car pool car. I glance at it hard for a moment, again putting on my detective's impression, filling the gesture with meaning, before handing it over to her.

She near enough snatches it from my fingers and then jams it into the lock. The mechanism turns almost silently, only the mere suggestion of a *click*. That's the standard of living a place like this affords. All the little things are taken care of.

She steps over the threshold, wiping her feet several times on the well-used doormat—so well-used that it resembles a scouring pad more than a doormat. I follow her in, already musing that the people that live here must have some sort of help, what to keep the garden in order, neatly trimmed, and the outside looking fresh. But when it comes to things like doormats, they really aren't all that interested. I guess most people don't see the doormat from the outside.

The house is a little gloomy, which is more the day's fault than the house's, what with this grim, grey overcast weather we're having—another excuse for a British summer.

The police woman clicks on a light switch with a smart *snap* and a steady orange glow shines on the hallway.

My heart jiggles just a bit, as I'm sure I've caught her out. "Aren't we supposed to keep from contaminating a crime scene?" I say, feeling my tonsils bob up and down as I speak.

She shrugs then heads on into the house.

As I follow her, brushing the impeccable, matted wallpaper against my forearm as I go, I suppose that—where one of Brian Mathewson's clients is concerned—there aren't so many rules. Their reputation comes first and, alive or dead, must be protected at all costs.

When I turn the corner, a steady, rusty stench of blood crawls up my nostrils. My stomach heaves and I taste bile at the back of my throat. But I keep the vomit down, covering my mouth with my the back of my hand. What a sight.

I T'S NOT that I'm not used to smelling blood, or even being around dead bodies. But it's more just the sheer out-of-place quality about the whole thing. This *nice* neighbourhood, this *nice* street, and this *nice* house. You can never quite get used to the horrible happening around *niceness*. But here it is, all spread out before me.

There is blood all over the place. In fact, when I lift my foot from the carpet and I notice the *squelch* it makes me cringe. I look over to the police woman, who's standing with one hand on her hip, a slight smirk on her face, eyeing me over the body. "You going to be all right?" she says. "Or should I put a call into your boss?"

I don't reply, instead turning to the task at hand. Namely, the dead body before us. I study the pattern of the dress she's wearing—the dead body—a blue, flower-printed number, that just shimmies an inch above the knee. When I say blue I mean that it was probably blue before whereas now it's been permanently stained purple, what with the mixture of her blood and the material. Her arms are sprawled and her eyes are open wide, her mouth even wider. When I look up from my studies, I notice the police woman still there, the same petulant look on her face.

"Well?" she says. "Deduced anything?"

I straighten up, and then, seeing an opportunity to defuse the tension in the air, put on my straightest face and hold out my hand to her, across the dead body. "I don't think we got the chance to formally introduce ourselves."

"I know who you are," she says, her eyes smouldering like hot coals.

"But I don't know your name."

She pats her pocket, sending some unseen coins or keys jangling. She squeezes her lips into, what's fast becoming, her trademark pout and then reaches out across. Our palms clasp together, I note her slightly sweaty, but otherwise chilly skin, and then we break it off. She sniffs a little, apparently not completely immune to the stench of blood here, then says, "Name's Officer Douglas."

I jab my tongue into my cheek, taste the bumpy, soft skin there, then say, "Right, Officer Douglas, let's get something straight, okay? I'm going to be honest with you. I really don't have the foggiest clue why Brian's sent me here—had me come all the way down here—to look at some dead client of his, but that's what he asked me to do."

We lock eyes, then I continue, "I'm not a police officer, and I've got no plans of treading over your domain, just as you've got none, I hope, of treading over mine. So, with that in mind, can we just cut the frosty, cat-fighting bullshit and get on with our respective jobs?"

She cocks her head to one side, looking at me askance, then says, "And what exactly is your *domain*?"

"Precisely none of your business."

"Oh come on, now, if we're going to be honest—have a fresh start—then you need to let me in on what it is you're doing for Brian Mathewson."

"If I told you I'd have to kill you."

She arches an eyebrow, shakes her head in disbelief and then, with a sigh, looks back down at the body. "Looks like you've been watching a few too many films."

"Maybe," I say, then can't think of anything more witty to say —perhaps I *should* watch some more films.

After another of those long, pregnant pauses, Officer Douglas returns to looking over the dead body. Apparently finished with her gander, she looks up at me. "Look," she says. "I'm not a detective any more than you are. You know why he chose me—why Brian decided to trust me?"

"Nope."

"It's because I've done this before." She pauses a moment, thinking and then adds, "Well, that and him and my dad are close—pretty close—friends. He knows he can trust me."

"And who's your dad?"

"Charlie Branwick, Chief Constable of Police around here."

"And what does he think of his daughter running around, doing grunt work as an officer?"

She colours slightly, and, naughty me, I take a little pleasure in having got a rise from her. But, a moment later, any flush is gone, and she says, "I want to work my way up—show that I can do it just like he did. I don't want any family favours."

To be fair, I'm quite impressed by her measured response, not to mention her modesty. But I can still see where she's angling, what information she wants, so I say, "And what's that supposed to mean, that I can just break down and tell you what it is I do for Brian? You do realise that it affects him too, if anyone finds out what it is I do?"

She looks at me long and hard, those penetrating, sapphire-blue eyes and a slight scent—that I'm only getting just now—of strawberry-scented perfume, maybe that was what I caught a whiff of outside the house. I get the taste of strawberries in my mouth, which is better than the taste of blood, I suppose.

She wiggles her nose, like a bunny rabbit, then says, "You're an assassin, aren't you? Brian pays you to kill people."

I guess my mouth forms one of those cartoon strip *o*'s because she smiles back at me, satisfied. "That's it, isn't it?" she says. "You're the one they were talking about. I mean, I've heard Dad and Brian talking about you—talking about a *she*. You're the one who does Brian's dirty work."

"I'm *one* of them that does Brian's dirty work."

"But the only girl?"

It's been a long time since someone's referred to me as a 'girl' before, but I guess I get over it fairly sharpish, because I manage to say, "Officer Douglas—"

"Call me Amy," she says.

"All right, *Amy*, don't you think we should get a move on here? I mean, whatever muscle Brian pulls with your dad, don't you think that your dad would appreciate a fairly quick assessment of the circumstances here—give him a chance to get this back into the proper protocol for handling scenes like this?"

Again, she flushes slightly, and I can see that there's still more than a little bit of naivety about her, and think that her earning her stripes probably is a good thing. And it impresses me that she notices her own lack of experience too. Her own short-comings.

"So," I say, "any ideas on this thing—anything that I should let Brian know about?"

She measures the scene, long and hard, then steps around the body. She ventures over to the large front window, peering out into the street. The clouds are rolling over now, getting darker, and I know that when I step outside it'll smell like rain. She pulls back from the window then heads over the blood-sodden carpet, and through a door.

I follow her through and the next room turns out to be a kitchen. It has marble surfaces, chrome finishings and emerald-green tiles. Quite a nice kitchen, if a little dark. Not that I can make any comment, considering my own kitchen would probably win any nationwide prize for darkest and pokiest going. Then again, I don't suppose the owner is going to put up much of a defence to my verbal remarks, let alone the mental ones.

Amy stares out through the kitchen window, into the back garden. She scans the place with a slight squint.

"Do you wear glasses usually?" I say.

As she turns to face me, I notice a strand of her blond hair has gone rogue, that it dangles down from beneath her hat. She's still got that rosy, slightly warm, colour in her cheeks. "Yes, why?"

"Just the way you're squinting."

She shrugs, then returns to her staring out the window. "I wear contacts, actually, better not to wear glasses on duty, too many horror stories of getting them broken—getting glass in your eye." She smoothes down her navy-blue jacket then takes a step back, still eyeing the back garden through the window. "But forgot to put my contacts in this morning—Brian called pretty early and I had to head down to the station to check out a car." She glances back at me then gives me a nervous smile. "Sometimes being the chief's daughter doesn't make you so popular with the more bureaucratic aspects of the force—takes quite a bit of brown-nosing to keep everyone onside, make it seem like you're not getting special treatment. And then, well, a case like this comes along, and I've got no choice." She shrugs again. "I guess as much as I try I'll always be Chief Charlie's daughter."

"Yes," I say, feeling myself warming to Amy by the second, then I meet her gaze and look out the window. I let loose a sigh, feeling the urge for my mid-morning coffee coming on. "So, anything else we should take a look at here, or are we done?"

She closes one eye, continuing to peer out into the back garden. "There is something," she says, then she motions for us to head out the back door.

5

I'M AT A LOSS for quite a while about what she's got in mind.

Amy walks over to the fence and crouches down, running her fingers along the base of the wood. She busies herself there, not bothering to give me any explanation.

I go over to her, look around her to the fence. There, at the base of the fence, I can see a scrap of material. And then, moving closer, I can see that there's a hole at the base of the wooden posts. The earth is all dug up, and there's enough space for someone to crawl under.

She glances back at me and gives me the sliver of a smile.

"Maybe you should get your eyes tested again," I say.

Leaving the scrap of material there, she gets up, then brushes the earth off the shins of her trousers. "Long-sighted," she says. "I can see things further off fine—better than most in fact." She grins. "It's kind of like a superpower."

"Yeah, I guess it is." I shift my weight from one foot to the other, still examining the scrap of material there. I think back to the dead woman in the sitting room. "So what does this mean?" I say.

Amy looks me up and down then says, "Well, I guess it's up to you to go and find the killer—bring him to justice, isn't it?"

I shrug. "Could be, I guess, but it's never that simple."

Just as that thought shoots through my mind, my mobile buzzes in my pocket. When I pull it out I see that it's Brian. Of course it is.

"What's the situation?" he says.

I explain to him about the lady's body, the scrap of material we've just found beneath the fence, snagged against the wood— the obvious direction in which the murderer has escaped. As I speak, I roll my eyes at Amy, who giggles back in response. I'm definitely warming to her as time goes on. Anyone who laughs at my jokes—or attempted jokes—is okay in my book.

However, what Brian has to say next certainly doesn't have me laughing.

"Right," he says, with that insanely pragmatic tone of his, "this is what you're going to do next. First, I want you to go about the house, with Amy, and scrub the whole place top to bottom, then—"

My heart pounds a couple of times, and the smell of the flowers—I think they're petunias—gets a touch too strong for a moment. I break off eye contact with Amy. "I beg your pardon," I say. "What do I look like to you, a cleaner?"

And then, a beat too late, I think of how—if I was a normal person—the question I would've asked was why the hell we weren't calling the police. Thankfully Brian's an understanding boss, not all that out of step when it comes to dealing with sociopaths.

Brian continues, "After you've scrubbed the house up I'll have someone come by for the body—I'll let you know closer to the time what their cover is, but"—and here I'm sure I can hear a smile in his voice—"I'm playing around with the idea of refriger-ator salesmen. What do you think?"

My heart beats in my ears, thick and booming. I feel sick again, Amy's strawberry scent making my mouth water. In the distance I hear a lawn mower choke into life. A bird squawks as it passes overhead.

"Now," Brian says, "I'd like you there the whole time, just to keep an eye on the place, make sure everything goes smoothly. Don't worry about Amy, she's well onside, anything you can see she can see. One-hundred-per-cent trust."

I look over to Amy, who's picked up on my uncertainty and is now watching on anxiously. And then I have a churning in my gut, and I know that it's my conscience, my *damn* righteous conscience, and I have to ask the question or I won't be able to live with myself. "What about the . . . the murderer. What happens to him?"

"Hmm?" Brian says, as if he hasn't heard me.

"We found the scrap of clothing. Shouldn't . . . I mean, shouldn't we tell the police?"

Brian stays quiet on the other end of the line. When he comes back, his tone is bright, and I imagine him standing there in his office, gazing out the window across the London skyline with a glass of whisky in his hand, perhaps his breath is creating a light mist on the glass. "That was the fridge men. Should be there around an hour or so. Enough time to clean up don't you think?" And then he hangs up.

I bring my mobile down slowly from my ear, staring off into space, thinking.

Amy looks to me eagerly. It's almost as though she's a vibrating ball of energy, just ready to burst from the seams. "What?" she says. "What did he say? Does he want me to put a call through to Dad?"

I just eye her and then look back down, to that scrap of material stuck to the fence.

6

WE FINISH UP cleaning the house about forty-five minutes later. It's funny, once we find the cleaning stuff in the cupboard it's quite a quick job. We can't quite get out the whole stain, and no cleaning product on Earth will, but I guess the idea is to make it look a little less like a blood-soaked carpet. And I think we've succeeded at that.

While we've been cleaning, Amy's stayed totally quiet, just going about her work, unmoved. Us cleaning around this dead body, getting all the blood out. I'm just getting up off my knees, wiping the thin layer of sweat from my forehead with the back of my hand, when I hear the rumble of an engine outside, feel the vibrations passing through the floor.

"Right," I say, to Amy, "looks like they're here."

She doesn't reply.

The doorbell chimes, one of those hideous pieces of music played just half a step out of tune. I have no idea what particular piece of music this one is but it sounds familiar—familiar enough and annoying enough to suggest that it might be a kids' tune.

I answer the door and two men stand on the doorstep with a large container between them. This, I guess, is what they use to transport fridges, or at least that's what the average curtain twitcher sees. They both look in their mid-forties—judging by the thinning hair and the stages of their beer bellies. Both nod to me and then, me stepping aside, they lug the fridge box in through the front door. They seem to know where they're going, although they might just as well be following their noses, drawn to that pungent chemical smell coming from the sitting room.

I stand about in the hall, listening to their *grunts* and murmured remarks to one another as they go about the business of loading the body into their fridge box. Approximately five minutes later they lug the box back out again, straining under-standably a little more this time round. I watch them off down the gravel path, their boots crunching along it, and then see them load the fridge box into their van before driving off.

I smell that familiar strawberry fragrance. My mouth waters, and I start thinking about the last time I ate—thinking fondly of my breakfast several hours ago. I turn my head to see Amy standing there. Her eyes skitter about their sockets before coming to rest on me. She can only make eye contact a brief few moments before she looks back to the living room, to that discoloured blotch on the carpet, and the cleaning hatchet job.

When Amy touches me on the arm, I flinch as if she's just run a blade between a pair of my ribs. In turn, she flinches at my flinch, taking a step back as she does so. When she speaks it's with a tired, almost whiny voice. It takes me a moment to place it and when I do I realise it's just the same tone my daughter takes when she's pining for something.

"So," Amy says, "that's it?"

"What's *it*?"

"We're, you know, not going to call the police in—nothing like that. I mean, someone murdered the woman, don't we have to find out who? They could be dangerous, still running around."

Although I have a heavy heart these little injustices are fairly typical for me. To be honest, someone with my job description can't really afford to grow a moral compass—not if they want to remain employable. I turn to make my way out of the house, my job now done.

Amy's sudden, strong, grip on my shoulder stops me before can walk another step. She wheels me around and stares into my face with a new steel in those azure eyes, an icy blue fire. "It's not right," she says.

I realise that for all Amy's little-girl tendencies she's much stronger than me and I'm not going anywhere till she physically allows me. Or one of us loses an eye. My shoulders rise and fall with a profound sigh. "Look," I say. "This is how it is, okay? This is much bigger than the both of us, there's no point in us complaining about it. It's just the way it is," I add, unconvincingly.

"What are you doing the rest of today?" she says.

"What do you mean?"

"The rest of today, do you have more . . . work to do?"

"Not really any of your business."

Her eyes flash and she smiles. "Didn't think so. What about if the two of us look for him? Find the killer and bring him to justice."

"Uh, what do you mean by justice?"

She reaches up and grasps a loose strand of that blond hair between finger and thumb. She jabs it back up beneath her police cap. Her smile widens, a touch deviously, I think. "Well, if we can't call the police then . . ." she pauses a moment, her grip on my shoulder draws tighter ". . . you're an *assassin*. You've got a gun, haven't you?"

I try to squirm out from beneath her grip, but, just like I thought before, she holds on strong, and there's no chance of me getting away. Annoyed, I look back at her. "If you're so hopped up about justice then why don't you do it yourself?"

"What?"

"Don't act like that, you know that you can do it on your own." I shrug my shoulders to indicate her vicelike grip there. "Look at that, if you get hold of him you can do him in yourself, with your bare hands. That's more than I can do. I usually work with a pistol and, more importantly, cover from Brian. Without either of those I don't kill anyone. If you really want some proper assassin, why not go down a pub and round up some mobsters, being police I'm sure you know the places, one of those'll be just as happy to help you out I'm sure. If the money's right, that is."

Her grip tightens on my shoulder and then, all of a sudden, just loosens completely.

I take the opportunity to get a few steps away from her. I step out the front door and set foot on the gravel, already preparing myself psychologically for the ride in the car back home—I'm deliberating whether I'm going to listen to the classical station or the rock one, that's about the stage my mind's at right now.

"I know who you are, Anna Harris."

I sniff a laugh. "Right, that's what it says on my driver's licence, congratulations. If there's anything else then you can reach me through Brian Mathewson. Got it?" I say as I turn and walk back toward the car.

"You think that Brian protects you?"

I keep walking, putting her out of mind.

"What do you think, if it comes down to it, who do you think he'll protect if it comes to a choice between you and his best friend's daughter—his *life*long best friend's daughter?"

I shake my head slightly, knowing that this has all the hallmarks of an impending tantrum. I feel the car keys in my pocket and slip them out. I press the button and the lights flash and a *whip-whap* sound comes from the car.

"Anna!" she says, sounding more frantic now.

I reach the car, open the door on the driver's side and turn around, prepared to humour her for one last moment.

She drops her voice, and there's no trace of hysteria now. Thinking about it there's a slightly maniacal look in her eye. But it's calculated, she's weighed up the risks and reached her conclusion. "If you go now I'll turn you in—make it known who you are."

I roll my eyes and step into the car, allowing myself to sink into the plush cushion of the driver's seat, to breathe in that new car smell, to cleanse my pallet of its bloody strawberry taste.

"Brian won't be able to save you—not with the people I

know." She breaks into a wide grin. "Don't you think that there's a reason Brian's friends with my father, why he keeps him close after all these years?" Her smile straightens out. "It's because he could destroy Brian in a moment and don't think Brian will stop to save you if it comes between him saving face and him saving you."

I think this through, look at it from all the angles. Then, finally, I glance back at Amy, standing there on the doorstep, her features a little in shadow now that the sun's come out. I curl my fingers around the steering wheel, and close my eyes, shut them as tight as I can until I see little purple stars. I haven't really got much choice, have I?

7

BACK IN THE HOUSE, Amy puts her policing head to good work on that piece of material. Without so much as blinking an eye she digs out a photograph on the mantelpiece, a photo of the dead woman and, who I presume to be, her husband. She matches the material up with the jacket he's wearing in said photo and from there on declares him to be the murderer. And, really, I'm just ready to go along with it. I try not to think that I could quite easily be back home by now, feet up on the sofa, watching crap on television with my cat in my lap purring as I bury my hands in her warm, fuzzy belly. But instead I'm getting blackmailed by a blond rookie cop, albeit one with connections . . . or at least balls enough to stick the wind up me.

We get done with all the evidence shifting and finger-pointing, and Amy makes a list of the various places that the man—this man who we've established is called Peter Williamson—might have run off to. She has a bunch of places she hooked together from out of, I don't even want to ask how many, pieces of paraphernalia dotted about the house—a membership card to a sports club, a library card and an identity badge to some laboratory, which I guess is where he works.

Why someone on the run would ever think, after killing his wife, of running to one of his regular places where he'd be likely to be seen is beyond me. Then again, I guess anyone who is psychotic enough to kill his wife in the first place might well have some other mental deficiencies.

Before I know it, we're driving in the police car—with Amy promising to drop me off back at the house when we're done—and headed for the sports club. I have to give it to her, despite her showing fang back there, threatening to blow my cover as an assassin, she's become quite chirpy all of a sudden about the prospects of catching this Williamson guy. And why shouldn't she? She's not the one that's going to have to kill him.

We roll up at the entrance to the sports club car park. And a guard appears from within a booth, signalling for us to roll down our window. He wears a light beige uniform with a pillar-box hat perched on his head. He reminds me of the bellboys in posh hotels—and that probably tells me all I need to know about this place.

I let Amy do the talking, catching a whiff of the guard's cologne as he leans over into the car. She gets through with him, getting hold of a temporary parking permit, or some such nonsense, and then we're inside, heading for a space near the entrance to the building.

The place opens up into a large glass dome and through the sheeny windows I can make out the Olympic-length swimming pool inside, and the gym a little further beyond that. On the cusp of entering the building, Amy reaches out and touches my arm.

"What?" I say, just wanting to get through with this and be on my way—back home with my cat.

"I think it'll look a little odd if I wander in there—in uniform. Maybe it's better if you go and ask."

I roll my eyes, but can't see any good logical reason not to do what she says, well considering that I'm being blackmailed, that is. And so I strut on inside, that stench of chlorine and floor polish making itself known to my nostrils, and the faintly muted splashes coming from the pool through the reinforced glass.

I approach the reception desk and lay my hands on the plasticky surface, feeling it cold and strangely bumpy beneath my fingertips. I take in the receptionist who's a brunette with heavy blue eye shadow. She has the top three buttons of her light blue blouse undone which exposes her faint line of cleavage. I guess her at being about nineteen, maybe twenty.

I stuff my hand into my pocket and come up with Peter

Williamson's passport which Amy snaffled from the house. I peel it open to the back page and slide it over to the receptionist. "Have you see this man coming in today?" I say.

She squints at the passport, then looks up at me, closing one eye, reminding me a little of Amy and her long-sightedness. "No," she says. "I don't think so."

"But you recognise him?"

She slides the passport back across the desk to me. "Sure, that's Mr Williamson. Comes in here just about every day."

"But he didn't come in today? This morning?"

She pouts then shakes her head. "Don't think so."

"Are you sure?" I say, feeling my tone take on a sharpness.

"Yes."

I allow myself to transition back into a light smile then, snatching the passport back and stuffing it back into my pocket, I head back out to the car park where Amy's waiting, leaning back up against the car with both hands behind her back.

"Well?" she says.

I toss the passport back at her, and she catches it at chest height. "Hasn't been in there today," I say, getting into the other side of the car.

She sighs then gets in her side. She brings the door shut with a *slam* and her strawberry-scented perfume wafts back over to me —not unwelcome following that chlorine stench. And I can almost taste the strawberries on my tongue. Strawberries, I think with a touch of bitterness, like the ones in my fridge back home. The ones I might just as easily be scattering over my cereal right now.

8

AND SO we go about on our way, to the library, of course, Amy getting all excited again, and then we head off to the laboratory, with that identity card Amy dug out. We turn up absolutely nothing. It's a complete blank.

We sit in the car park of the laboratory, me with my head propped up on my fist, forehead pressed up against the freezing cold inside of the window, and Amy staring at her mobile which is slowly vibrating its way across her dashboard.

After a few seconds I turn my head to her, my neck now aching like nothing else—crying out for a hot bubble bath. "Aren't you going to get that?" I say.

She just continues to stare at the mobile.

"Amy?" I say.

She shoots me a sidelong glance. "It's Daddy."

"Well, won't he get angry if he finds out you're screening his calls?" I stretch my arms out and hear a light click of some bone or other before my fingertips brush against the plastic dashboard. "Anyway, I thought, what with you being the chief's daughter, it wouldn't be much of a problem for you to go missing for a while."

This time she eyes me for longer, her look taking on a bit of that little-girl gaze again.

The mobile stops buzzing.

When I catch sight of the display I see that it's the fifth time that 'Dad' has tried to call Amy. I glance out through the windscreen to the brick wall before us—there's a pipe there that's sprung a leak and that's spraying dirty, brown water into a puddle. "So what now?" I say.

Amy just shakes her head and keeps staring into space. I take in those relaxed muscles, all bunched up beneath her uniform and I start thinking about taking opportunities. But then I remember these 'friends' she's got and I don't want to push my luck. If I play it lightly here, manage to talk her down from this game she's playing, I might be able to get away all the sooner.

And then the mobile buzzes again, and I make the snap decision that softly-softly just isn't going to cut it. I lurch over the handbrake and grab the phone off its spot on the dashboard, evading Amy's flailing arm as I do so. And before she knows it I've got the phone pressed up against my ear, and I can hear a gruff male voice on the other end. "Chief Constable Douglas, I presume."

I eye Amy who's falling back into her seat, apparently defeated, knowing that now she's got to sit there and be patient, for the time being anyway, then I listen to what it is that Constable Douglas has to say.

"Who's this speaking?"

"Anna," I say. "Anna Harris."

There's a long pause on the line, I can't be sure but I think I hear him mutter some remark to someone in the background. If he does I have no chance of hearing it. Maybe he's tracing the call. "What is it?" he says. "What's happened to her?"

I'm more taken off guard by the tone of the question rather than its content. The way he says it is so matter of fact, no sign of any emotion for the daughter that might be in trouble. "She's fine," I say. "In fact, she's sitting right next to me."

"Then why didn't she report for duty?"

I decide, at this point in the conversation, that I'm not going to be filling the role of some middleman, and I locate the button which places the call on speakerphone. Chief Constable Douglas's heavy breathing and that sound of amplified static fills the car, and I look to Amy to answer this question.

Her eyes fly from me to the phone outstretched toward her. "Um," she says. "Daddy?"

"Yes, *Officer* Douglas."

She widens her eyes, apparently recalling the role she's supposed to be playing, then says, "I . . . I got a little side-tracked."

"Whatever do you mean?"

I look out the window, across the car park, and out into the main road. I'm just trying to be somewhat polite about this private conversation when I spot, quite clearly and distinctly, a man sitting on a motorbike, all dressed in leathers with a long grey beard, watching us. My first thought is *perv*, and then, as he notices that I've caught sight of him, he puts out the cigarette he's smoking, stamps it beneath the heel of his calf-high leather boots and mounts the motorbike. This is one of these gut things —a real sense that something's odd.

Not really caring what stage of the conversation Amy and Chief Constable Douglas are up to, I shove the phone back at Amy and tell her to start the car, to follow the motorbike. With a wavering voice, she curtails the call with her father, and she starts the car. With a couple of deep-throated *va-rooms*, we're away, sweeping out of the car park and toward the main road. In hot pursuit.

9

AMY'S NOT A BAD DRIVER at all. She screeches around the corners with the blue lights flashing and the siren blaring. I find myself gripping the sides of my seat, feeling that unpleasant rough weave of the fabric. That strawberry scent of hers has taken on a burnt quality. And I think I like it.

The motorbike is about six or seven cars ahead of us and is rapidly overtaking traffic, often swerving onto the other side of the road. The rider himself, though, doesn't bother to look back over his shoulder to check on us, or seem at all perplexed or surprised we're chasing him.

Amy jerks the car out onto the other side of the road and really puts her foot down, so far that the engine just becomes a nasal *whine*, and I can feel my stomach sinking, being left in the boot behind us.

She nails a roundabout, which is to say, she shoots right over it straight between a car coming from the right and one about to join on our left, just swooping right onward.

There're only two cars in front of us now. The one directly in front is a steel-grey estate, with a middle-aged woman driving— from the puff of hair I can see poking out behind the driver's headrest. And the one in front of the estate is a smaller hatch-back—a cherry-red colour, the cheery colour they seem to love making hatchbacks.

Amy gets right up the backside of the estate and the woman soon pulls over to the side of the road, allowing us to go past. As I watch the road ahead I see the motorbike slip from sight around the corner, the rider almost touching the asphalt he leans so far over. As for us, though, we've got this hatchback to contend with.

When we get up close the first thing I notice are the prevalent 'L' plate magnetically attached to the back of the car. The next thing I notice is that the car's barely brushing thirty miles an hour on the road. The third and final thing I notice is that a chain of caravans are turning the corner on the other side of the road.

Amy does her best, driving right on the bumper of the learner car, flashing her lights several times and blaring the sirens several times. But this doesn't have much of an effect.

As I look in through the hatchback's rear window I see a lady —about my age—gesticulating wildly at the boy in the driver's seat—her son, I guess—who's stiff with tension, eyes locked before him, and clearly terrified about the whole thing.

To be fair, on our left, there's no space to pull over, just a seemingly endless row of cars stretching along the street. As I lean over to check Amy's speedometer, I see that the learner driver's actually slowed down by about five miles per hour. I glance back over my shoulder. No options there either. The cars we overtook have caught up now, and there's a long tailback. In short, we're completely stuck.

The learner driver keeps on going along at that steady twenty miles per hour, and I'm growing restless, knowing that we're losing the motorbike.

On the other side of the road, through all the caravans, I spot a turn off. "Over there!" I say, pointing it out to Amy.

She flips the indicator and pulls across the road. The caravans, though, have no intention of letting our marked police car through. They form up a barrier, staying bumper to bumper. One of the drivers even has the nerve to flick Amy his middle finger as they trundle past. And much to his surprise, instead of following him, Amy just gives him it back.

Seconds later and, not quite able to believe what I'm witnessing, Amy pulls out into the constant stream of caravans —grazing the front bumper of the next in line as she goes with a tongue-chewing *scrape*—and before I know it we're into the side street and motoring away from the gridlock back on the road.

With one hand on the wheel, steering us around another sheer corner, Amy reaches out for the radio handset which, until then, I haven't noticed sitting innocuously in its dock. She twiddles the knob on the radio and a backlit blue screen lights up some frequency or other. The car speakers spray static, and then Amy jams her thumb on the button and speaks into the handset. "This is Car 49A, I'd like to get a direction on one motorbike." She pauses looking to me, and then I feed her the description, as much as I saw of the guy while he watched us, which she, in turn, relays to the dispatcher.

The radio burbles something or other and then a response comes, telling us of the location of the motorbike. A little bemused, I look up at her GPS screen and see that—apparently back at the station or wherever they keep the dispatch office— they've drawn on a neat little circle of the motorbike's approximate whereabouts onto the real-time GPS map.

Amy flies along the back road, and I watch as our paths are inevitably intersecting. In fact it's near enough perfect. We might just—

My hearts fluttering in my throat as Amy shoots right over another intersection, pulls a ninety-degree turn and lands us right on the motorbike's tail. This time the motorbike rider does glance over his shoulder, and I can see the wide open cavern of his mouth, the look of total surprise in his eyes.

Amy doesn't let up and I squeeze the sides of my seat all the more, increasing my grip and preparing for impact ready for us to bump up against his back wheel at any moment, sure that we're going to do so.

The motorbike stays just a hair's length ahead of us. Now I can make out the seams in his leather jacket, the slight scuff mark he has on the back of the left elbow. I think that I can even smell that dirty stench of exhaust coming out through the car's air vents, that ashy taste burning itself into my tongue. And then, all of a sudden, Amy catches his steel back plate.

The motorbike wobbles a couple of times, the rider zigzagging over the road, before he, inevitably, flies off to one side and tumbles over a grassy verge, falling out of sight into a ditch.

Amy jams on the brakes and we squeal to a halt in the middle of the deserted road.

For a long moment I'm just totally speechless. I find myself looking at Amy, who still has her fingers, white at the knuckle, wrapped around the wheel as she stares out of the windscreen straight ahead, as if we're still pursuing the motorbike.

After another second or so, once my heart's under enough control for me to put words out there, one by one, I say, "Have you . . . have you ever done that before?"

Still staring forward, blue eyes wide open, she shakes her head.

10

I LEAVE AMY BEHIND in the car, seeing that she's in shock, still not quite sure exactly what she might or might not have done. I should be so bold because when I step out of the car I feel myself sway on my legs, my stomach too not quite sure whereabouts on planet Earth it is and a light ringing in my ears. Still, I manage to set one foot in front of the other and make my way over to the ditch, where I can hear the slight *crackles* and *hisses*, the unmistakable sounds of a dying engine.

As I peer over the ditch I get a scent of hot vapour, the radiator bursting, no doubt, and I can taste that sweet, icky taste of seeds in my mouth. When I take a moment to look around me I see that we're surrounded on all sides by golden fields—swaying in the light breeze.

The rider lies on his back, his limbs all hunched up in a way that reminds me of a dead wasp. But he does give some sign of life when he groans and he lifts his right arm up to feel his face, where blood trickles down from a cut at his forehead. Slowly and surely, he opens his eyes. First a crack and then all the way. He focusses on me. Before he speaks, he licks his lips, as if he was about to blow into a trumpet. "You," he says, steadily. "You have no idea who I work for."

That line resonates with me. The line that I've said to myself a million times before, the line that only I . . . well, me and a few choice others . . . would be able to recognise. And then everything, all at once, slips into place.

I have the urge to simply turn around, leave this guy here, to dry out for a bit with his motorbike, but I know that wouldn't do. That wouldn't be *humane*. So I glance back at the police car, signalling—what I think to be a signal, in any case—for Amy to call an ambulance. She seems to interpret my vague gesture just fine, since she immediately stoops over and yanks the radio handset to her mouth.

I stand on the verge of the ditch, feeling the long grass brush against the sides of my jeans. The sun appears from behind a cloud and I feel its strong rays hot on the back of my shoulders.

The motorbike rider, holding his hand to his bleeding forehead, tries to rock himself into a sitting position, fails, tumbling back over, and then seems content enough to lie there on his back while scowling up at me. "You'll be sorry," he says. "You'll be so sorry."

"Try me."

He shakes his head, his mouth almost as much a mean open wound as that one on his forehead, and then he stares off beyond me, above my head. "You have no idea who I work for."

"You said that already," I say, not bothering to hide the weariness creeping into my voice.

He simply nods from then on and his eyelids droop. His head slumps back and he lies stretched out, down there in the ditch.

I put my First Aid training to good use, checking his pulse—it's still there, strong, actually, considering his situation—before propping him into the recovery position. Then I stand back to admire my good work.

I sit on the roadside, on a comfortable grassy bank till I hear the faint wail of an ambulance in the near distance. I hold my hand up to shield my eyes from the sun and watch it slowly descending the hillside, coming toward us. When it pulls up, I simply jerk my thumb to indicate the ditch to the paramedics and then get back into Amy's squad car.

She still seems a little shaken, but apparently it's bad form to let someone like me drive a police car, so she is the one who drives us—me giving her the directions.

11

W E PULL BACK UP in that perfect suburban neighbourhood. Amy, almost absent-mindedly, crunches on the handbrake and switches off the engine. She sits there for a moment and then looks to me expectantly. "What now?"

I decide that it's time to spell it out for her. She looks to have recovered sufficiently to at least take something in. "The motor-bike rider, he was working for Brian. I guess Brian got the idea that we were snooping around—that was probably why your dad called up, trying to get you out of the way, extricate you as easily as possible."

She nods, again with that dead-eyed stare, impossible to tell whether or not she's absorbing what it is I'm telling her.

"But now it's too late," I say. "Brian knows that we were sniffing around." I turn in my seat and face her straight on. For the first time that day I feel totally and completely stern, stone-faced serious . . . and that takes some doing on a day when I've seen a body, cleaned up after a body. "Those friends of yours, did you say they'd even get Brian running scared?"

"Uh huh."

I reach over and touch her shoulder. When I feel her quiver beneath my fingertips I take hold of her, squeeze her lightly. "Do you think . . . I mean, could they get us, the both of us, out of this mess?"

Another nod.

"Fine," I say, sinking back into my seat, then turning my stare onto the house. "That's just fine."

We stay there, steeped in silence for a long while, and then Amy glances out over the hedge, to the house, as if she's only just now realised where we are—what our destination has been all along. "Why did you bring us back here?" All of a sudden her face changes, she gives me an extreme look and I see one of those biceps of hers bulge a little. "Don't tell me you're just going home, after all this?"

"Well," I say, then trail off with nothing left to add.

Then I watch as the realisation passes over her face. She turns back to look at that house, open-mouthed. "Oh," she says. "He's here. He's . . . in the house, isn't he?"

If I'd been in a less sombre mood I would probably have slipped her some biting sarcastic remark, I was thinking of something along the lines of 'some police chiefs' daughters do have 'em.' But I keep schtum as far as witticisms are concerned.

"But . . . but," she says. "Why. I . . . I just don't understand at all."

I stare at the bush beside us, and realise that there are wild strawberries growing there, the type that grow too small to eat, that give you a stomach ache if you eat them. And with Amy's perfume in my nostrils it's a strange sensation, looking at the strawberries growing under glass and yet smelling them at the same time.

I glance over to her. "Isn't it obvious?"

She shakes her head.

I guess I should really celebrate her naivety, sometimes I wish I could be as naïve as her—not have seen the things I've seen, come to know the things I know. I breathe a long, sturdy sigh and stare up at the roof of the squad car. It's beige with a few dirty marks on it. Most likely from scuffles with various crooks, getting them into the backseat. "These two—the Williamsons—they're a couple, right?"

She nods.

"Okay, so what does that suggest to you?"

"I don't know."

"Well, we know that the wife was one of Brian's clients and, as is protocol, whenever one of Brian's clients gets into any bother, doesn't matter which side of the law, the police know to go to Brian first . . . if they know what's good for them. Just so that Brian's got time to clear up any . . . unpleasantness. Anyway, in this case, as with most of these husband-wife things, I think it's fair to say that the both of them were Brian's clients. It just wouldn't have made sense any other way."

She blinks a couple of times, then says, "What you're saying is that Brian is protecting the husband—Peter Williamson."

"Yes," I say. "That's exactly what I'm saying."

"But he *murdered* his wife."

"That's what it seems like, yes."

She nods in the direction of the house. "And you're saying that he's just inside there, back in his house, as if nothing at all's happened?"

I nod.

"That he's never going to face justice and he's just going to . . . just going to go on living like nothing's ever happened."

I shrug.

She stews on that fact for a long time. Again I get a waft of the strawberry scent and it makes my stomach grumble. I can't quite get comfortable in my seat anymore, it's as if the rough fabric's scratching me through my clothes. I decide that the time's right now for me to step back, to get out of the car and go on home. And so I unbuckle the door, set one foot outside. Amy reaches out and grabs hold of my coat. "Wait," she says, her blue eyes ablaze once more. "I want him to know some justice—he deserves it."

"So why don't you do it?"

She looks to me seriously, and then down into the foot well, where she has her feet on the pedals.

"Yeah," I say, "thought not," then step away from the car, pad my way around it, noting the mighty gash on the side, where Amy had a close miss with one of those caravans . . . if you can call scraping its front bumper a miss at all. I run my fingers through the scrape, feel the raw, scratched-up metal beneath. She calls out to me, stopping me before I step back into my own car.

"Anna?" she says, then gets out of her car, saunters around the side of it. She looks me dead-on, in the face, then says, "Have you got your gun?"

"I'm not doing it—say whatever you want. Tell those friends of yours what you want."

"But you've got a gun?"

I think this over for several seconds and—the thick-skulled girl that I am—I only then get it, understand what it is she wants. Without really thinking, I unlock the car, reach in, unlock the glove box and then remove my pistol—wrapped in its strawberry-red velvet cloth—and hand it over to her.

I STAND OUTSIDE, leaning up against the bonnet of my car as she rings the doorbell. I watch on, heart in throat, as Peter Williamson looks first confused, certainty more than a little paranoid, before stepping aside to allow her in. I think I can hear her mutter the words, "Brian Mathewson," which in this case are akin to 'Open Sesame.'

The door slams with a woody *thud* and I watch the glass panes vibrate a little before settling. The house then just stands completely still, like the rest of the street, frozen in normality.

I get into my car, sitting in the driver's seat, facing forward, looking at the police car in front of me, waiting to get away from this thing, out of this nightmare.

Amy returns about ten minutes later. I expect to see her coming out with a ghost-white complexion, but she looks assured, even business-like, as she brings the front door to a close behind her. I spot her hand stuffed in her pocket as she walks toward me. As she draws closer I see the faintest outline of a smile on her lips. She bends over, down to the window, and passes the gun through it.

Working quickly, I check it over—see that she's used four of the bullets—and then stuff it back into its velvet cloth and return it to the glove compartment.

We stand there for a while, regarding one another, clearly with neither one knowing what to say to the other. As the senior partner in all this I take it upon myself to be the one to speak up first. "Are you going to tell your daddy about this?"

She shakes her head. But there's none of that childish nature to her, none of that indecision, her mind's made up and I for one believe her. And, at the same time, I think that the threat she stuck me with, telling on me, that it was all part of her adolescent game. Now she's all grown up. For better or for worse.

"I guess I'll be seeing you around," I say.

Her smile widens. "Yeah, I'd like that."

I stick the keys in the ignition and turn. Then, out of nowhere, I give her a little mock salute. "Take care, officer."

As I drive away, I look back in my rear-view mirror, regard her there, standing on the roadside, on the pavement beside her police car. I think about calling this in to Brian but somehow I get the impression that he already knows, that he's already taken provisions for this whole thing. Somehow he's *always* one step ahead.

13

I ONLY START to wondering where the day went when I step out of the Tube station near my house and see the sky darkening overhead. And then it seems like, all at once, my body catches up with me. As I pad along the chilly street, picking my way through crisp packets and bits of broken glass, I let loose an enormous yawn.

I hoped to see Brian back at Mathewson Media. I don't know what I expected, maybe that a group of five armed men would appear from the shadows the moment I pulled up in the underground car park. But there was no one. Just the box where I dropped the keys, the half-asleep guard in the booth to murmur a goodnight to me. Those old, exhaust smells of an empty car park, the shrill taste of blood in my mouth after a long day's work.

Back home my cat Lizzie winds her way around my legs, purring her head off, clearly delighted that I'm home. Mainly because I'm going to feed her, but I'll take love where I can find it. I dish her out a plate of rancid-smelling cat food, set it on a floor with a porcelain *tinkle* and then have a paw through the fridge for those strawberries. It should be a nice dessert to complement that burger and chips I scoffed from the fast food place before taking the Tube.

When I pour the strawberries out into a bowl, I notice that quite a few of them have gone bad, that they're now covered in brownie-black bruises. Still, I've never been a picky eater and I don't plan on starting now. The seeds all get stuck in my teeth, but the fruit juice is just what I've been craving just about all day. Only now that I realise it, though. I'm not one of those people that goes out of their way to get their five a day.

I set the bowl down in the sink and, seeing Lizzie still making significant headway into her plate of cat chow, I pick my way through the darkened house, not bothering to turn on any of the lights. I slide back the French doors and emerge onto the patio outside.

When I breathe my breath makes mist. About five seconds later and I'm shuddering all over, jumping from one foot to the other to keep warm. My self-imposed punishment done, I turn to go back inside, back into the warm house for the long-promised crap TV and fuzzy, purring cat . . . or maybe just to drop into bed.

Just as I set one foot inside, I note movement out of the corner of my eye. I stop dead and look closer. Yes, I'm sure there's something there. More than that. A person. My heart leaps into my throat, I think about the pistol, which I left on the kitchen table. If Brian's going to bump me off then this is the perfect time.

But, when I calm myself down, realise that a gunshot's not forthcoming, I make out the familiar shape, the business-like dress sense of AA—one of Brian's most-trusted assassins. Why that should put me at ease is just another piece of evidence of the messed-up world we live in.

He pulls a pack of cigarettes from his pockets, plumps a cigarette between his lips and lights it as he saunters out of the shadows. His face looks a shade of pale blue in the moonlight. He puffs away several clouds of smoke, then says, "Heard you went against the boss's orders today."

"Yeah, well," I say, crossing my arms over my chest, to give me a little warmth. "Sometimes a girl's got to let her hair down."

He chuckles, a smoker's chuckle. "Lucky for you it all ended pretty neatly, or I might've had to come here for some other reason tonight."

"Lucky for me."

He takes another long suck on his almost fresh cigarette and then drops it on the patio. He crushes it with his shoe, then turns to leave whichever way it was that he got in.

Just as he's about to make his daring exit, I say, "You're not planning on littering my garden, are you?"

He turns, gives me a slight smile as if he'd expected me to say as much. "Annie," he says. "I wouldn't be worrying so much about your patio if I were you. This time it was close. I'm not joking." He blinks a couple of times then says, "That girl. You didn't need to get her involved. Not in all this."

A shudder passes through me and I look to the cigarette butt, still smouldering a little, sending a little coil of smoke upward, and then to AA. All I can think to say is, "Don't call me Annie," then I turn to go back inside, sliding the French door shut behind me.

I return to the kitchen where Lizzie's polished off her supper and she's looking at me expectantly for some more. I stand still a couple of moments before making all manner of nonsense noises —noises that I suppose I've decided cats like—and I sweep her up in my arms, holding her warm, furry body to my bare chest. And together we plod up the stairs and to bed. Another day's work wound down.

And perhaps a monster created.

HOTEL PARAISO

1

I TRY NOT to sink too far into the saggy springs all coiled up beneath the fabric of the back seat of the taxi—a battered-up shell of a hatchback, barely worthy of the name, but I hand over the euros anyway.

Most likely it's just to get myself clear of the driver: a slick-haired man with a bushy black moustache and a devil of a gut. I wonder why he hasn't given any thought to growing a beard to go with that moustache of his, what with those acne scars all over his leathered cheeks.

He wears his lavender-coloured shirt unbuttoned down to several inches below his nipples, too far for a man of his size and shape and age.

But who's going to tell him, not me, not out here in the sticks, what must be a good ten miles from any known civilisation, and a solid twenty-minute drive from the airport where my flight back home to rainy old London was cancelled not more than an hour ago.

The greasy, oil stink of the car is the worst thing, and I spent most of the drive over trying to divine whether it was the driver or the car that caused the smell . . . talk about a chicken-egg scenario.

So, all things considered, good thing that I saw fit to invest in some fruity sweets to suck on for the duration of the drive. I'm currently sinking my teeth into one that's vaguely lemon flavoured, but it does the trick, just about.

The driver goes fishing in the breast pocket of his shirt, and he comes up with a wad of curled-up, grease-stained euros that I would tell him to keep if I could only speak Spanish. He licks his browned-up fingernails and then flips through the notes, finally peeling off a couple of fives. I take them from him with a vague smile, though my mind's already very much fixed on the place he's brought me to.

I gaze out from under glass at the façade.

A series of complicated looping neon lights: purple, pink and white, shine up the name of the place:

Hotel Paraiso

Well, at least the name's jolly, even if the hotel itself is smoke-stained red bricks with an unconvincing corrugated steel roof perched on top, way up—six or seven storeys up. The place in general looks like it could do with more than a lick of paint.

Maybe a wrecking ball would be more up its street.

I thank the taxi driver with a quick-fire "Gracias" just about the only phrase I've managed to master during my stay in Spain, and I tug down on the frail plastic door handle of the taxi—turns out it was just shiny plastic, not metal at all—before stepping on out into the warm night air.

Too warm for me. So warm that it immediately brings a fresh sapping of sweat drooling on out of my skin, and gets to work soaking my simple white travelling blouse: only undone by one button for consideration of the situation over comfort.

My grey-and-white-striped, floaty tracksuit bottoms, some sort of brainwave I had years ago for travelling in planes, don't do all that much floating considering there's no breeze to be had about here, what on this . . . looking around . . . desolate dusty plain that stretches out far as the eye can see. The sucking sound of a plane taking off in the distance the only hint of life for miles around. And it annoys me not a little to think that my little plane just couldn't get its little self off the runway while that one, apparently, has had no trouble.

Still, guess it'll teach me to fly budget airlines . . . or not, as the case might be.

Thrifty is as thrifty does.

I realise that we're away from tarmac here, too, as I take my first step towards the boot, which obediently clicks open as I approach it. I hear the crunch of gravel beneath the soles of my strappy, leather sandals. The ones that I'd thought would be wonderfully airy up there in the compressed cabin of the plane.

And the ones that now seem just a touch unpractical to be wandering about desolate places like this late at night.

Once I've got my luggage: a little, bulky silver-grey, hard-case, up onto its plastic wheels, I trudge away from the departing taxi and onwards in the direction of the laminated, rectangular sign which sits in the window of the hotel and which reads: RECEP-CIÓN, all spelled out in block capitals with red letters within a neat blue frame.

Guess I've found the right place.

The door to the reception is made out of flimsy, termite-infested wood, and has that sun-faded, peeled grey shade to it that always reminds me of back garden sheds.

I shove on through it, hearing a dampened bell clang out a flat note above my head.

All at once, a sharp smell of polish mixed with something sharper still—vomit?—hits my nostrils without pulling a punch. Just what I needed after that stomach-crunching car journey over here, to be greeted with eau de puke.

I rummage through the pocket of my tracksuit trousers, manage to fumble out that packet of sweets and deposit one of those glistening, sugary lumps of gunk onto my tongue. As I suck on it, it tastes vaguely of strawberry, and it does enough of a trick on taking my mind of the stench about this place.

I look to the desk of the reception, made up of that cheap, office-furniture wood, the kind that's been shined down to its atoms.

I hope you don't get the idea that I'm a snob, because I'm

really not, you should see the state of my own house . . . but in the circles I move in, I think I've subconsciously developed a good eye for the finer things in life, and that's just made everything else seem blunt, bulky and, for want of a better word, *ugly*.

There's one of those beaded curtains to keep the flies out that leads into a darkened area behind the desk that I guess is some kind of a backroom.

And if there's anything that I've learned from a lifetime of going to see films, that's where all the *really* horrific stuff happens.

So . . . perhaps better to steer clear of there, maybe?

From within aforementioned back room, I hear a throaty, almost consumptive, cough.

I blink a couple of times, not really having any other way to register my discontent. Because, honestly, there are a thousand places I'd rather be right now than the Hotel Paraiso, located precisely in the centre of No One Gives a Damn . . . Population Five.

Wait, make that a *million* places I'd rather be.

Finally, this rakish girl emerges from behind the beaded curtain. The beads all dance about on the ends of their threads, and make a *clickety-click* sound as they bounce off the walls. The girl has blond hair, and is wearing too much blue eyeliner. She has a fair complexion, and lots of freckles all across her cheeks. Her expression is dour, to say the least. She looks at me as if I've just broken a window to get into the reception area here.

"Si?" she says, nonchalant.

I take in just what she's got on today: a light-blue, strappy top that just about covers her tight breasts and a small region of her midriff. Her belly button is pierced with a silver hoop, though the skin about it has gone all bloated and red. She wears a pair of cropped denim shorts which cling to her bony thighs.

As I raise my eyes upwards, to take in her eyes, I see that

they're puffy, and red, like she's just been crying . . . or doing something else that I really have no interest in knowing about.

"Uh," I say, not really a promising start, "have you got any rooms for tonight?"

"Eh?" she says, staccato.

I decide that I'm going to have to put my international communications to the test, and make a job of miming my clasped hands are a pillow, and I'm setting my head down onto it.

"Ah," she says, apparently *now* understanding . . . I guess the context helps her out just a touch too, given that she *is* running a hotel reception here . . . or at least doing her best impression of doing so.

She ducks on down, below the desk, rifles through some drawers, striking lucky once she's brought open the third one with a teeth-grinding *creak* of its runners.

She slaps a wad of papers down on the desk before me then looks at me with profound expectation.

I read over the form, because that's what it is, laid there before me. There's a bunch of Spanish scrawled across it, with various fields that apparently need to be filled out. Luckily, I also see, etched out in greyscale, an English translation of each field.

"Uh," I say, "have you got a pen, please?"

"Eh?"

I take a breath, not too deep, and then give her a pleasant smile as I mime just what I need from her.

She gets my drift and delivers me a chewed-up black biro.

As I fill out the form, I make a pitiful attempt at conversation. "Full up?"

"Eh?"

"Lots of people?"

"Eh?"

"Guests? Many guests?"

The girl shrugs. "No. No many guests. You only."

Well, I have to say that that's reassuring . . . because if there's anything worse than a full hotel, it's a completely vacant one, that's the stuff of horror films.

I get the form all filled out, and, a quick scan of my credit card later, I'm the proud recipient of a key card with a number—503—scrawled out in permanent marker across it.

I trail my luggage through the quiet hotel, and then up a cranky lift with dented doors, before I locate where I'm going to lay my head down for the night.

At the door of my room, out of habit, more than anything else, I pat the front pocket of my luggage, feel for my gun: A pistol.

.45 calibre.

Semi-automatic, single-action.

A sleek chrome.

This one's a recent acquisition, from this holiday.

I was planning on ditching it before I set foot in the airport, of course.

It's not like, me being an assassin and all, I wanted to draw any undue attention.

Gun in hand, I slip my key card through its slot, wait for the out-of-place, merry *beep*, and the merrier flash of a green light, then I shove my way inside.

2

THE ROOM IS, all things considered, just about what I expect.

Twin beds with lime-green spreads that have gone all fuzzy from being washed too much. Old grey-green curtains, but nice and thick, and probably quite pleasant after a thorough clean. I guess that they block out sunlight quite nicely.

And stop anyone from looking in.

The carpet is thin, but feels warm beneath my now-bare feet.

I guess that the heating, or the hot water, runs beneath the floor of my room.

The air is dusty to breathe, but that's okay, because soon enough I get those windows opened wide . . . or as wide as I can get them, having to slip my hands between the black, iron bars which cover them.

Most likely, this being the fifth floor of the hotel, those bars are to stop people getting out, rather than to stop people getting in.

A slight smell of disinfectant clings to the place, but, in my book, that's better than the vomity smell of the reception area, and one which I can live with for a night.

I roll my shoulders and then allow myself to fall onto the bed. The springs sound like Slinkies beneath my weight, and I sink on down into the mattress.

But, for me, I've never had much trouble with overly soft beds.

'Better an overly soft bed than a bed of nails,' as I think maybe my mother—or was it my father?—might once have said.

Ah . . . the working classes, if only good old Mum and Dad could see me now.

I give my strawberry sweet the coup de grace, and swallow,

leaving me with that faint strawberry taste lolling about my saliva, then I reach for the front pocket of my bag once more, withdraw the pieces of paper I've carelessly stuffed in there.

The pages are just about held together by a single staple through the top left-hand corner. It's the confirmation they gave me back at the airport. My voucher for the next flight out tomorrow morning at five minutes past nine.

For some reason I get all neurotic about flying, like I have to have absolutely everything laid out and ready the night before, otherwise I'm liable to collapse into a nervous heap.

And, I have to say, from my experience so far of the Hotel Paraiso, I'm feeling even more tightly wound about catching the next plane out of here.

Of getting back home, back to Blighty.

I leave the pages there, on my bedside table, which isn't really much more than a rickety wooden stand, seemingly that same cheap office wood they used on the reception desk downstairs. I remove my passport from my bag too. Place it there on top of the pages.

That's another thing, the night before a flight, I'm liable to wake up a solid dozen times, if not more, and the only way I've found, from experience, of me slipping back off to sleep, is the knowledge that everything's all laid out and ready to go at a moment's notice.

Just a load off my mind.

Done with my resting, I trudge on across the carpet to the en suite bathroom. That standard hotel fare of white porcelain all over the place, and white plastic where they're not able to use the porcelain: the bathtub, the toilet seat, the toilet paper dispenser.

Just as I pad up to the sink, to give my hands a good wash before stepping in the shower—don't ask—I get a glimpse of the contents of the toilet bowl.

Though there's nothing solid in there, the water is an unnatural *brown* colour, that colour that makes me think that the water's been standing there, in one place, for quite a long while.

I breathe a quick sigh, then turn the tap for the sink.

After a bunch of gargling, a silty brown paste oozes out from the tap, accompanied by the occasional bright burst of water coming through. And the water coming through looks clean enough, and if it wasn't for that brown stuff then the water would work just fine.

I leave the tap running a good five minutes, and when I come back it's still spitting out more of that brown paste than water.

With another profound sigh, I step over to the bath, yank back the mouldy shower curtain, and try *that* tap.

Same problem.

Same brown gunk spilling out.

Another sigh, and then I'm off across my room, back over to where I left my bag. I think things over for a moment, eye my passport and my flight confirmation, pocket the two of them in my tracksuit trousers. And then, just because I can, I stick my gun into the waistband.

Some people may call it paranoid, but I prefer to think of it as being prepared.

3

BACK DOWN in the reception area, my friend the consumptive anorexic is conspicuous by her absence. I eye the dulled, scratched-up brass bell on the desk and then give it a good old press with the heel of my hand.

A not-too-flat tone rings out about the reception area—a tone much brighter than I expected.

I pull up my trousers just a little, feeling them slip with the weight of the gun tucked into the waistband. I guess whoever designed these trousers never spared much thought for making the elastic strong enough to sustain a serious firearm.

I listen out for more of that coughing, but hear none at all.

I lift my shoulders in yet *another* sigh, and tell myself not to get carried away.

I drum my fingers on the desk as I wait, hearing that satisfying *clink-clink-clink* as my nails bounce off the heavily lacquered surface.

I pound the desk bell again.

No response.

This is getting ridiculous.

Or maybe this is all just a customer relations strategy: the customer shows up, receptionist takes the credit card details, and then promptly goes AWOL when customer comes on down complaining about the sewage / water eking out of their taps.

I stand there for another moment, think this thing over, try to work out just what I'm going to do now.

I *could* go on back up to my hotel room, brave the water . . . most likely it's actually safe, just not very pleasant to look at . . . take my shower, and then tuck myself into bed in order to get some sleep before shipping back out to the airport in the morning.

214

Or . . . well, not much point in thinking it, seeing as it seems like I'm already *doing*.

I duck beneath the fold-down wooden flap that bridges the gap between customer and receptionist, and just like that I'm behind the desk.

There's nothing much of note.

A computer with one of those CRT monitors that instantly tags it as 'nineties,' a notepad with a bunch of scrawlings in Spanish written all over it, and an emery board from which it seems the receptionist has been trying to extract maximum value.

I mean, seriously, the damn thing lost any of its filing abilities many moons ago.

Aside from that, there's a beaten-up, light-blue, steel filing cabinet which might've been placed alongside the order for the desk, and a coffee pot that is fogged up with coffee grains and still has a sad little puddle of coffee sitting stagnant in the bottom.

I wonder how long that coffee's been there . . . but not for too long.

It's not healthy for anyone to begin thinking in decades.

I skip on by all that miscellanea, anyway, and find my way through the beaded curtain, go on through into the back room.

An exposed light bulb hangs down above my head, shedding a far-too-bright lemony glow over just about everything. The level of light reminds me of a smoker's complexion, and, to be honest, seems to make my gut squeeze in on itself.

The air smells strongly of nail varnish remover—a smell I *really* can't stand. Just breathing in the air right now, I can feel its burn at the back of my throat, and how it strips away the last of the taste of that strawberry sweet I polished off back up in my room.

A black-and-white TV monitor shows the car park outside the hotel, and the desolate road which sweeps on beside it. Then again, it's close to midnight now, so I guess that there's not really much reason for anyone to be driving on out into the middle of nowhere.

A calendar hangs from the wall, and even me, with my rudimentary Spanish skills, can work out that the page hasn't been turned for several months, that it's well out of date.

The tanned, bikinied babe with barely suppressed plastic tits, pouts out at me provocatively. Her lips full and clearly as augmented as her mammary glands.

Or maybe it's all just post-production tricks.

When I take a step to my right, I feel my sandal squidge on down in something wet and sticky. And I guess, before I turn my head downwards, I should know just what it is that I'm in for. But, silly naïve me, I always miss the clues.

The metallic stench in the air.

Or that biting taste on the tip of my tongue.

Blood.

A great big pool of it.

The light bulb sheds a shimmer across the surface of it, turning it a deep purple colour, but it's unmistakable just what it really is.

I step out of the puddle, already thinking just how I'm going to get the blood off my sandal in the shitty water that spews from my bathroom taps.

But that little quip slips away as I peer on around the corner of the back room.

And see her lying there.

On her back.

Eyes wide in fear.

And very, very dead.

The blonde receptionist.

4

NOW, I've seen my fair share of bodies in my time, but there's a thing such as context, and coming across one now, especially one that I've had no part in the demise of, catches me way off guard.

So much so that I can feel my heart beating hard in my throat. And that wafting stench of vomit from the reception area at my heels becomes almost overwhelming, smothering even the high-pitched odour of the nail polish remover.

I suck on my tongue, trying to see off the swirling nausea, and I manage to keep myself just about upright.

Instinctively, I reach for my gun, still sitting snug in the waist-band of my tracksuit bottoms. I click the magazine into place and hold it down at my side, not wanting to shoot anyone's eye out if I can help it.

No one who doesn't deserve it, anyway.

As I prowl about the back area of the reception, I realise how tight and small it is. The only thing that catches my attention is a door which leads out to the back of the hotel, and which, I have a good idea, is most likely where the killer, or killers, fled to.

Before committing myself to anything I'm likely to regret, though, I double back on myself, check over the girl's body.

I look her over, stare at the bullet hole in her throat, see another one in her chest.

That might well have stopped her screaming out.

Because one thing's for certain, with my highly attuned hearing, the hearing which has kept me alive on more than one occasion, I would've heard so much as a mouse's *squeak* down here in the reception area.

I hold my ground, not wanting to make a sudden movement

in case the killer might still be watching, might be lurking some-where waiting to pop off another victim.

And I have no intention of being a victim.

I force myself to take a deep breath of the vomit-stinking air, take it right down into the pits of my lungs, telling myself that it'll do me good, that it'll get me thinking straight again.

Then it strikes me.

Do I really need to do anything?

Is this really my issue at all?

. . . Why don't I just go and phone the police?

After all, it's not like *I'm* going to achieve much seeing as I'm only here for the night—taking the plane out bright and early tomorrow morning.

And I'm sure that I can handle myself just fine with the handgun I'm packing.

I'll be anonymous and safe up in my bedroom.

So, with that thought on my mind, I step over the reception-ist's body, venture on back behind the desk and I locate an aged, plastic, beige phone sitting there. It's one of those ones that, I swear, can be found in just about any nurse's office across the entire face of the earth.

Gun still dangling from my right hand, I lift up the handset, take care to keep the dangling cord from getting knotted, and I dial out the number for emergency services, the one which is written out in clear block capitals on the phone itself, the one that reads: *EMERGENCIAS* with the number beneath.

Only when I've been waiting for what seems like a *very* long minute do I realise that the handset isn't making any sound at all. None of that foreign chirping in my ear that I've become accus-tomed to. And I realise that the line's been cut.

For a moment my mind gets the better of me, it starts to unravel, maybe it's the stress of the day finally getting to me.

Or maybe it's because I'm demanding that it give me something to do next.

Finally it does.

My mobile, up in my room.

Simple.

Simple solution.

So I sleuth my way through the quiet hotel, deciding to take the stairs rather than the lift . . . if there's one thing about finding dead bodies, it's that it really puts your hackles up about voluntarily shutting yourself into enclosed spaces.

At least for me, I prefer to be out in the open.

And preferably armed.

Back in my bedroom, I stick my gun back into my waistband, and get my mobile out.

Finding that the battery is pretty much dead, I dig out the charger too—along with the foreign adapter—and then I plug it into the wall.

Finally I manage to get onto the phone—onto the emergency services using the same number I dialled downstairs in the hotel reception.

I hear a couple of those pleasant, foreign-sounding chirps when I hear the *click* of a gun, and the gentle, not-unpleasant, Spanish-inflected male voice.

"Hang up now."

The phone rings another couple of times.

I think it over for another fraction of a second before allowing my phone to drop down to my side, out of sight to my gunman.

I don't hang up the call, hoping that the emergency services won't hang up on any call of distress.

Then I look over, in the direction of the voice, to the man with buzz-cut brown hair who stands in the open doorway of my hotel room. He wears thin-framed glasses, has a narrow face, a pointy chin. And he's wearing just about the smuggest smirk I've ever seen.

"I am sorry," he says, and I hear the trigger *creak* beneath the weight of his finger.

5

THOUGH I HAVE TO ADMIT that I've not given it much thought, all things considered I might have made a pretty good cowgirl, you know, out in the Wild West.

That's how quick my draw is right now. The way that I make to show him my hands before I tumble on over, onto my side, reaching for the gun in my waistband.

I hear a couple of suppressed shots.

Feathers or dust, or something, puff up from the mattress where the shots go in.

But he doesn't hit me.

Doesn't even come close.

And now it's my turn.

With the gun in my hand, I aim at his gun-holding hand, his left hand in this case, and let loose.

My shot finds its spot and he drops his gun with a cry of pain.

I watch as it bounces a couple of times on the ground then settles there.

The guy stands up tall. Makes no sudden movement to reclaim his gun.

I guess he might've been in a situation like this before.

On instinct, I glance down, at my mobile, see that the call is still going on, can just about hear the mumbling on the other end, someone trying to speak to me.

Keeping my gun fixed on the guy, I strafe over to my mobile, swoop to pick it up, and then hold it to my ear.

The guy looks at me with wild eyes, and I can see the blood dribbling through the cracks in his fingers of his good hand as he holds the one I shot.

His lips are trembling and his complexion has taken on a bruise-blue colour.

I turn my attention to the voice on the other end of the phone. "English?" I say.

On the other end of the line, there's some scuffling about, maybe they didn't expect an answer at all . . . I guess they heard a shot and, most likely, a police car's already on it way.

"Yes?" goes the voice on the other end.

A female voice. Sure and confident.

Business-like.

The type of person I like to deal with.

"Someone's been killed here," I say, and then, guessing that they'd like just a little more to go on than that, "two shots, one in the throat, another in the chest, I'm staying at Hotel Paraiso."

I pause for a moment, trying to think of anything that might resemble an address—Hotel Paraiso isn't one of these places that leaves one of those laminated folders with breakfast menus, room service and guest activities all laid out inside.

"It's, uh, near the airport," I say.

There's some mumbling on the other end of the phone, and I make sure I keep a good eye on my friend here, and his shot-up hand.

"Are you in danger?" the voice says.

As I watch the spot between the guy's eyes down the barrel of my pistol, I allow myself the slenderest of smiles. "Not now."

"A car will be with you shortly. Please stay on the line."

I look to my phone, and then to the cable plugging it into the wall. I don't think it's charged up enough yet for me to unplug and go wireless.

Then again, I guess I'm pretty much stuck here, facing off with this guy, while I get the whole thing straight.

"Stay there," I say to the guy, covering the microphone on my mobile, "You move a muscle and I shoot you, got it?"

The guy mumbles something under his breath, something between a groan and a complaint.

Not much he's going to get his way about in the near future, though, unfortunately.

I lay my mobile down on the bed, and then shuffle over to his gun, to where it sits on the carpet. He watches on with bulging eyes as I retrieve it, check it over, see that he's not used any shots in the magazine.

Next I conceal my own gun back into the pocket of my bag, not wanting to get myself into trouble with the police, and I ready my cover story for them, that I managed to disarm the guy and shoot him with his own gun . . . purely out of self-defence.

I reckon, if I really lay on the tears and the wobbly voice I'll be just fine.

And so, I sit there, waiting, the guy still quivering as he stands before me, with his own gun being pointed at him.

I pay attention to my mobile, waiting for any sound on the other end, any signal that they want to speak with me some more, but it stays pretty quiet, and I can only hear breathing—no doubt the business-like woman on the other end is putting all the information I've given her through to her people on the ground.

I wait, feel myself sinking down on the mattress.

Somewhere, off in the hotel, I can hear footsteps.

The police?

Would they come on in here without announcing themselves?

. . . I *did* tell them that a murder took place.

I wait out the time. Count the beats of my heart in my eardrums. And I bide my time, prepare my story for them, and tell myself to make it just as convincing as I possibly can.

If there's anything I've learned about men, and female tears, it's that turning on the waterworks can do wonders in *all sorts* of situations.

The footsteps get louder. I hear a few floorboards creaking.

I look to my hostage, see that he's still holding that bleeding hand of his, and that his head is bowed as if he's soaking up the pain.

If he makes so much as a whisper, I'll give him a whole lot *more* pain to soak up.

But he keeps still, like a good boy, and I find my thoughts turning more to those sounds off in the hotel. I try to identify them, try to picture the policeman . . . just *one* . . . all dressed up bulletproof gear and lugging a semi-automatic about.

Clearing the shadows as he goes.

It's only then that I think that I forgot to tell them just which floor I was on, but I guess, as the footsteps get louder still, that, soon enough, they'll be able to tell for themselves.

As I sit there, on the edge of the mattress, my brain running all sorts of situations and scenarios, the last thing I expect is a grenade to come rolling on in across the floor.

6

LIKE A BIMBO, I stare right at the grenade for several seconds. My heart *thump-thumps* hard in my chest, and for the life of me I just can't get my thoughts straight.

And, as it turns out, that's just as long as I've got.

Because the grenade puffs out a thick, grey cloud.

A smoke grenade.

I just about get myself up onto my feet, and firing before the smoke has turned the room into a great, big impenetrably foggy mess.

I hear no response to my bullets and I know, right then, that my hostage has escaped.

That he has a friend along with him.

But of course he does.

I counted the bullets in the magazine, after all.

Whatever gun it was that killed the receptionist, it probably wasn't the one I'm holding right now . . . which is both reassuring and horrifying, because it almost always turns out better to keep yourself as far away from a murder weapon as you possibly can.

The smoke quickly fills the entire room about me. It gets up my nose. Seems to drown my tongue with its bitter taste. Fills my lungs.

Soon I start to feel woozy, and know that I need to get down.

That I need to get *below* the smoke.

So I do just that, dropping down onto my front.

I count the bullets in my magazine and see that I've got plenty.

Enough to be getting on with.

If there are only *two* of them, that is.

Using my elbows, I crawl my way across the carpet of my hotel room, constantly keeping an eye out for any sign that the smoke might clear, and my ex-hostage and his accomplice standing there ready for me.

So far so good.

So far the smoke won't clear.

And, for the time being, that means that *I* benefit from the cover just as much as my friends do.

It seems to take me forever to get to the doorway of my hotel room, and when I do, I hold back, I check my position, look about my surroundings the best way I can.

No sign of anyone else here.

Tears sting my eyes and I rub them away with the back of my hand, determined not to let them get one up on me . . . determined that I'm *not* going to die here.

Not in a dingy little airport hotel.

I finally reason with myself that I have to get out of my bedroom, that's the key, I have to maintain the element of surprise. And if I simply stay put I'll lose that—they'll know *just* where to look first.

So, still crawling on my belly, I emerge out onto the landing of the fifth floor and, using the wall as a guide, I feel my way along it, hoping that I might just stumble across a fire escape . . . something like that would be extremely welcome right about now.

I guess that my ex-hostage's accomplice let off another smoke grenade or two out here, because the smoke is just as thick as it was back in my bedroom.

After what feels like hours of crawling, I find myself up against a dead-end.

A long window that looks down at the steep drop to the car park below.

I blink back tears trying to the bring the image down there into focus.

After a couple of attempts, I succeed.

Down there I can see a police car, pulled up, a pair of uniformed officers, armed with those semi-automatics I promised myself.

They make their way towards the reception of the hotel, and I see their eyes darting about, looking up to the building, apparently scouring the place for anything that looks unusual. Maybe they've seen the smoke from the smoke grenades, but, most likely, it being night and all, they can't make out the fifth floor from where they stand.

If only there was an open window, something to show them, a *signal*.

It hits me at once.

But I don't think.

I act.

I grab hold of the gun I stole from my ex-hostage and, using the grip, I bust a hole in the glass, listen as the glass tinkles out of the frame and plunges on down to the car park.

As I lie on my belly, not wanting to get in the way of any panicked shooting, I watch as the smoke plumes on out through the glass.

Perfect.

They'll have seen now.

And the smoke on the landing is clearing too.

Victorious, I help myself back up into a standing position, and guide my way along the smooth cornice which sticks out of the wall.

But, just as I reach the stairwell, just as I stare on down it, I hear gunfire breaking out over my shoulder. Back in the direction where I broke the window.

I drop to the ground once more, wondering just how many dozens of bruises I will have collected by morning.

7

THE FIRING GOES ON for what seems like hours. There's a burst of fire, from what I recognise as the police's semi-automatics, which is then greeted by a few pops of a handgun . . . what I guess must be the murder weapon—the gun that was used to kill the receptionist.

I hold my ground, right there, reasoning this thing out.

If I just keep where I am, if I just stay right here . . .

Another gunshot puts paid to that thought.

It blows a hole in the ceiling above me. Sends plaster and paint sprinkling down through the air. It lands on me like very dry, oddly warm snow.

Another gun?

It seems that way since the shooting match between the police and one of the other men inside of the hotel continues.

Another shot blows the banister of the stairs into splinters.

I just about duck out of the way of the flying, needle-sharp chunks of wood, deciding that I might be better off a little way away from the stairwell.

The smoke has almost all gone now, and I guess that might be partially responsible for those gunshots.

With my cover gone, I'm something of a sitting duck for them.

Maybe I should be flattered that they've made me a priority target even considering the pair of police officers outside with semi-automatics.

I bound my way over the landing, and arrive at the shelter of the other wall where I press myself flush up against the surface.

That's one of the first rules of survival.

You've got to blend in.

I stay there for a few moments, feeling my chest rising and

falling against my blouse, seeing that my blouse has been a little discoloured what with all this woodchip and plaster flying about.

I don't even want to think what kind of a state my hair is in.

I think about warning shots for a while—whether or not they'd be a good idea.

I decide, given the circumstances, that they're probably not.

It's not like I want to attract those police officers' semi-automatic fire to me.

Another few shots come up from the floor below. Some more plaster flies. A little more wood from the banister splinters up. It's only when I get a second to really think about it—to really think about the sound coming out of the gun that I twig that it's *my* gun that's being fired.

I think back, think back to my bedroom, and to where I hid the gun.

My ex-hostage obviously saw where I stowed it away.

And he returned to fish it out when the smoke in the room cleared.

Well, that was wily to say the least.

My heart beats harder still as I wait for the next shot. For another bullet from my gun to blast its way up the stairs. But all the shooting goes quiet for a moment . . . a long moment.

I allow myself to breathe.

One.

Two.

Three.

I count out in my head, trying to bring myself back to some degree of calm.

I listen hard to the hotel, try to pick out any sounds that might give me a clue as to what's going on right now about me.

But I can hear nothing.

Just the *slush* of water through the pipes hidden beneath the wallpaper I lean on.

A V IAIN

I take one step forwards. Then another.

Feeling a little more assured that I'm not going to get myself gunned down immediately, I continue on. Get myself back to the stairwell.

But that's when I hold back.

I don't want to look over the edge.

Now that *would* be an idiot move.

I continue to listen in.

I can hear voices, speaking in a tone just above a whisper. But, since they're speaking Spanish, there's very little I can make out. Only individual words that really mean nothing to me without the context of a sentence to fall back on.

I wait a little more. Gun primed. Ready to sling it round.

To point it at anyone who needs it pointing at them.

I decide the time is right for me to make my move. For me to see if there's anything I can do to help the police out.

I get the feeling they'd be glad to have these two dead, however it happens.

If there really are only two of them.

I take hold of the banister and I guide my way down the steps, taking care to use the outside of the steps so as not to make the wooden floorboards creak beneath me.

I keep my eyes primed, fixed on the furthest space I can see up ahead, ready to react to any object that comes into my vision.

My finger rests on the trigger of the gun, and I can feel the weight of it tugging down my arm, keeping all my muscles there primed and ready.

Dangerous.

I take another few steps down.

Now onto the fourth floor.

It looks pretty much like the fifth though without any smoky residue from a carelessly tossed smoke grenade.

No sign of either of my two friends.

So I stalk onwards, keep myself flush against the wall, as small a target as I possibly can.

Off, somewhere deep down in the hotel, I hear the front door splinter, and then some shouting in Spanish.

I guess the police officers have finally got themselves into the building.

That they've finally got around to doing their jobs.

Something inside of me tells me to look down, and whatever instinct it was, I guess I have my life to thank for it, because it alerts me to the drops of blood on the carpet at my feet. I follow them with my gaze, then step carefully on my way along the trail.

Soon enough the trail halts at a closed door.

Room number 401.

When I inspect the doorknob I see that it too has a smattering of blood.

No mistake that I've tracked down the troublemakers.

I hold back, listen into the police, far away off in the hotel, apparently going through all that dull protocol of clearing rooms before getting up to where they saw the smoke coiling out of a broken windowpane . . . still, what exactly *did* I expect from police?

Thinking about this now, allowing myself to reflect on just what's gone on, I can see just how I can manipulate this situation to work out perfectly for me.

First things first, I grip the gun tight in my fist, then, sure that I've got a good, tight hold on it, I use the butt to hammer up against the door.

A steady *thwump-thwump-thwump* sounds.

Next, I hurl myself against the wallpaper, well away from the door.

Just as I expected there's a spate of firing, from the guys' handguns inside the room.

I watch, side on to the door, as the bullet holes snap through the wood as if it wasn't even there. Wooden splinters fly and I hold my forearm up to my eyes to keep them from damage.

The shooting stops. There's muttering from inside.

One of the men calls out something in Spanish.

There's no response of course.

I listen into the rustling sounds inside, the scruff of shoe soles crossing the thin carpeting.

The door opens a crack.

Right then I let loose a blood-curdling scream, a scream loud enough for anyone in the faraway airport to hear me, and then I rush past the door.

Right as a man I haven't seen before stands in the doorway, looking slightly dazed and holding a gun down at his thigh, I toss my own gun past him, and rush on down the staircase before he can so much as blink.

I keep up my screaming act so that when I do almost bump into the police officers—all body armour, and semi-automatics, they quite happily turn side on and let me rush past them and continue on down the stairs.

Only when I get back to the reception, back into that vomit-stinking reception with the body lying in the back room, do I finally feel safe.

I hold myself upright against the front desk and tell myself to breathe.

I listen in on the ruckus that goes on upstairs as the police go through the motions with the two gunmen . . . and their three guns.

In the end, it's all worked out rather tidily, or so it seems.

8

ONCE I'VE GIVEN my statement to one of the police officers, the one who has deep brown eyes and high-arching cheekbones, I see that the sun is already up on the horizon.

Since I don't have my phone with me, it still being up there in my bedroom, I ask the police officer the time and he tells me dutifully in his charming accent, and perfect English.

Pretty much time for me to be heading for the airport.

Off to see if I'm going to be able to get away finally.

The police officers get a touch grumbly when I get to talking about going back into the hotel, despite the fact that they've locked up both gunmen in the back of their car—maybe they've got some orders from on high not to contaminate the crime scene —but I manage to convince them with a few doe-eyed smiles, and some batting of the eyelashes.

Soon after, I've got permission to go up to my room for the sole purpose of retrieving my luggage, and all my personal things.

As I get back down, back to the car park, I'm just in time to see them zipping up the confiscated guns into transparent plastic pouches. Just in time to see my gun being laid down on the hood of their car alongside the other two.

I guess the officers have got their work cut out for them in terms of deciphering which one is the murder weapon.

When I make noises about having a plane to catch, the officers get quite accommodating once more, and no sooner have I asked before another police car rolls up into the car park of the hotel . . . though I imagine that it was called out long ago for backup.

My deep-brown-eyed, high-cheekboned officer has a quick word with the driver of the recently arrived car, and then he opens up the door for me.

As I sit there on the back seat, my luggage drawn up beside me, the officer ducks down into the interior of the car, and says, his breath smelling slightly of cinnamon, "We have your contact details if we need something else, yes?"

I try to work out whether that slight hop at the end of his sentence is because of his Spanish-inflected accent or because he's suggesting something entirely different.

I get my answer soon enough.

He digs into the front pocket of his armoured vest and produces a business card which he hands over to me.

It's basic, just black and white lettering, and it has the name of the police force, or at least that's what I think it is, and the name of this rather nice specimen leaning over me.

I give him a smile. "Gracias," I say.

He gives me a cheeky wink, and then withdraws from the car, straightening up and adjusting the belt of his combat trousers. "No problem, Mrs Harris. We shall be in touch, yes?"

He shuts the back door, raps on the roof with his fist, and we're off, en route to the airport. Just me and my, apparently, mute driver.

As we pull out onto the main road, move into the middle of the empty carriageway, I shift a glance back over my shoulder, look out through the rear window of the car.

The officer is still standing there, watching us go, and I decide to give him a friendly wave.

Once he slips from view, I console myself with his business card, which I'm still holding in my hands: Eduardo Geraldo Sanchez.

And I can't help wondering . . . just *wondering* . . . whether the number that's written out there only works for emergencies.

After all, from here to London, it's only a two-and-a-half-hour flight.

HEAR ME

1

I LAND WITH A *THUMP*, then a jarring *snap*.

Pain flushes through me. Up from my right ankle. Dancing its way up my calf muscles.

My breathing comes shallow. Eyes awash with the blackness. My lungs fill with soot. Cool ash layers up on my tongue, stealing away not just any taste I might've had, but any taste I might be able to think of.

Like Father Christmas, I thought the best way in was down the chimney. That *seemed* like the best way in when I studied the blueprints of the place. Scoped my target. Readied to kill them in their own home.

But if Father Christmas is out there—and rumours of his omnipresence are proven not to be overblown—then I bet he's laughing his arse off right now.

At me.

An amateur.

Just a poor, little amateur.

A stupid girl.

Because I've gone and got myself trapped in the midsection of this chimney.

Or someplace like that.

And hurt.

I shift my crumpled-up legs beneath me. I whip off my black leather gloves, leave my hands bare, and then I feel for the smooth bricks which surrounded me. I wonder if they're like those glazed bricks that are often found in fireplaces—those ones which are a kind of rich, burgundy shade.

Then I realise that—really—I should be thinking of other things right about now.

Like how I'm going to get out of this obsidian pit.

Out of this darkness.

And escape.

As I ease the muscles in my legs, I try my best not to scream from the pain which flies through me. And the best way I can come up with to battle that is to dig my teeth into my lower lip. To feel that dampened, gentle, throbbing pain which burrows through my jaw as if answering the sharp prods of sensation from my ankle.

It's made worse by the sooty air. That, even when I feel these flushes of pain, I can't so much as gasp in response. Doing so would only bring yet more ash into my lungs. Make inroads on smothering out my breaths from the inside.

Snuff out my life in this dark, tight little hole.

And I'd quite like to go on living, thank you very much, at least for a little longer . . .

I try to put the pain out of my mind, to scope my immediate surroundings by using my fingertips to feel out the bricks about me. To work out just how large this prison I find myself inside of is. But I struggle to do so. I've never had the greatest of imaginations in the world, and now only serves to push home that fact, to demonstrate, once and for all, that I'm almost certainly a lady of the senses, that I need all my senses about me to have a hope of dominating my environment, and not becoming lost to it.

Still, I do manage to find a hole in the brickwork.

Somewhere I can at least jab in my fingertips.

Get my fingernails into.

I work quickly, using the hold to help myself up, onto my afflicted right ankle, hoping that I might be able to get into a standing position. Might be able to hoik myself upwards. To see if I've got the strength to climb up the way that I came in.

But, just as I get about half the way to standing up, I hit my head on the brickwork above.

More pain.

This time from the top of my skull.

Hard and fast and fizzing.

It drives my teeth deeper into my lower lip.

Draws blood.

Brings up that metal taste onto my tongue, coupled with its lolling, warm ooze.

I slump back down.

The pain in my ankle flames up.

And I know that I'm in trouble.

This time I'm in *big* trouble.

2

ONE THING NOBODY appreciates in this business—if they can really be said to appreciate anything at all—is the waiting.

The interminable waiting.

Oh, most think that the hardest part is cornering your prey, looking into the eyes—into the *soul*—if you're that way inclined, and then pulling the trigger anyway.

Snuffing out human life.

But, no, at least for me, that's never been the tricky part.

Maybe I'm just a monster.

That could explain an awful lot, actually.

Or maybe it's just because I can block it all out. That I can simply press a button—my *kill switch*—and make it all disappear, and all at once.

Now, though, sitting slumped here in the darkness of this fireplace, that faint odour of fires long-ago burned out, I can't help but think that I'm doomed. That this is my last job. That, sooner or later, dead or alive, they'll drag me out of this fireplace.

I listen hard, doing my best to forget the ticking pain at my ankle, to tune myself out from the incessant doomed thoughts which form themselves in my mind.

If I concentrate—*really* concentrate—I can hear the house sounds on the other side of the brickwork. The *fizzle* of electricity. The churning of a dishwasher—a little further off in the house—and the creaking floorboards of the place.

I know that—realistically—there's only one way I'll ever get out of here.

It seems like my instincts are ahead of me on this.

I pad my black fleece—the one I put on for my killings—and

I feel the lump of my mobile there. Its thick shape there. I fish for it. Bring it out. Illuminate its screen.

And my surroundings.

That's better.

A little better.

At least now, I can make out something of my setting.

But I can't say that it lifts my heart at all.

From the bluish-white light I make out the brickwork of the chimney. See that it's stained with black ash. Then I look downwards, at my feet, see that they rest on a ledge. That the chimney bends its way over it at a ninety degree angle. And that there's hardly enough room for me to snake my arm through that space, let alone somehow bend the entirety of my body through it.

Maybe if I was a gymnast.

Maybe if I hadn't been stupid enough to think this was *ever* a good idea in the first place.

But retrospect is really a fine thing.

And often a luxury.

I'll start immersing myself in retrospect once I get myself out of this tight spot.

If I manage to get out of it at all.

3

I FLIP through the screens on my mobile. But it's only just when I've illuminated AA's number on my screen—my immediate superior, and all-around go-to guy—and I'm readying to give him a call that I note there are no signal bars remaining for me.

Apparently no possibility for a call to AA working out.

I think back to this place—to this house—way up on a hill, at the end of a winding dirt road, right out in the sticks really.

To get here I had to hike through about three miles of woods, had to navigate my way over several rabbit holes. The irony was that I spent a long time worrying about those rabbit holes, worrying that I might turn an ankle in one of them.

Well, look at me now.

Guess I never put too much thought into turning an ankle while going in through the chimney.

I parked the car up in a layby, pulled out one of those stickers the police use to notify the public that a vehicle has been abandoned—and, more importantly, *already* reported in.

That, I suppose, was the cover I was looking for.

What I thought would be so intelligent at covering my tracks.

And then to make my way to this place on foot—another stroke of genius, or so I believed.

I can still remember clearly now, even with my extremely poor, pitiable imagination, the mansion up on the hill. How it stuck out like it was from some sort of a horror film. What with its pointed rooftops, its slatted tiles, the framed windows.

And, of course, the wide-open chimneys.

I think back to being in my kitchen, at home, and looking through the blueprints for the place. It just made so much sense for me, looking over the plans. How the rooftop jutted out in such a way into the forest, over the six-foot high fence with the barbed-wire coiled about the top of it. And how it would be so easy if I could only find the right overhanging branch, and somehow toss myself straight onto the roof.

A shortcut *and* a way around having to sleuth my way in through the grounds, navigate the guard dogs, and the search-lights hanging off just about every nook and crevice.

Perfect.

Clever.

Just a little *too* clever, perhaps.

It didn't stop there, though, because I'd also seen the way the line of the chimney would snake about, down through the house, and to that fireplace, to the bedroom of the target.

It would be so easy.

Just a matter of sliding my way out, shooting, and then making my getaway just as quickly—back up through the chimney, clambering my way upwards, onto the roof, then back out through the forests.

I'd estimated that I'd get back to the car parked in the layby before the sun had so much as licked its first ray up on the horizon.

And I would be away.

Fee in my account.

The job done.

But now . . . now—*here*—in this chimney, *trapped*, I know that there's no way out.

I hold my mobile up a little higher, trying to catch just a single bar of signal, something that'll give me some hope. Something that I can cling to.

But, no, fate just laughs in my face.

Yet again.

4

I WONDER if that's the point where I'm meant to slump to the ground, thoroughly beaten. To give up on my life. And, to be honest, I do have one of those dark moments where the pain in my ankle tingles into a hot sensation. It near enough freezes every conscious thought from my mind. But I hang on. I sink my teeth into my tongue.

As if time passing might've helped things, I glance back at my mobile screen. Look to see if I have any signal *now*.

No luck, though.

What did I *think* would have happened?

I check the battery.

That's still fairly full.

At least there's *one* good thing to hang onto with the very edges of my fingernails.

I flip through the screens, find the thing that stops the back-light from fading out, and then I set my phone down at my feet. On the fairly level ground I'm crumpled up against.

For a few seconds, I lose myself in that light blue glow all about me. I think that I can hear the tiny microprocessor of my mobile humming away to itself, but, at the same time, I know that that's impossible.

I try to get my mind back on track.

Chimney.

Gotta get out of here.

Somehow.

I reach about me, brush my palms over the bricks once again. Feel the knobbly edges of the end of each. Where they're mortared together. My finger dips down into the crack. I feel for the rough material. It's brittle and I can feel it flaking away as I make contact with it.

The dust tinkles down the wall before me.

I breathe in and catch it in my lungs.

It's rough in my mouth—on my tongue.

And, before I can stop myself, the tingling gets too much to bear, right at the back of my nostrils, and I feel the sneeze building within me.

Then it bursts right out.

It sounds like my sneeze is dulled.

Like the bricks around me have somehow absorbed the sound.

I really hope that's the case.

I pull up the neck of my fleece so that it comes up to cover my nostrils and mouth, and then I continue to work at that little niche I've managed to whittle on out of that space between the bricks.

Just a tiny hole. A *tiny* hope.

But it's all that I've got.

I keep working away. Feel the rough material against my skin.

I think, for a moment, that if I was one of those uptight women, the ones that worry about *manicures* and *nail varnish*, I might well be freaking out right about now . . . but I'm *not* uptight, or, at least, not in that sort of a way.

That's normal, right?

Just as I'm sawing at the mortar I feel a large wad give way. Skitter down the bricks. Tumble down somewhere at my feet with a dry *crunch*.

I work harder with my finger. Realise that, if I push hard, if I poke my tongue out through my pursed lips *just so* I can fit a couple of fingers through the gap.

And . . . *yes*, all the way to the other side.

Or, at least, to some *other* gap.

I bring my fingers back out from the hole I've created.

I try to keep my wits under control.

I crouch myself around, feeling my ankle screaming out in pain as I go, to the hole that I've created. And then, with those same *pursed* lips of mine, I blow hard.

Dust flies through the air.

I'm pretty sure that I hear some more mortar drop out of the crack.

I wait a couple of moments for the dust to clear, and then I can see through the hole I've created. I reach down, flip off the backlight of my mobile. Then I can see light streaming through the hole.

Moonlight.

5

FOR A LONG WHILE I just slink back, against the wall of the chimney, trying to catch my breath as best as I can. This basically involves tipping my head back and gulping at the air above me, hoping that it'll be mostly free of that mortar dust I've dragged on out of the wall.

My heart thuds dully in my chest. Blood throbs through my cheeks.

And down at my ankle.

My ankle feels almost like it's on fire now.

Like, with every heartbeat, my ankle is blazing with pain.

I know that I'm still in trouble—deep trouble.

Even if I can work out *some* way to get myself out of this chimney, onto the other side of these bricks.

Because, though I might be on the slender side, I really can't see myself fitting through a hole just about big enough to fit a couple of fingers.

For some reason it's then that I think back to that mug of hot chocolate I'd been sipping back at my kitchen table. Looking over the blueprints. Checking—and *re*checking—the place for a good point of entry. Just having that gooey chocolaty paste flowing about my mouth. Lolling over my tongue. Warming me from within. It seems so far away from where I am right now.

It's weird, even though I know this is a point of pretty great danger, I can't help letting loose just a tiny cackle under my breath.

I feel it sort of vibrate in my chest. Almost send my lungs jangling about.

A fresh waft of dust and ash steals that cackle right off my tongue, and threatens to send me into another coughing fit.

When I do cough, I cough into the neck of my fleece.

Time for me to get to work on this hole.

So I work at it. A long while. Just my fingers. Every so often, I check my phone, look over the time. It takes me about an hour—till around two o'clock in the morning—before I've managed to successfully remove all the mortar surrounding the single brick.

I *am* just using my *hands*, okay?

I bring the brick out carefully, lay it down at my feet, and then I stare on into the room on the other side.

Moonlight continues to stream on into it, and I think a little dizzily over the blueprint—wonder about bringing it back up on my phone to check it over.

But I don't like to do that.

More than anything else, I know how good my memory is, and know—from experience—I'm almost always better off just trusting my senses than doubting myself.

Yeah, that and technology is notoriously unreliable.

I mean, in my line of work, swimming through lakes, or wading through waist-high mud isn't out the question . . . and most mobiles I've run into don't seem to do such a great job in those situations.

And if it's not water, then it's almost always the *battery* running out on you . . . just when you most need it.

This, I think to myself, should be the study . . . or what was marked as 'study' on the blueprints.

Right on the other side.

Strangely, with this house, the master bedroom—my target's bedroom—is on the bottom floor of the place. And this study is on the next floor up.

If I can just manage to get myself through this wall . . . the *rest* of this wall . . . then maybe—just maybe—I can manage to make a good job of this impending disaster.

Yeah, and pigs might fly.

That's what I think as I try to help myself into a standing

position. Try to put weight back onto my right ankle. Feel the pain flush right through me, causing my teeth to crunch together, apparently unwilling to unseal themselves till I take the weight back off again.

But I push the pain away.

Pressure it into a distant corner of my skull.

Crouched over, I worked at the space I've opened up. Work at the bricks which surround it. Find them flimsy. Think to myself that they'll be quite easily knocked over. If there was no one home—hell, maybe if the target wasn't sleeping *right beneath* this room—I probably wouldn't have any qualms about just shoulder charging these bricks.

Way it is, though, I have to be a little more subtle about it.

I slip my leather gloves back on.

Not really wanting to add a broken hand to my list of ailments.

I work at the bricks.

They feel like loosening teeth—just like I remember being a little girl, working at a baby tooth that just wants to be set free from the gums.

It's a tedious process, but I finally get a couple of them loose.

Remove them from their places.

Lay them down beside the other brick.

Thirty minutes later, I see from my phone, and I've managed to clear a space that looks like it'll be just about big enough for me to fit my head through. If I can just manage to crunch my shoulders right then I might be in business.

Guess we'll see.

I've got to the stage where I'm shaking pretty much all over from the shimmering pain rushing up from ankle.

But I make the effort to stay still—still long enough for me to get my head through the gap I've created and then, not without a little swearing under my breath, to manage to get one of my shoulders through the hole too.

I breathe in deep. Try to catch my breath on the other side. Away from the ash and dust. Though I'm sure there's no open window in the room on the other side, the air feels infinitely fresher, more nourishing. Every time I breathe out, it's like I'm breathing out a cloud of smog. As if with each exhale my lungs are lightened.

I squeeze my eyes shut and try to get my other shoulder through the gap.

. . . Nothing happening.

The gap's just not big enough.

I breathe in deep, try to think myself thinner.

I mumble another few swearwords.

Taste a little blood . . . maybe I've been nibbling away nervously at my tongue *just a little* too hard.

I push myself back on my haunches, allowing just a little weight to drop back into the chimney which I'm trying so hard to escape from, and then, with a great big effort, I shove myself towards the hole. Everything at once. Wanting to push my *whole* body through.

And I manage it.

But not without that jarring grind of brick on brick, and the tumble of what must be half a dozen of the aged bricks.

They all tumble loudly onto the stone fireplace on the other side.

Falling down beside me.

Seeming to ring with a sustained echo all about the room.

All about the study I find myself in.

6

M Y BRAIN is overwhelmed for a few moments. My mind just goes blank. It feels strange to be able to move my limbs freely. To no longer have the limits of the chimney oppressing me. But that sensation only masks the intense flurry of pain from my right ankle for so long—because soon it's back, and worse than ever.

I feel the pain pulse its way up the backs of my calf muscles, wrench its way through my bloodstream, almost seeming to cut off the blood flow to my heart for a couple of moments.

But I screw up my eyes, try to forget about it.

When I finally get the pain under control, blink away the daze the pain has set drifting over me, I see that the dust is still clearing from the study I've emerged into.

And I see that I really have made quite a dramatic mess of the fireplace here.

Managed to bust my way through its back wall.

I crawl my way off the hearth stones and onto the wooden floorboards.

I ache all over now—and I'm sure that my ankle must be broken, at the very least.

Only as I try to stand up again, this time without the restrictions of the chimney, do I remember that my mobile's still stuck inside.

Another swearword later, and a bunch of loping from side to side, just about keeping myself upright, pretty much hopping along on my left foot, I manage to retrieve it.

I fire up the screen.

Somehow wishing for just a scrap of signal here, now that I've emerged from the chimney.

But . . . nope.

What was it I was saying about technology?

I pocket my phone, maybe just a little too strongly, and then I stagger my way across the creaking wooden floor of the study knowing that—no doubt—I've woken half the house with these escapades of mine.

The study has a large oak desk, the kind that looks like it would be just about big enough to host a thirty-person dinner . . . though I imagine they've got an even *bigger*, and far *fancier*, table for that purpose.

Bookshelves punctuate the wall space with those big, expensive-looking, hardbacks all stuffed into them. The spines of the books appear sun-faded even in the moonlight. And, though my nose is still reeling with the scent of dust and ash, I'm pretty sure that I catch a whiff of that stale smell of yellowing pages.

My eyes fall on a glass case which stands up on a small footstool, over by the enormous window which looks out over the grounds of the house—to all those bustling trees, and to the bristling lawn.

A pair of dead birds—pheasants?—stand proud inside.

Their marble eyes gleam sickly in the moonlight.

I feel for my handgun—strapped down at my thigh.

Feel the grip.

Then I unclasp the holster.

Slip the gun out and hold it firm.

Check the suppressor.

Ready for anyone who wanders on in through the darkened inner doorway of the study.

I keep my eyes fixed on that doorway, what with its thick wooden beams about it, and the clean, cream-painted door.

I've got to have no reservations about painting that door red with blood if it comes to it—if I've got any sort of interest in self-preservation.

And, I suppose, after thirty-something years on earth I have got just a little attached to this body . . . along with its beating heart and all.

When I reach the other side of the study, and the door doesn't fly open, I press myself up against the wall.

Waiting.

Listening.

Heart ticking by.

Ankle flaring with pain.

The stink of ash still thick in my nostrils.

Footsteps?

I listen harder.

Sure that I can hear that unmistakable sound of muted footsteps.

Out there. On the landing carpet.

I stand my ground. Keep my shoulders pushed up against the wall.

On the other side of the door, a floorboard creaks.

A shudder runs up my spine.

I grip the gun tighter.

Feel the blood pumping through my hands.

Right to the tips of my fingers.

I need to stay focussed.

One mistake here and . . .

The doorknob jiggles. Just a little.

I hear the almost silent *crunch* as the mechanism engages.

I ready myself.

Squeeze my eyes shut so I won't have to blink again.

Risk missing something.

The door opens out on well-oiled hinges.

It opens towards me.

I watch a large form—a *man*—step through into the study.

Large . . . yes, that's right, he has that slightly unwieldy aspect to him, the one that tells me, instinctively, that I can easily outfox him.

He must be approaching twenty stone.

He has that fat man's waddle.

In the moonlight, I can see he's dressed in a sleek suit, a crisp white shirt nestled beneath with a tie which dangles down too and which seems, to me, like it's almost too short for a man of his stature.

With the rolls of flab he has.

The man doesn't scout about the room. Doesn't look back over his shoulder to the wall where I'm hiding.

He stares out ahead.

Apparently transfixed by the study.

He takes one step.

Two steps.

Three steps.

Staring at the fireplace.

What's become of it.

I wonder if he thinks a pigeon took a fall through the chimney, landed down here, brought all those bricks tumbling on down with it.

A plume of dust flying up and concealing the room for just a few seconds.

But it doesn't matter what he thinks.

Because I shoot him through his back.

Pierce his lung.

Watch as he slumps to his knees and then onto his front, arms sprawled, breaths snatched and high-pitched.

Dying in silence.

I work quickly. Pad his suited body. Find a gun. A Taser. His wallet.

I hold my fingers to his neck, feel for his pulse.

It's weak.

Fluttering away ever so gently.

Soon it'll be gone for good.

As I straighten up, an odd slippery sensation grips hold of me.

Maybe it's the pain in my ankle that steals away my rational thought, or perhaps it's just because I spent a good few hours trapped in that chimney, but I've neglected to notice that twinkling neon-red light on the security camera which hangs from the corner of the study.

And I can't help but wonder if it's pointed right at me.

If they've got my face in close-up.

If they're all on their way *right now*.

7

QUICK THINKING is all I have now.

So that's what I do.

I ship on quickly out of the study, not bothering to take the time to hide the body.

How stupid would *that* look, me hiding a body while that camera's filming me?

I draw my gun again, stride my way out of the study, onto the landing.

I breathe in a slight smell of waffles . . . not really sure *why* waffles, but that's exactly what I smell.

I wonder if the target here gives their security guards the run of the kitchen.

One of the perks of the job.

Suppose they need to balance the ability to make waffles against the definite disadvantage of being killed in the line of duty.

Being killed by someone like me.

I'm glad for the soft carpeting on the landing and a quick glance about reveals that there are no cameras about here.

When I peer over the banister, I see down into the front hall.

Now, there *is* a camera there.

Pointed right at the front door.

I guess the target feels like they need *some* degree of privacy.

I think back to the blueprints.

There was nothing that said *anything* about there being security guards, or security, *inside* the house.

The only real info I got on the place had to do with the exterior.

I guess they thought I'd have the greatest trouble in entering the house in the first place.

Guess they were half right.

I know, from where I stand, that I'll be forced to head through the front hall to get to the master bedroom just about underneath where I stand now.

But I wonder if I'll somehow be able to avoid that camera.

If I can figure out some way to disable it.

Then again, if there's someone on the other end of that camera—if that fat man I popped in the study has some buddies —then that might be the least of my troubles.

I reason the thing out.

Think it over.

Most likely, in a case like this, with an intruder detected in the house . . . an intruder that's *killed*, no less . . . some sort of an alarm would be triggered by the person watching those security monitors.

At least that's my line of logic.

And so it stands to reason, if there's no alarm sounded, no stamping boots heading their way towards me at a brisk march, then perhaps my fat man *was* the only one on duty.

Then again, this does present another problem.

It doesn't *quite* leave me in the clear.

Because that camera definitely *did* see me. And I was just about dazed—or *stupid*—enough to stare right down the barrel of it.

I need to take care of whatever's happened to that footage.

And that means finding the base of operations as soon as possible.

Easier said than done.

I glance about me.

Listen for any other sound.

When I hear nothing at all, I reach for my mobile, giving a little internal sigh, and then I boot up the blueprints I have stored there.

Maybe it's the pain, or maybe it's the stress.
But I know that I have to have another look here.

8

AFTER CHECKING OUT the blueprints a few times, I establish the likeliest place for the bank of security monitors. And, unfortunately, it happens to be somewhere down in the basement.

I've had a look at this tiny little room which is right beside the wine cellar.

That seems like an unsuspecting . . . and *quite likely* place to take a look.

So, gripping hold of the banister with my gloved hand, squeezing on tight so as to take the weight off my right ankle, I ease myself down the stairs—one by one—I grit my teeth at the vibrations that accompany each of my landings on the carpet, and the jangle of pain that it sends up through me.

When I reach the bottom, I stand there and glance about the front hall.

Slick, slate floors.

That really fresh, *cool* scent of slate when I breathe in.

It sets my gut tingling.

A slight flurry through my blood.

This is the sort of smell that money can buy.

I eye that neon-red light from the security camera.

I listen for any *whirr* from the camera, any sign that there might be someone zooming in on me. Trying to take another shot of my face . . . and not just for posterity.

Keeping myself as close to the side of the staircase as I can manage, I strafe my way about the front hall, all the way over to the stairwell leading to the basement—according to the blueprints on my phone.

I have to keep going.

Need to see this through.

Be professional.

Otherwise it'll be more than *my* neck on the line.

. . . It'll be my employer's too . . . and Brian Mathewson really doesn't take failure all that well—or at least that's the gist of the majority of the stories I've heard about him.

I glance up—to the door of the target's bedroom, knowing that it'll be my final destination.

The last place I'll visit before heading on home.

And collecting my fee.

9

ALFWAY DOWN the narrow spiral steps into the basement, I almost trip over my own feet. As I grab a hold of the banister, steady myself, I get a fresh flush of pain through my ankle, and it seems to hang—*wrench*—at my heart.

For a few moments I'm totally vulnerable, just standing right there on the staircase, unable to move forwards, or retreat.

Finally, I get myself back together.

I venture downwards.

Breathe in the smell of red wine—seemingly everywhere. Feel just the scent of it already drying out my tongue. Almost sending a swilling warmth through my blood. Making my brain begin to swirl. Though I don't drink, I feel my mouth salivating, and I guess that I must be thirsty after all of that being trapped in the chimney.

I hadn't planned on being stuck on this job for so long.

Thought I'd been so clever in my planning—that I'd be straight in, and out again just as quickly.

Shows how good plans can be sometimes.

I find the wine cellar. That's just a matter of following my nose. And the boxy little room beside it follows.

There's a multi-digit lock on the door, and I know, even without glancing at the make or type, just what I've got to do.

Ten seconds later, I spring it open, hear the hinges creak.

Guess that the target doesn't think much about expending so much on oil down here in the basement where they're not likely to bring that many guests.

Also guess that they never gave much thought to some intruder managing to get *this* far into their home without their noble fat security guard taking good, clean care of them.

Guess they were wrong.

The room turns out to house the monitors—just as I hoped.

They're all stacked up.

Dozens of them.

All black-and-white footage.

A squidgy, reclining black leather chair sits unoccupied before them.

I catch sight of the stained coffee cup there too.

The coffee rings well ingrained into the desk.

I guess the recently deceased security guard spent an awful lot time down here.

Maybe that's one thing that me and him had in common.

That whole *waiting* thing.

I work quickly, not really knowing all that much about surveillance equipment, but knowing enough to fiddle my way through the computer which sits alongside. To find the file where the videos are despatched to. To open it up. Have a poke around.

Before long I've deleted every scrap of footage from the last week.

Then I have a quick glance about the place for any extra hard disks that might be hooked up to the monitors here. Finding none, I get the feeling that the job's a good one, and I make to move off.

I'm just about standing in the doorway of the little room when I catch movement on one of the monitors. Out in the front hall. I see the shape on the black-and-white, flickering screen. A figure carrying what seems to be a fishing pole.

Or a gun.

And it's then that I finally twig . . . maybe my mind's more befuddled that I thought . . . and I realise that it's the target.

The one I've got to take down.

10

A LL THINGS CONSIDERED, I would've liked to have another quick look over the monitors there—you know just to cross the *t*'s and dot the *i*'s . . . but I guess it's most likely something that I should call in later, get someone to come by the house and clear up before the police arrive. After all, I really know next to nothing about surveillance.

I'm a *killer* after all, not a voyeur.

Back out in the basement, and the stench of red wine still thick in the air, I turn my attention upwards, concentrate on any sound that might be coming from the front hall of the house.

From my target.

I think over the information I've got on them.

Vague, at most.

Like sometimes happens.

The only thing I really know is that the target lives alone— out here, all alone . . . give or take a few security guards, cameras, and dogs . . . that already gets a little shudder passing through me at the thought of just how I'm going to extricate myself from this.

The pain in my right ankle has reached that peak where it's more or less numbing every nerve in my body—as if my brain just can't cope with the level of sensation.

I'm kind of glad about that, even if I still have to hobble about all over the place.

I feel for the wall which runs up the steep stairs out of the basement.

I keep my gun down at my thigh.

Shudders run through me, attempt to jangle my nerves.

But I keep my wits about me.

Tell myself that—really—this isn't the time for me to have a breakdown . . . to submit to pain.

I grip tighter. Try, mostly in vain, to keep the sweat from seeping of my palms, sleeking up my hands beneath the leather gloves.

I listen for any sign that'll give my target away.

Give away their location.

When I finally reach the top of the stairs, feeling like my ankle is pretty much on fire, I can't help but let loose a hard exhale. It took something out of me to suck up all that pain. I give myself just a quick second to recover, to keep myself from simply flopping over myself—collapsing right there and taking a tumble down the basement stairs—and then I turn my attention back to what's ahead of me.

The *hit* ahead of me.

I glance about the front hall.

See no sign of the target.

At least not now.

My mind flurries a little. I scope out the shadows—it plays tricks on my mind. I think that I can see all sorts of things here.

But then, all at once, it comes into focus.

The darkness slips back into the corners as my eyes grow better accustomed.

And I see the shape.

See the *long* shape pointed at my chest.

"You move, I shoot," the voice says, hardly above a whisper.

11

I RESIST the natural urge to turn my head.

Though the voice sounds fairly together—fairly even and unflappable, I've always had this strange sort of gut feeling that whenever someone's pointing a gun at me I should err on the side of caution.

Guess it's kept me alive thus far.

Till this moment.

So I stare forwards, at the staircase which leads upwards. Stare at the ornamented cornices on the banister. To the pictures all hung up in a diagonal ascending pattern with the designs that I have no chance of scoping considering the gloom.

The smell of the slate about me keeps me better awake than a shot of espresso.

The tingling, lingering pain at my ankle, daring me to put some more weight on it, constantly makes its presence felt to my jabbering heart.

I can taste blood in my mouth.

The target's breathing is husky—a slight *wheeze* to it.

But I can't note anything else.

"Put the gun down," the target says.

I blink a couple of times. Feel some muscle at my temple twitch.

Then I do what they say.

The gun skitters onto the slate floor before me, almost instantly sucked into the shadows. And I think—right away— that, all things considered, I might've made a better job of letting the gun fall a little closer to hand . . . then again, I guess I don't want to piss off the person with the gun . . . not while they're pointing it at my chest in any case.

"Who sent you?" the target says, voice still firm—unruffled.

I'd like to say that it's the first time a target has got the opportunity to ask me that question, but that would be a lie. That said, I answer the same way I did before.

"Never saw his face."

The target scoffs in disbelief.

Though I have no intention of moving so much as a muscle in their direction, I'm pretty sure that I catch a slight jiggle of the rifle out of the corner of my eye.

"Brian, it was *Brian*, wasn't it?"

That sends my blood tingling.

I'll be first to admit that I've never been the best liar in the world.

And I guess that—even in the darkness—the target can sense that.

"Yes," the target says, "it was Brian—you don't need to say anything."

I hold my breath a few seconds as if I'm punishing myself for having allowed the target to reach a conclusion of their own.

But then, with a slight jump of my heart, I remind myself that I've got to find a way out of this . . . and, preferably, a way that'll mean the target ending up dead, and me alive and, even more hopefully, me driving away from here at top speed.

"Take two steps to the left," the target says.

I hesitate. Just long enough. And then I break from my stasis.

Tell myself that it's better to comply.

I take the steps.

My ankle blazes with pain.

I crunch my teeth together till I get that dry taste of enamel.

Then I wait on my next order.

"With your left hand, reach out and brush the wall, at about chest height."

HEAR ME

Again, I do what I'm told.
Feel a light switch there.
But I don't do anything else till I'm told.
"Turn them on," the target says.

12

THE FRONT HALL fills with an orangey glow. When I glance upwards I see that a crystal chandelier hangs above our heads. That the light reflects in the ornate pieces of glass.

Directly across from me a lamp blinks into life too.

One of those *lawyers'* lamps, you know the ones with that kind of semi-transparent green, glass shade at the top.

I try everything in my power *not* to look at the target—to look at the gun pointed at me.

But then . . .

"Look at me," the target says.

I hold off—again just a couple of seconds—then I glance at them.

I take in the target.

A woman . . . no, a *lady*, there's a distinct difference.

She wears one of those baggy, fleecy jackets that looks like it's simply been culled directly from some sheep then thrown about her shoulders. It has all sorts of discoloured stains marking the once-white, but now-grey, wool.

The greyed wool, in a way, echoes her own wispy grey hair.

Her face sags—she has jowls, just like those men that spend too long down the pub.

And her complexion is mottled.

She has a pink tinge to her cheeks.

Her black eyes never leave mine.

Then I look to the gun.

A hunting rifle . . . never been pointed at another person before, or so I hope . . .

It looks a little like a blunderbuss, but I wouldn't swear to it.

Not with the fiery pain crawling its way up my leg and crushing my every discernible thought into Pablum.

I look beyond the target—to the front door, and then, quickly, about the rest of our surroundings. When I turn my attention back to the target, I see that she's wearing a faint smile on her cracked, bloodless lips.

"Don't worry," she says, "there's no one else around. Not now that you've taken care of Nigel."

Nigel. So that was the fat man's name.

It seems to suit him somehow.

. . . But, then again, from what I've found, most names seem to suit the dead.

It's as if—the minute they stop breathing—they take on this everyman personality.

Or maybe I'm just heartless . . . an irretrievable *destroyer*.

"Quite ingenious," the target says. "I mean, sneaking on in through the chimney like that. Breaking in through the fireplace. Avoiding the grounds." She sighs full-bloodedly, and then jigs the rifle just a little in her hands—just enough to send my stomach crunching in on itself. "Yes, I can tell that *Brian* sent you."

Now that I think about it, the lady has something of a lilt— something of a *snap*—to her accent, and it marks her as a member of the upper class. And I wonder if this place, this coun- tryside mansion where we stand now, has been handed down over many generations.

For a long while, there's silence between the two of us.

I'm left alone with the pounding—*pulsing*—pain in my ankle.

"A shame," the target says, but adds no other explanation.

I take the hint that I'm meant to pick up the slack in the conversation. "Why?" I say, my throat suddenly dry, the pain in my ankle suddenly overwhelming.

"I was so *ready* to die," she says.

I'm not really sure what to make of that and I think, under different circumstances, I might have said so much.

Like this, though, there's not really anything for me to say.

So I keep schtum.

"Cancer," the target says, still holding tight to her rifle. "Six months, that's all they say I've got to live." She sighs again. "But Brian couldn't wait *that* long, could he? No, I imagine he *had* to make sure—had to make sure that even that *one* percent wouldn't get a chance."

Out of the corner of my eye, I get the impression that she shifts the rifle closer to me . . . or maybe she takes a step nearer to me.

"Do you realise *why* Brian wants to kill me?"

"No," I say, answering honestly and thinking about adding 'and I don't *want* to know' but stop myself short.

The target draws breath again, and I'm sure that I hear a slight *snick* to her breathing, something which keeps her from functioning normally.

"No," she says. "I don't imagine he ever does—*tell* you, I mean."

I feel my ankle throbbing a little more. I think about this. Start thinking about my escape from the house. But, somehow, just can't manage to get it straight in my mind.

I know I still have a job to do.

Unfinished business.

A life still functioning.

"I'll tell you what, *Anna*"—I flinch just a touch when she says my name . . . but, at the same time, get the feeling that, deep down, I knew she knew who I was—"I'll give you a fighting chance—another opportunity to *finish* what you came here to do." She cocks her head to one side, and adds, "Does that sound fair?"

I swallow hard. Stare down to the table opposite me. Eye the gun there.

Where I tossed it.

And then I say, "Yes."

13

ABOUT TEN SECONDS pass before I can fully absorb what the target tells me.

"... Go on, then," she says. "Pick it up."

Still, I hold back, just for those few moments, wondering if this might be some sort of a ruse, a way to get me into a vulnerable position so she can shoot me—so that she'll have a *rock-solid* reason for shooting me.

I *was* armed, after all.

Only when she takes a step towards me do I break out of my daze, make a move for my gun. Duck down beneath that table and sweep it up.

I take hold of the grip, aware that I'm showing the target my back, and that, if she chooses to do so, she can quite easily terminate me here and now.

But she doesn't.

There's no gunshot.

And when I turn around she's got her eyes closed. Still gripping her hunting rifle tight. Her knuckles turned white from the effort.

I only stop staring so hard at her when she crinkles open one eye, smiles that gentle smile of hers once again, and says, "Well, then, Anna, I'll count to a hundred." She pauses a second, then adds, "I promise not to peek."

When she closes her eyes again, I can't quite believe what's going on.

It just seems so ridiculous.

Like a game ... well, actually, what she's proposing *is* a game.

Doesn't she realise that I could shoot her, right here, right now: between the eyes while she's doing this counting thing of hers—mouthing the numbers as she counts them off in her head?

For some reason, though, I feel that tweak at the base of my spine, something that—for want of a better way to put it—is my sense of good sportsmanship.

Though I was sent here to do it, I can't simply shoot this woman between her eyes.

End her right here in the front hall.

But, then again, surely I can't afford *not* to?

I didn't *ask* to get wrapped up in this game of hers.

To play along like this.

I just came here with a job to do.

And now's the time for me to do it.

. . . Yet, I can't bring myself to.

Can't help but stare long and hard at the lady's face—see her eyes gently fluttering beneath their mauve-veined lids.

I read her lips.

See that she's just reached thirteen.

Maybe it's some sort of an ominous sign.

But that's when I take off.

Limping all the way.

Off to go hide somewhere in this big house.

14

I DON'T EVEN ATTEMPT to climb stairs and yet the pain from my ankle still flurries through my every thought.

I pad on over the slate floors, quickly leaving the front hall—and the counting woman—behind.

Why couldn't this just have been easy?

Why couldn't *I* just shoot her right between the eyes, while I had the chance?

Have been a professional?

. . . I think I know the answer, deep down, that if I'd gone through with it, if I'd shot the woman right there, in her front hall, while she was in the midst of proposing a *duel* with me, I'm pretty sure it would've haunted me for the rest of my life.

To say the moral code of an assassin is a minefield is putting it mildly.

Or maybe it's just Anna Harris's moral code . . .

In the end, I pick out a pair of double doors, the doors which I know, instinctively, lead to the master bedroom. To the place where I'd *hoped* to take care of the target in her bed.

. . . Best-laid plans and all that . . .

I slip in through the doors. Feel my way along the thick wallpaper. Inch my shoulders along the way. Stare at the enormous four-poster bed which sits in the middle of it all. It has everything: even those flimsy drape things that hang down about it.

It makes me think of the bed of a king, or a *queen*, as the case may be.

As I'm scoping out the place, a pristine white envelope lying on the bedside table catches my eye.

Well, to be honest, what really catches my eye is the flowery, blue-ink handwriting on the front which reads: *For Brian.*

And though I know that there's a woman with a hunting rifle

just about to bear down on me, to try and *kill* me, I can't help slipping it off the bedside table. Tucking it into my pocket . . . though I stop short of giving it a little pat . . .

I turn my attention back to the bedroom door knowing that I've got the vantage point here—that I'm in control. That if the woman thinks of coming in through those doors, even with her rifle blasting, that I'll be able to take her out right away.

But, pretty much as I've just decided to turn my *full* attention to the doorway, and to the approaching woman, I hear a loud, percussive . . . and *final* gunshot come from the front hall.

For a couple of moments I listen to it echo about the mansion.

Try to make sense of it.

To work out just what it *means*.

And then, just like that, I snap into motion.

Realise what's happened.

15

BACK IN THE FRONT HALL, I find the target right away.

Lying on the slate tiles.

Prostrate.

A puddle of blood forming about her head, where it lies on the ground.

Mouth appearing to whisper something.

Rifle discarded, off at her side.

I see right away that she's shot herself in the head . . . or at least *tried* to.

When I get closer, I see her eyes swivelling about their sockets —moving quietly over mine, jiggling just a little.

I see her mouth rather than hear her voice.

And, still stunned—or at least stunned enough to forget the twisting pain in my ankle a couple of moments—I tread over to her. Bend down. Bring my ear close to her lips to hear what will surely be her dying words.

"The . . . the *letter*," she says.

I strain a little harder. Feel almost as if my brain might melt.

I manage to draw back, to nod at her.

A smile forms on her lips.

She blinks slowly.

Once.

Twice.

And then she's gone.

16

MIRACLE OF ALL MIRACLES, I manage to get some signal in the front hall.

One bar, that's all.

But it's enough.

Just after I've placed the call to AA—told him that I'll need just a little bit of help down here in this mansion after all the events of the evening—I turn my attention back to the letter that I snaffled off the bedside table.

When I turn it over in my hands, I notice that it hasn't been sealed—that the target didn't think to lick it shut . . . on purpose?

So, flipping the flap open, I slip the letter on out.

It's doubled over.

I unfold it.

Simple.

Just a couple of lines.

Nothing else:

Dear Brian,

I knew you wouldn't have the guts to do it yourself—to do what needed to be done.

But you never did hear me, did you?

I look it over again, wondering if I might've missed something.

If I might've missed a signature at the bottom.

But—nope—no signature.

Though, all things considered, I guess it's pretty obvious who *wrote* this letter.

For some reason I find it difficult to shake those lines of the letter—as simple as they are, and as unenigmatic at they seem.

Because they're saying one thing.

Very loudly.

And very clearly.

That my employer—that Brian Mathewson—is a *coward*.

. . . And if Brian's a coward, then what does that make me?

But my train of thought, maybe for the best, gets cut off right there and then by an extremely unsubtle and reverberating ring of the front door bell.

AA arrived to help me out.

To help me finish this thing.

I don't go to answer right away.

I read the letter over another couple of times.

Then I fold it up—in two—and slip it into my pocket.

Most likely Brian won't even notice it's missing.

That it even existed.

WHITE OUT

W HEN I CRY, there seems to be no end to it.
Just one of those things about keeping everything bottled up, I guess.

But, right now, there seems to be no other option.

I clench on tight to the steering wheel of the four-by-four. My fingers squeeze into the rutted plastic mould. I feel the engine tremble through me. I can smell the exhaust pumping on in through the air vents of the vehicle, and it's almost dizzying. I have the dry, almost-there taste of mint at the back of my throat, on account of those sweets I bought a good few hours back from the last touch of civilisation—this independent garage selling petrol at, quite frankly, *extortionate* prices.

I push down on the accelerator. In first gear. I listen to the wheels—all four of them—spin out of control against the icy surface below.

I'm stuck.

Well and truly.

And this just *would* be a Christmas Eve for Anna Harris, wouldn't it?

When it becomes apparent that I'm not going anywhere fast, I let off the accelerator, but keep the engine ticking over. Anything else would be madness. The engine also serves to keep warm air pumping into the interior of the car. Keeps the foggy condensation off the inside of the windscreen.

Keeps me from freezing to death.

Outside, everything is white.

Snow bundles down.

Gales blow against the side of the car.

Send its suspension shaking.

And make me tremble all over.

But not from cold.

From *fear*.

Because, where I am now, is, quite simply, somewhere which is beyond help.

I've been sent here, to this location in the middle of nowhere, to kill.

And, despite my predicament—despite my *tears*—I'm determined to get the job done.

Anything else, by definition, would be failure.

On paper, everything seemed simple and, indeed, looking up at the GPS screen which is plugged onto the inside of my windscreen, things still seem that way.

The cocky screen shows that I have only to go on for another three kilometres and I'll be there.

At the target's location.

What the screen doesn't take into account, though, is that although the route marked out by the greyish, purple line seems easy enough to follow, all the roads here are covered in—what I estimate to be—a good metre or so of snow.

Neither does it take into account the ability, or mental state, of the driver.

I thought that this would be a Christmas to spend with my family.

I thought that the silence on Brian Mathewson's end was something of a Christmas bonus. That he was giving me some slack over the festive period.

Apparently not.

It was only the eye of the storm.

I try not to think of the cooking turkey, or the roast potatoes and parsnips which warm you up from the inside-out. Or of the central heating and—in theory—the fireplace roaring with hardly contained warmth.

All those smells.

All those tastes.

The flashing of fairy lights.

Tittering remarks from my children.

Gruff reprimands from my ex-husband.

All so far away.

On another continent, in fact.

I won't be back till New Year's, that's for sure.

To be with the ones who stayed behind.

As my pity party reaches its pinnacle, I gaze on out into the Great White stretching away from the bonnet of my vehicle, and wonder if I should just cut my losses, get out and walk.

That's an option.

I have the gear.

In the back.

A thick, thermal snowsuit—white for camouflage, of course.

And then there's the hefty boots.

Those'd come in handy too.

But this approach to the target's house has more to do with planning than comfort.

To make the hit, I'd wanted to get parked up outside his luxury mountain cabin a good few hours before he returned home. That would give me time to break into his house. Set myself up for the killing. But if I can't ease my car on over there, and I have to trudge my way through the snow, then I'll lose a good chunk of my planning time.

And that's a recipe for mistakes.

And I don't like to make a habit of mistakes.

. . . As far as I can help it.

With another vain press on the accelerator, and more spinning wheels, I decide that there's nothing for it now.

I have to take the walking option.

I wipe my tears away.

Switch off the ignition.

2

O F COURSE, it's more complicated than I imagined.

Since this is the only road which leads up to the target's cabin, I can't just leave the car here. For one, it would block his own access to the cabin. And, for another, it would mark out my presence here right away. That something about this is *Just Not Right*.

Again, that's when mistakes happen.

A spooked target is never a good prospect.

Taking the initiative, I recover a shovel from beneath a patch of detachable carpet in the boot of the four-by-four. And, by God, I get shovelling.

In the constantly falling snow, and in the gales which just won't let up, I manage to dig away a good portion of the snow bank to the side of my four-by-four.

It'll be enough.

That done, I turn my attention to digging out the wheels of the four-by-four, too.

So that I can, at least, back up and swivel the vehicle into place.

I grab hold of all my gear from the boot before getting back into the driver's seat.

There's no telling just how this'll go.

If I'll actually make a *success* of it.

It's one thing to be resourceful, but quite another to be *competent* too.

I back up the four-by-four and—far more easily than I imagined—manage to slot it into the hole I dug out of the bank.

It fits.

Leaves the road clear.

That done, I switch off the engine once more, grab my bag of stuff, and venture off around the back of the four-by-four. Time for me to get digging.

3

IT TAKES ME, by my best estimate, about an hour to get the four-by-four covered to my satisfaction. And, even then, as I trudge away from the buried car, I can't help but glance back over my shoulder, a slight squint in my eye, and wonder—*wonder* —if I've actually done a half-decent job of concealing it.

My mind flurries with paranoid imaginings along the lines of the target returning to his cabin and noticing the track for my four-by-four coming to an abrupt halt.

It'd only take a little digging to uncover the white paintwork of the vehicle.

And my cover will be blown.

The job blown.

Hopefully ice will set in. Make it so that the snow turns into a kind of rocky consistency. Never to be seen again until the springtime sun arrives to melt it.

I turn away from the burial mound for the final time and tell myself—*again and again*—that everything will be just fine.

Brian will have some people out to recover the vehicle sooner or later.

But I'll have to think through my escape following the hit a little more clearly.

Later.

Getting through the snow sends unbearable pain up my calves.

Guess I should spend more time at the gym.

To walk, I need to bring my feet right up and out of the surface of the snow.

I have to bring them almost up to my chest.

With the GPS in my hand, I glance back over my shoulder

far more than once to check up on my tracks. But I can't see any more than about five metres behind.

This falling snow is transforming into a blizzard.

Even as I find myself in this situation, about to break into a house, and kill somebody on Christmas Eve, I can't help wondering what my family are doing right now.

Thinking about the time difference just does my head in.

As far as I know, it might already be Christmas Day.

My brain is so frazzled from the constant travel to get to this point that I can't quite believe that my home exists any longer.

There is nothing but this moment.

Right now.

The GPS emits a tiny *ping* indicating that I'm within a kilometre of the destination, and I keep my eyes fixed on the screen. Looking for any clues that might indicate a crevasse awaiting me below thinly layered snow.

But the resolution of the GPS doesn't seem to quite cover that level of detail.

I squeeze my eyes shut. Hold my gloved hand—the one which doesn't grasp the GPS—up to cover my eyeballs from the constantly falling snow.

I can just make out, through the veil upon veil of snow, an enormous cabin peeping through the otherwise perfectly white landscape.

Just need to keep going.

Keep on.

Almost there.

. . . Christmas Eve.

4

THE CABIN presents few obstacles.

Oh, there's a decent alarm system, but nothing that the tech I'm packing can't take care of in less than fifteen minutes.

And I'm in.

Thankfully, and perhaps in anticipation of my soon-to-arrive target, the heating has clicked on. I can feel waves of warmth oozing through the house.

Bringing me out in *sweats*.

I take off my boots.

Pack them into a waterproof separate pocket of my bag.

In my socks, I walk across the curly, impossibly soft carpet.

This is surely the retreat of somebody who doesn't have kids.

Just the thought of extracting long-ago spilled cornflakes from between the long, furry strands is enough to send a chill up my spine. And I really don't need any more chills for tonight.

The sitting room is all decked out in Christmas glitter.

A Christmas tree: a verdant pine strung with tinsel and silvery lights.

Stockings hanging down from the oak fireplace, currently unlit.

And a whole host of Christmas cards dangling precariously off a string.

I can smell something cooking.

Not turkey.

Nut roast?

And a tinge of gravy there, too.

When I take another few steps about the sitting room, thinking through how I'm going to approach this hit, I can't help but catch a sweet flavour at the back of my throat.

My mind twirls about for several seconds.

Call it nostalgia, whatever you want, but I lose myself to *it* for a brief while.

Then I snap my mind back to the matter at hand.

The killing.

I pry through the rest of the house, up the stairs, to the next floor.

And then the next.

In what appears to be an attic, there's a very useful window which affords a view of the entire approach of the road to the cabin. Crouching—or squatting, take your pick—up here will give me a very nice big picture of whereabouts the target is.

If only I'd brought a rifle, I might be able to take care of him in his car.

If only the snow wasn't falling so thickly.

. . . If only I had *some* level of competence with a rifle.

But I'm much more of a handgun girl.

In the attic, with the eerie, brushing sound of the snowflakes settling on the roof just above my head, I set all my gear out, unpack the bag I lugged through all the snow dunes.

I look at my gun.

The one that I've Christened *Mrs Claus* . . . original, I'm sure you'll agree.

.45 calibre.

Just how I like it.

Working quickly—I like to think *professionally*—I screw on the suppressor, and then check that the extreme cold hasn't had any effect on my trusty companion.

It hasn't.

At least as far as I can tell.

With everything done, I sit there, by the window, and stare out.

Waiting for the man I need to kill.

5

THROUGHOUT MY CAREER as a hired assassin, I've often had trouble with what might be considered in the Trade as *fidgeting*.

It's a kind of nervous apprehension that's most likely going to take some expensive psychiatric work to take care of completely . . . and, right now, I'm not really feeling like splashing that amount of cash on something so self-indulgent.

There's how I'll untie, and tie, my shoelaces.

I have this thing where I'll need to do the loop first one way, and then the exact opposite. Kind of bordering on a sort of tribal ritual, I'm sure you'll agree.

Then there's the buttoning—or *zipping*—of my jacket.

For some reason, I just can't seem to keep my busy hands from constantly going through the motions. Making sure that I'm tightly—*snuggly*—fitted into whatever garb I've opted for that particular day. I'm sure that any self-respecting therapist would have a field day with that one . . .

My very worst habit, though, is how I'll constantly take my gun apart, before, piece-by-piece, putting it back together again, as if now—*somehow*—I've fixed something that wasn't quite right earlier. And it was just after I'd gone through that little cycle of *fidgets* that I heard, unmistakable against the nearly silent soundscape encapsulating the cabin, the *rumble* of a car engine approaching.

I keep myself still as I can, staring out through the attic window, down onto the path.

I know I have to concentrate.

Down at my thigh, I grasp tight to my handgun—to *Mrs Claus* —and I do my best to ignore the constant rapping of my heart at my tonsils.

A large black four-by-four with tinted windows.

If the target was looking for subtlety, he sadly lacks it here.

The driver's door levers open and—*immediately*—I recognise the target.

Bald.

Tanned complexion.

A little under six foot.

And the beer belly he's growing is not to be sneered at.

He wears a black bobbly fleece, and a pair of black, leather driving gloves.

As he turns his head, to glance back at the cabin, I duck down.

When I look back, though, he's no longer turned around.

And now that I catch him in profile, I see that he has a pair of thin-framed glasses perched on the bridge of his nose.

The fact that he wears glasses has been overlooked in the profile.

As has the next fact . . .

First, the passenger door opens to reveal a leggy blonde, surely a good few inches taller than the target. His wife?

What catches my attention all the more, though, is the target venturing around the back of his car.

Him going to the back door, and then opening it up.

A little girl—maybe six or seven years old, and dressed in a frilly, ice-white dress—bounces down into the snow. She grasps hold of the target—*her daddy's*—hand, and the two of them tread towards the front of the cabin.

That isn't where it ends, either.

The target's companion helps another little girl down from the other side of the car.

She might be eight or nine.

Not much older.

Right as I feel my heart bouncing all about my throat, something deep within me tells me to duck down. So I do.

As I disappear from view, my mind remains impressed with the vision of the girl looking up at me. Did she see?

6

HOLDING MYSELF UP against the wooden wall of the attic, I can feel the chill of the snow, piled up on the roof. It keeps me awake. Keeps me alert.

All these things that're—*right now*—imperative.

I listen for any words from the little girl outside.

The one that *surely* saw me.

I hear nothing.

Perhaps I haven't been seen.

. . . Yeah, and wishful thinking *really* got me where I am today . . .

I work quickly, knowing that I need to keep a low profile. That I have to prepare for the very worst. The first thing that I get to doing is hiding the bag I brought with me—the one which contains my clothes, and all my travel documents so that I can get home *after* Christmas.

I eventually conceal it behind what looks, to me, like a grandfather clock covered in a dusty, white sheet.

My mind switches.

What next? What next? What next?

The loop of words ebbs through my brain.

I glance about.

I need to hide.

I have to hide myself.

Can I hear footsteps?

Coming up the staircase?

With no time to waste, I dash across the attic floor, paying no attention to the squealing floorboards as I do so. I find a large wooden crate there. When I peel back the lid, I'm almost delirious with happiness that it's empty.

I wonder if it's where the target stores his Christmas decorations.

Forgetting my deliberations and speculations for now, I pile on inside and hoik the lid up over the top to hide inside.

And it's not a second too soon.

Because the hinges of the door to the attic creak.

I am not alone.

7

MY HEART is beating so hard that I believe—I *know*—that anybody who's standing vaguely in the vicinity will be able to hear every last beat.

I peer through one of the cracks in the wooden crate.

Almost like watching a film in widescreen.

The attic door opens up.

A light shines out behind the figure.

Behind the target.

Makes him into nothing more substantial than a silhouette.

I grip my gun tight.

Know that now—*now*—is the time.

With a house full of people, I'll never have a better chance at getting the target alone.

I'll need to bust out of the crate.

There's no way I'll be able to fit the barrel of the gun through the crack in the crate.

If I squeeze the trigger I'll be liable to blind myself with splinters.

And then it really *would* be impossible to get away.

The target continues to step over the wooden floorboards.

He treads over to the window.

Where I was crouched, looking out, only moments before.

The target bends down, apparently to inspect something.

And I hope I've been professional.

Haven't left any traces.

The target straightens up.

Is he holding something between his index finger and thumb?

Or am I just deceiving myself?

Whatever he was doing, the target loses interest in the

contents—or *non*-contents—of his hand, and he shifts his attention back behind him.

For a heart-stopping moment he sweeps his gaze over me.

My hiding place.

But he moves away.

Turns his attention—*not much better*—to the grandfather clock covered with the dusty white sheet.

With a quick glance around, the target pulls back a little of the sheet near the top of the covered grandfather clock. Of what I *think* is a grandfather clock.

In profile, I watch on as a smile grows out of his lips, and up the side of his face.

It brings out wrinkles.

A little way off, I hear a shout.

A *little girl's* shout.

High-pitched, squeaky, *demanding*.

For some reason, I get a little smile, thinking about how my daughter Josie sounded something like that at some point in the past. Funny how time just marches on . . .

The target's attention moves away from whatever lies beneath the dusty sheet. He glances back over his shoulder briefly, and then, a little hurriedly, he replaces the sheet over the object beneath.

For a second, he glances downwards, to where I have stowed my bag, but he has little chance to consider what he does or doesn't see, because the youngest of the two girls—the one wearing the dress—now stands in the doorway.

"Father?"

"Hmm," the target says, bringing his head all the way around, and refocussing all his attention, apparently with some degree of finality, onto his daughter. "Yes, dear?"

"Come help us put the star on."

" 'The star' ?" the target says, sounding somewhat distracted.

Even though I can't quite get a clear look at the little girl's face from my hiding place, I'm fairly certain that she's glaring at him.

Despite myself—*despite the situation*—I break out in a smile too.

Hey, if you can't have a little fun at Christmas, when you're murdering somebody's father, then when *can* you have some fun?

"Yes, Daddy," she says, "just like every year, remember? We wait till Christmas Eve to put the star on top of the Christmas tree."

If the target's mind had been elsewhere until that moment, it suddenly switches to be totally engaged in what his daughter says. He scratches his scalp a pair of times, and then grins back at her. "Oh, yes, that's right. Silly Daddy forgetting, huh?"

"Yes," the little girl says, seizing her father's hand. "*Silly Daddy*, always forgetting."

And, without having the chance to so much as glance back over his shoulder, the little girl drags the target away. The door slams shut behind them.

I allow myself to breathe.

Tell myself not to breathe too quickly.

Don't want to give myself a head rush.

When I pop the lid of the wooden crate, I realise that it's gone dark in the attic now.

My night-vision goggles are over in the sports bag.

Beneath that cloaked object.

I wait in the wooden crate, wanting to see if either the target or his daughter returns.

But I can hear nothing.

Only the muffled voices from down below.

The very gentle *rustle* of snowflakes.

Taking care, I step out of the wooden crate.

I tread with extreme caution over the floorboards—telling

myself that so much as a misplaced toe might bring the entire wrath of the house upon me.

I remind myself of all those security systems I had to bypass to get into the cabin. That can only mean that the target is expecting visitors over the Festive period. That, even out here, in the middle of nowhere, he expects his enemies to be able to find him.

And *kill* him.

I reach the cloaked object.

I snatch up my sports bag and have a dig about inside.

Everything's still there.

Though the reason why it *shouldn't* be escapes me.

I place the bag down at my feet, convinced now, if not before, that nobody is going to be visiting the attic imminently.

Then, thinking again, I reach into the bag, unzip a side pocket, and withdraw a torch from within.

I flip it on: the light a tiny bluish-white glow.

Even though I'm fairly confident I've got inside undetected, it really doesn't pay to set up a light beacon irradiating the place.

I tug back a little of the dusty sheet and I peer at the object which is concealed below.

My eyes flicker forwards.

And then back.

Forwards again.

It takes me a moment of staring at just one section of the object to really understand what it is. To have made sense of just what it is that I'm looking at here.

But, still, even then, I can't quite get my head around it.

A coffin.

8

NOW, the last thing that I thought I'd be dealing with on Christmas Eve was vampires. But, then again, I guess this is why I get paid the big bucks to do what it is I do.

Still, I have a gut feeling that dealing with vampires might be somewhat beyond my skillset.

I sort of vaguely know that I can kill them with a wooden stake to the heart, that, for some reason, they aren't all that partial to silver, and—somewhat more far-fetched—that they have a definite *dislike* for holy water.

I brush the dusty sheet back a little more, hoping to get a better idea of just what this is.

Now, I'm no expert on coffins, but the coffin looks like it's made of something like ebony.

Well-polished.

And standing in an upright position which suggests, to me, that, if there was somebody inside, they would've long ago tumbled out onto the floor.

Or, perhaps, there's some sort of a catch system which negates that particular effect.

I listen out for any other sound in the house, hear that gentle babble of conversation coming from—*I suppose*—the sitting room.

Nobody coming to check.

But then, why would they?

If I've done my job right then there's no reason for them to check . . .

I work my hands down the side of the coffin, looking for some sort of a clue, but eventually come up with nothing.

No catches.

No release handle.

Nothing that suggests a way into the coffin.

But, then again, why do I need to get into the coffin at all?

It's way beyond my basic brief of taking care of the target.

I always did have a nosey nature.

Telling myself that I need to get my brain back into the hit, I shift away from the coffin standing upright, making sure that I pull the dusty white sheet down so it's like it was before . . . before I disturbed it.

Just as I put the last piece of the dusty sheet back into place, though, I notice something etched into the wood, near the base of the coffin.

A serial number?

That's what it looks like.

E9-67HJK

I wonder if it should elicit something in me.

If that chain of numbers and letters carries significance.

But there's nothing that I can gather from it.

I bring the dusty sheet down to cover the coffin. I move gently across the floorboards. I take care not to cause them to squeal out. And I return to my previous hiding place in the wooden crate.

As I bring the lid down over my head, I hear a final peal of laughter from downstairs.

Girlish laughter.

And I know this'll be the last night they spend with their father.

9

MY MIND gets one over on me. I find myself drifting away into a kind of half sleep.

I wake with a jolt.

Bad dream.

All my dreams are bad.

I breathe in the attic air, as if smelling it for the first time.

The dust.

The cut of the wood.

And that plusher—*more expensive*—odour of the ebony coffin beneath the white sheet.

I bring my hand up to my temple.

Give it a rub.

Try to release an iota of the tension there.

No such luck.

I try to piece together my surroundings.

Listen tight.

I can hear a slight *creak*.

Floorboards.

Footfall.

And I have just enough time to grab for my handgun before light rushes into the attic.

It blinds me.

In the panic, I squeeze the trigger.

Safety's—*thankfully*—on.

I compose myself.

Breathe as quietly as I can.

As *deeply* as I can.

I peer through the crack in the wooden crate.

See him there again.

The target.

I squint, feeling the harsh light burning the backs of my eyeballs.

I'd like to shut my eyes.

Get some strength back into them.

But I know I need to keep my eye on him.

Maybe he's feigning.

Maybe he's *discovered* my hiding place.

He wants to lull me into a false sense of security.

And then strike.

Take *me* out.

The rest of the house, as far as I can tell, is steeped in silence.

Waiting for Santa Claus.

And the target—*unsuspectingly*—awaiting a visit from Mrs Claus.

The target seems a touch hurried.

His hands shake as he removes the sheet from the coffin.

He takes extreme care to peel the sheet back, and then to place it down at his feet. Then he stands, almost in reverence, before the coffin. Almost as if he is expecting higher instruction. As if he's speaking to some god, unseen to me . . . or anybody else, for that matter.

His hands move almost so quickly that I have no time to trace their movement.

But I *do* trace their movement.

His fingertips smooth the outside of the coffin. They slip and slide over the well-polished veneer.

Looking for something.

For a way in?

Finally, his tongue jabbing out the corner of his mouth, the target finds what he's looking for. He leaves his fingertips in whatever it is he's discovered for several seconds. He glances about.

Into the attic.

For a horrible second I convince myself that his gaze lingers right over me. Over the crack in the wooden crate I peer out through.

But then his focus shifts back to the coffin.

All the time, his fingertips remain on the coffin.

In that place which took him time to find.

With a single, slick movement I have no time to trace, there's the sound of hydraulics decompressing—or whatever it is they do when they go *hiss.*

The target stands back a little.

But retains his touch on the coffin.

As if it might disappear if he lets go.

The coffin lid hisses all the way open.

It reveals *something* inside.

In my limited, cramped space, I struggle to see past the target, but what I manage to see suggests—at least to my mind— some sort of a large, elongated canister.

The chamber of a bomb?

Do bombs *have* chambers?

Again, I scold myself for having—*surely*—dozed off at some point during some briefing or other in the army when we were, no doubt, given detailed description on explosives.

Only now, with the coffin lid-slash-door fully open does the target remove his finger from the point on the outside case. He glances about again as if he sits right on the point of discovery.

Or the point of death.

I squeeze the grip of my handgun a little tighter. More as a nervous gesture than a definite decision, I flip the safety off.

I ready myself to pop up—*hello!*—at any moment.

I see the target reach for a red hose which snakes across the floorboards.

He fiddles with the nozzle which may, or may not, be made of brass.

Not like what my mind imagines as a firehose.

No *pointed* end to it.

Just a brass ring.

The target bends down. He gets into a crouch. And he works to fasten the hose to something at the base of the coffin.

I have no idea what he's doing.

But I know that now's the time.

That now I have to move.

I should've done so about ten minutes ago.

If I hadn't dozed off, got my brain all mixed up, I probably would have.

Mind made up, I flip the lid off the top of the wooden crate.

Hear it clatter down behind me.

Straighten.

Aim for the spot just between the target's shoulder blades.

His spine.

"*Freeze*," I say, thinking—a little dizzily—that I sound something like a policewoman from some terrible eighties TV show.

All the same, it has the desired effect.

The target remains on his knees.

Fiddling away at the base of the coffin.

"*Stop!*" I say.

The target *doesn't* stop what he's doing. In fact he seems to speed up. But, at least, he deigns to reply to me over his shoulder. "I knew you were coming—I knew you were up here, in the attic, waiting for me."

This takes me a touch off guard.

And, though it's strictly forbidden, I find myself speaking with the target in something other than the imperative. "Aren't you going to call for help?"

The target continues, as if stuck on some other track. "When I got out of the car, I saw you up in the attic window. I saw your face there. Like a ghost. Just like a ghost."

There's a slight *snick* within the canister he's working on, and it seems to add a certain urgency to the target's tone when he speaks again.

"Or an angel of death," I say, aiming for the back of his head now.

"I wouldn't fire if I were you. It shall not be a peaceful death if you happen to miss. And that is what I least wish for my family."

"I never miss," I say, sounding far more cocksure than I feel.

The target doesn't respond. His fast hands just work at the canister within the coffin.

"Do you understand English? I said *stop* what you're doing."

"Or else you'll shoot me?" the target says, a nervous smile clearly in his voice. "Isn't that what you're going to do anyway?"

Not really much I can say to that . . .

"No," the target goes on, "I've known that you were after me —that *somebody* was coming for me . . . people talk, you know? I hear things ahead of time." This time he glances back at me. Meets my eye briefly. He taps his glasses a little up the bridge of his nose. "I made peace with dying a long time ago, but I won't allow my family to be put through pain."

"Why would they go through pain?" I ask.

The target gives a wry smile. "Because you want information, do you not? That is what they all want from me. All that I am good for. And to get it out of me you will surely hurt my family."

Now he gets to his feet.

Wipes his, no doubt, sweaty palms on his jean pockets.

I resist the temptation to tell him to get down, knowing that so much as a misplaced fingernail might tip this faceoff over the edge.

And I could do with a clean kill.

He stares right back at me. "You want to know it all, don't you?"

I shake my head. "No," I say, "my only orders are to kill you —nothing to do with your family."

He freezes at my words.

A kind of almost inexplicable reaction passes through him.

He seizes up.

He stops blinking.

I watch as a single bead of sweat squeezes out from his brow and then ekes its way down the side of his face. It hangs on his chin for a couple of long—*long*—seconds before finally tumbling down to the floor.

Where it splashes at his feet.

I hear only one word, clean and clear, and *piercing* the air, as he ducks and rolls away from me.

"*Liar!*"

10

THOUGH I KNOW BETTER, I can't resist a pair of snapshots.

Both miss.

Cause chunks to fly out from an exposed wooden beam.

Splinters fly.

Several dig themselves into my forearm.

I just about turn in time to see the heels of the target's shoes skitter on out around the doorway, and onto the landing.

Outside the attic.

I go quickly.

I know—*from experience*—that it's bad enough to have to take somebody out with their family all sleeping in the house around them. But to do so with everybody wide awake, and scared . . . that's another matter altogether.

I pursue the target.

Know that, at any second, one of the little girls might peer out into the corridor.

Want to get a look.

See if Santa's here.

And get a bullet in the forehead for their trouble.

I push that thought down deep.

But it still makes my stomach swell.

It's almost enough to make me tumble down and curl into a ball.

Just wish this whole nightmare away.

But it's not a nightmare.

This is happening.

Really happening.

I barrel along the landing and down several flights of steps.

I don't know if my mind is deluding me that the target is just

ahead of me; that I'm always on the brink of catching him . . .
No *time* to know.

By some kind of horse sense, I reach the sitting room on the
ground floor.

Spot the motion in the kitchen.

See the target there.

Leaning up against the counter.

Panting slightly.

And then I see the blood.

He's doubled over.

Holding a place just below his ribcage.

Blood oozes out from between his fingers.

Black and thick.

I bring my gun up.

Aim for the headshot.

Now is the time.

This won't be anywhere near the clean job I hoped for.

Right as I feel my finger squeeze the trigger—take the weight
of the shot at the other end—he murmurs something beneath his
breath.

I spot his other hand.

See the switch he holds there.

The almost *comical* red button.

As I squeeze the trigger, I hear his words tumble out from
between his lips.

"My family . . . they won't . . . won't *suffer* . . ."

11

THE TARGET CRUMPLES DOWN.
To his knees.

Dead.

I wait a second.

Two.

Then, breath finally caught, I turn my attention to his hand.

To where he holds that device.

The one with the red button.

I see that he has depressed it with his thumb.

That a bright-green light is now lit.

And—*right then*—I think that it's the last thing I'll see.

To think my last moments on Earth will take place in the early hours of Christmas morning . . .

I await the explosion.

The sound of the bomb in the attic being triggered.

But . . . *nothing* . . .

I can hear my breath coming in through my nostrils.

Going out through my mouth.

Relaxation 101.

Is there . . . can I hear something?

I close my eyes, wondering if something's gone wrong with the bomb in the attic.

Surely something *has* gone wrong with it.

I wonder what to do.

Rush upstairs?

Try to make an escape?

My thoughts turn to the target's family.

To his sleeping wife.

And his two daughters.

Innocents . . . yet more innocents.

Left behind.

'Collateral damage' . . . whatever it might be called.

I stare down at the target, lying on the peachy, white kitchen tiles.

I see the dark blood ooze out, spoiling the material forever.

This cabin—this *place*—will never be the same again.

Once death has touched a place it loses its innocence.

Its *virginal* quality.

I make my mind up.

I holster my gun.

And dash up the stairs.

12

ONLY WHEN I ARRIVE on the landing upstairs do I realise that I can hear a gentle blowing sound coming from somewhere. Like the sound of a draught.

As I make my way along the landing—past the closed bedroom doors—I note the ventilation ducts which appear at regular intervals.

Is that where it's coming from?

The air smells a touch stale.

Almost like helium now that I think of it.

. . . But I know it's something *else.*

Subtlety goes out the window right then.

I break into a run.

I bash my fists against the doors as I go past.

When I reach the end of the landing, I stand there, and I wait.

I turn my attention upwards, back to the attic, wondering if there's anything vaguely technical I might be able to do.

Too late for that.

Surely.

All the doors, one at a time, open on their hinges.

Frightened expressions turn on me.

Mouths yawn wide.

Ready to scream.

But I raise my voice above them all.

Drown them out.

"Run!"

13

MOMENTS LATER, and despite the panic, I take pains to guide the family away from the kitchen. So they won't have to see their father—the target . . . their *murderer*—in his final, unflattering pose. We emerge into the midst of the fallen snow.

The silent, majestic, towering snowbanks piled up all around.

The car is half buried.

I turn to the wife.

Tell her to get the keys.

She trembles.

But does as I say.

I almost have to scream out at her again as she goes in through the front door.

I think she's delirious.

But she sets foot on the Welcome mat.

Returns bearing a clinking set of keys.

The locks on the car disengage with a flourish of bright, orange indicators.

And a broad *snick*.

Nobody speaks.

I work to free the back doors with my gloved hands.

Then the front doors.

That done, we all pile into the car.

I get into the passenger seat.

The wife sits—*frozen*—in the driver's seat.

The car keys tinkle in her grasp.

Her expression is frozen.

Almost like a china doll.

I want to reach out and shake her.

Know that I can't.

She might attack me.

Go ballistic.

I take a chance.

I speak to her.

"Do you have somewhere to go?" I say.

She doesn't respond.

I glance into the back seat, to the girls there.

Both of them have dark bags hanging down beneath their eyes.

But their expressions are panicked.

And why *shouldn't* they be?

Then I make a judgement call.

I shift off the passenger seat, emerge outside the car.

Slam the passenger door shut.

Then I run.

Run away.

14

I MUST'VE run a good ten kilometres before I manage to stop myself.

Before the cold which surrounds me becomes too hard to handle.

No snow falls now.

Everything is quiet.

In the distance I think I can hear the *rumble* of a car engine.

Of the wife, and the two daughters, making their getaway.

I fumble about inside my coat, locate the emergency radio, and then I tap the button which sends the signal. Which bleeps some control mast somewhere.

Which'll bring a helicopter on standby to my rescue.

An hour away.

That was what Brian said.

Just an hour's wait.

Try telling that to my legs . . . they soon crumple beneath me.

I drop down, into the snow.

And I rest there.

Heart beating hard in my ears.

Lungs filling and then emptying.

A frost seeming to layer my chest.

And then calm.

Knowledge . . . that I did the Right Thing.

I could've told her . . . could've told *them* . . . just what the target had planned.

How he wanted them all dead.

But I didn't.

I did the Right Thing.

As I hear the beating chopper blades approaching, I wipe

away the tears that've somehow sprung up again. The ones which—it seems—just won't go away *this* Christmas.

I put on my game face.

This is Anna Harris.

Professional murderer.

Ready for action.

317

VIAL DEBT

1

THE NOISE of the football crowd is all around me. Nearly deafening.

The air smells strongly of grease and lager and sweat.

In short, this is a stadium.

A stadium filled—*mostly*—with men.

Supporters wheel green-and-blue striped scarves through the air, above their heads, willing their team on . . . whichever team that happens to be. Vibrations pass through the concrete; the endless stamping—the jumping up and down.

Has someone just scored?

Has one of the *teams* just scored?

I couldn't care less.

Because I didn't come here for a sporting spectacle.

I came here to kill.

It being a winter's day, a brisk, chilly wind floats in over the top of the stadium stands. It tugs at my hair, teasing it gently from the tightly bound ponytail. I shove my hands deeper into the pockets of my thick, woollen jacket. As always, I dress to disappear; and today has been no different. I picked out the warmest black item of clothing within my wardrobe.

And I settled on this little number.

As I press my leather-gloved hands deeper into the coat pockets, I feel the shape of the glass vial within; the method with which I am required to carry out today's hit.

Today's *murder*.

An overweight man in a fluorescent jacket—a *steward?*—brushes past me, turning side on and apologising as he faintly rustles my coat.

I eye my destination, the door to the executive boxes, currently manned by a skinny, young man in a tight-fitting suit.

He is half-hypnotised by the football match taking place down below, and he hardly bothers to give the credentials I flash at him a second glance. He leans on some button, or some buzzer, and the door flips open on an automatic, hydraulic arm.

I'm in.

The hit is on.

I T'S LIKE entering another world entirely, to be within the executive boxes. The biggest change is the atmosphere. The singing—*the chanting*—is gone. The sound-proofing apparently taking care of it. Gone too is the smell of lager, sweat and grease, replaced by richer odours of sizzling steak, and the refined scent of bubbling champagne . . .

Underfoot, there's no sign of the bare concrete that I'd grown used to outside in the stadium. A well-shampooed, obviously cared-for, regal-red, thick carpet has appeared now. Sepia-stained framed photographs hang down from the corridor walls.

As I pass by the executive boxes, I can hear the muttered conversations of those in attendance. Of those who are *inhabiting* these spaces for the duration of the football match.

Kept well clear of the Great Unwashed.

My heart begins to beat a little harder.

My pulse quickens.

The thinnest of thin layers of sweat lines my forehead.

I restrain the urge to reach up and wipe it away with the back of my hand.

My hands still stuffed in my coat pockets, I feel for the reassuring form of the glass vial containing the liquid which will steal life away just as efficiently—and much more *quietly*—than any self-respecting bullet.

When I reach the room I was briefed on—the one which the target has hired for this particular day out—I pause. Think things through.

I *wonder* if everything is okay.

If the coast is clear.

If I'm *ready* to kill.

I turn side-on when a waiter bearing a silver tray appears at my elbow, with a trio of white porcelain plates on top, each of them bearing what looks to be an elegantly arranged salad dish. I watch him step into the room containing the target, and silently curse myself for having arrived slightly late. For having got here just a *little* too late.

The liquid—*surprise, surprise*—needs to be ingested by the target.

The way I'd been planning it . . . the way I'd been *briefed* to plan it . . . was to somehow get the liquid into the target's food. But things got more complicated when I started asking questions —silly *moral* me—enquiring as to whether or not there might be others accompanying the target . . . others who might also ingest the liquid.

And my client gave me the answer I dread.

Just get the job done.

The waiter brushes back out of the executive box, hardly noticing me there. I suppose that all the waiting staff have strict orders—*training*—to abide by . . . that they need to bow to the whims of their clientele. And it goes without saying that most upscale clients enjoy their privacy as much as the expensive champagne they drink. And the customer is certainly always right here.

I take a few steps forwards, so that I can just make out the interior of the executive box; the one which the waiter has just entered.

I hold myself still.

Peer within.

I make out the target. Almost right away.

A woman.

She wears a pair of blue jeans. A replica shirt tucked into the waistband. A silver necklace dangles down about her throat with what seems to be a cluster of diamonds at the end of it. I can tell that she has dressed down for the day; that she has decided to go with 'inconspicuous' as the theme for her styling.

And yet it won't save her.

It won't save her from someone like me.

A monster.

With the woman, there's a man—*her husband?*

He also wears a football shirt. He shifts about in his seat, as if he isn't quite comfortable.

To tell the truth, I can't see why he *wouldn't* be comfortable.

The executive box has more in common with a sitting room than with a sports stadium; what with the armchairs, and the sofas, and the coffee table in-between the furniture. It's certainly a long way from the plastic, fold-down seats which make up the rest of the stadium.

Which the *common* fans have to make do with.

There's another with them, of course.

A young boy.

Perhaps the woman's son.

No, I'm *certain* it's the woman's son.

That's when my heart sinks.

When I catch a skittish feeling in my stomach.

To tell the truth, over the course of the past few weeks, I've been having trouble in staying motivated; in getting myself into the *killer* mind-set.

Perhaps it was all leading up to this moment.

I just wanted to see.

Just wanted to make sure.

I wanted to *know* if I still possessed the will . . . the *ability* . . . to kill without discrimination.

To snuff out lives.

And now I know.

Now I know my limits.

Already, as I back away from the executive box, I'm drafting the explanation for my client; ready to tell him the reason *why* I couldn't go through with the hit. I wonder if I should make up something; whether I should create some *lie* . . . and that's when someone calls out to me. That's when I turn my head. That's when I look *back* into the executive box.

That's when *she* meets my eye.

3

M Y HEART STOPS.
          Just for a moment.

But it's enough that I feel the lack of oxygen.

The *lack* of movement in my feet.

The feet which're supposed to carry me away.

I stare into her eyes.

And she stares into mine.

The target . . . the one who I should kill.

My *payday*.

Even now, as I push my hands deeper into my coat pockets, I feel the thrill pass through my gut. And then, slowly, up into my chest. I feel the glass vial in my pocket; can sense the liquid stirring within. I shift my attention downwards, to the coffee table, and to the salads which they have laid out before them.

In the background—completely forgotten for the time being—the football match continues on its course. Someone has scored a goal. Everyone has leaped up. The players of one team have converged on one another. All of them embracing. *Celebrating.*

I feel like I'm a million miles away.

As if I'm completely detached from the scene.

Isn't this how I'm supposed to feel?

Because when does the assassin ever take centre stage . . .

"Hello?" the woman says.

I crush the urge to reply straight away; to give her something.

It's always been in my nature to hold things back.

Simply *offering* information is a weakness.

Once they know you, they can *beat* you.

The man is rising out of his seat, a confused expression on his face. "Can we help you?" he says. "Are you *lost*?"

It's then that I cast a glance down at the boy—he can't be much older than six or seven—as his wide eyes drink me in. As his wide eyes drink in *all* the details. I wonder if he hasn't come across a situation similar to this one in the past; if his parents haven't sat him down for roundabout conversations about 'Mummy' being in danger . . . that he should alert everyone nearby if he ever comes across a 'stranger' in the house.

But he's not in the house now.

And he's with his parents.

Does he still believe that they can protect him whatever happens?

I used to believe the same of my parents until, one day, I didn't . . .

The man takes another step towards me. His expression turns to one of concern. "You're lost," he says; a statement rather than a question.

I track him with my gaze.

And he stares me right back in the eye.

I wonder what he's thinking.

What *thoughts* are going through his brain.

Surely he's twigged that I am a threat.

That I am not to be trusted.

Or perhaps he hasn't . . .

Because there doesn't seem to be anything else obvious for me to say, I manage to utter, out of my dry throat, "I . . . I am."

The man seems to scan my words, to dredge through them for any secondary meaning; for any subtext that might be present.

If he does sense something then he doesn't let on.

He only keeps up the same expression.

I half expect the woman to make a grab for her son, to pull him close to her. But she does nothing of the sort. I suppose she's been given training; that she *knows* it would only make her son a target.

Especially if the assassin has just come for her.

The woman does, however, stand up.

She straightens her back.

And then she says, "What's that, in your pocket?"

4

I WITHDRAW MY HANDS.
   First the left.

And then the right—the one which is pressed up against the glass vial.

The man and the woman remain where they are, both of them closely studying my hands. My *bare* hands. But neither of them is easily fooled.

"Your right pocket," the woman says. "What've you got there?"

I hesitate—as if that's going to help me out in this situation—and then I realise that there's no other way. That I've come this far so I might as well show my hand completely; so to speak.

With my same right hand, I reach back into my pocket.

I grip onto the glass vial.

And I remove it.

I feel the three pairs of eyes on the vial.

All of them inspecting it.

All of them *working out* what it means.

Finally, breaking off her concentration on the glass vial, the woman nods to the man.

The man, without a word to his wife, crosses the executive box, and then he closes the door with a gentle *click*. He stands just to my side, his eyes narrowed, apparently trying to make sense of the vial, and its contents. He shifts a glance at me, asking permission—asking if he can pry the vial from my tightly gripping fingers.

I give him a nod—one which is so subtle that I can't say for certain that he even registers the gesture. He treads towards me. And he takes the vial from my fingers.

I stand still, feeling in some strange way as if I've been

stripped naked, and that I'm being paraded before them all; that I'm being *judged* by them all.

And why shouldn't I be judged?

Isn't what I do a sin in whatever religion?

Isn't it, without a doubt—without *question*—immoral?

The man glances up from the vial, then back to his wife. Perhaps she signals for him to explore further, because next he unscrews the lid and takes a whiff of the contents. He recoils slightly at the strength of the odour. Then he turns back to his wife and says, "Hazelnut essence."

His wife remains very serious for a long moment, and then, with a whispered word in her son's ear, she sends him towards the door to the executive box. The son, without hesitation, lets himself out. It feels as if every one of our eyes track his departure.

As if we're waiting till we're alone.

Till we're *truly* alone.

Well, we're alone now.

"So that's where my EpiPen got to this morning," the woman says, with a slight note of joviality to her voice. "I *was* wondering." She nods to the vial which her husband is now holding. "And you were supposed to spread this over my food." She glances down at the salads on the coffee table before them. "On this?"

I hesitate, distracted by what's going on with the football match beyond the glass.

Everyone is on their feet.

Clapping their hands above their heads.

I shift my attention back to the woman. "Yes," I reply, simply, succinctly.

The woman pouts. "Well, I have to say that it's a *personal* statement, at least." She glances to her husband. "It leaves me in no doubt about who sent you."

I say nothing.

I need time to think.

I need time *away*.

I need to escape the killing . . . perhaps forever.

The woman's pout goes through a whole sequence of changes becoming a wince for a moment then transitioning into a wry smile before finally settling on a sneer. "You do realise that my son has the same allergy, don't you?"

There's nothing I can do here except tell the truth.

And hope I'm believed.

"No," I reply.

The woman arches an eyebrow, then shifts her gaze once more to the man. "What should we do?" she says.

The man continues to stare at me throughout. "If we call the authorities—if we make a *fuss*—then he will know just what has gone on; just what has *happened*."

The 'he', and subject of this conversation, I take to be my client.

The one who's paying me to do the killing.

"On the other hand," the man continues, "he will find out eventually that he wasn't successful, and he'll send someone else." The man holds the vial up to the light and examines the liquid slopping about within. "But we'll know to expect them." He looks back at me again. "Just like we knew that we needed to expect *you*."

My stomach sinks.

And my heart halts for a fraction of a second.

A skittery ticklish feeling passes up my spine.

I know that this is wrong—that this is *all* wrong—but I thought that I had to give this thing one last go. I had to check for certain that my moral compass has somehow kicked in.

That I simply can't *do* this any longer.

Finally, I find the strength to raise my voice, though it is croaky—*wobbling about all over the place.* "I'm sorry," I just about manage to get out. "I'm *sorry.*"

As the pair continue to stare at me, I take a step backwards—towards the door—and when I reach for the knob, I expect them to stop me. For either the man or the woman to cry out for help.

To cry out for the police.

But neither of them makes a sound.

They just continue to eye me closely.

Watching each and every one of my moves.

At least this much can be said, I still have my assassin's nerve, if not the killer instinct.

I sense my opportunity, turn the doorknob, and let myself back out into the corridor.

5

I PACE AWAY from the stadium, my ears still pricked at the sound of any passing siren—at the high-pitched revving of any engine. Of someone suddenly calling out.

Demanding that I *stop*.

Call it fate—call it chance—but nobody approaches me; nobody demands that I return; nobody tries to halt my escape.

As I turn the corner, I hear a loud cheer from the stadium and I can't help but catch that fizzing feeling in my gut—the shudder which passes up my spine.

Because I know that this is the end; that whatever debt; whatever *karma* I've stirred through the course of my killing career, it all comes to a stop now.

Forever more.

Author's Note

Thank you for taking the time to read one of my books. If you would like to hear about my latest releases you can sign up for my newsletter here: www.aviain.com

Thanks for reading!

AV Iain

Dressed To Kill
An Anna Harris Short Story Collection

www.ingramcontent.com/pod-product-compliance
Lightning Source LLC
Chambersburg PA
CBHW030920050726
47498CB00003BA/834